While the body of the cat, its throat torn out, bled on the deck, Linda stripped. Falsen did not watch her change; nobody had ever seen him do it and he hoped nobody ever would. He stood facing the door. From behind him, he heard the tearing noises, the noisy slurping, the splintering and crunching of fragile bones to an assimilable sludge . . .

Then he felt her hand on his shoulder.

He turned around.

There was very little blood about her, only a few smears on her chin out of reach of her tongue, other smears on her small breasts. She looked . . . sated.

A. BERTRAM CHANDLER

FRONTIER OF THE DARK

ACE SCIENCE FICTION BOOKS
NEW YORK

FRONTIER OF THE DARK

An Ace Science Fiction Book / published by arrangement with
the author

PRINTING HISTORY
Ace Original / January 1984

ISBN: 0-441-25504-3

Ace Science Fiction Books are published by The Berkley Publishing Group,
200 Madison Avenue, New York, New York 10016.
PRINTED IN THE UNITED STATES OF AMERICA

CHAPTER 1

Nick Falsen had never liked cats, and cats had never liked him.

He was lucky that mutual hostility between himself and members of the feline species brought only marooning as its consequence. He could have been ejected from the air lock without his space suit, or shot with a projectile pistol, or disposed of in other ways more interesting than pleasant. But Falsen had once saved Captain Canning's life at some risk to his own. The two of them had been making an outer-hull inspection and, somehow, the captain's magnetically soled feet had lost contact with the shell plating and he had fallen out and away. If his lifeline had not snapped, this would have been a cause for embarrassment rather than alarm. As it was, the situation was serious. Falsen, using the tools from his belt holsters for disposable reaction mass, had taken off after his commander, had caught him and brought him back to safety. He had been obliged to sacrifice his suit's air tank to give the pair of them that last shove towards the ship.

Canning had not forgotten and—to the displeasure of the other officers—the second mate was not popular—had ruled that Falsen be given a fighting chance. The master of the star tramp *Epsilon Crucis* ordered that his second officer be marooned on Antares VI, an inhospitable planet barely capable of supporting human life and considered by the Federation not to be worth the trouble and expense of a colonization project. In those days, with the Third Expansion just getting under way, it seemed that the galaxy was overstocked with

1

highly desirable hunks of real estate just waiting to be snapped up by the first comer. Antares VI was not in that category.

So, at the appointed time, the whine of the Mannschenn Drive had sagged from the almost supersonic to the subsonic, and faded into silence. *Epsilon Crucis,* navigating now in normal space-time, had made a gingerly approach to the sixth planet of the ruddy sun, had established herself in orbit about this world. Number two boat had been readied, and to it, under armed escort, Falsen was taken. He could have broken free even then; he could have slipped out of the manacles about his wrists with ease. But what good would it have been to him? The others were ready and waiting for such action on his part. Both Wilbrahim, the chief officer, and Baynes, the chief engineer, were carrying projectile pistols, old-fashioned weapons, outmoded blunderbusses firing metal slugs—and Falsen knew what kind of metal they were. So he went into the boat, which was being piloted by young Kent, the fourth officer—acting third as soon as the necessary logbook entries had been made and signed. Wilbrahim, still carrying his ugly weapon, came along for the ride. Minnie, the ship's cat, spat one malediction before the air-lock doors closed.

There was no conversation during the journey from ship to planetary surface. It would have been hard to talk in any case; the sonic insulation around the inertial-drive unit was not very effective. Kent, forward, sat hunched over his controls. In the cabin, facing Falsen, Wilbrahim lounged at deceptive ease, the pistol, safety catch off, pointing at the prisoner. Falsen hoped that Kent, not the best of pilots, would be able to land without too much of a jolt. Fortunately the set-down was made on soft ground.

It was a spongy plain that was more than half swamp. The last of the daylight was almost gone and a thin, persistent rain drifted down from the overcast sky. Falsen shivered as they pushed him toward the air-lock door. "You might," he protested, "have let me bring some stores, some warm clothing. . . ."

"*You* won't need anything," Wilbrahim told him. "You're lucky," he added as he gestured with his pistol, "that I didn't find some excuse to use this. If I thought that you had the ghost of a chance of surviving, I still would."

"You still could, sir," volunteered Kent, the obnoxious puppy. " 'Shot while attempting to escape,' or something . . ."

"Escape?" Wilbrahim laughed harshly. "To what? He's welcome to all that he finds here. Mind you, I do think that the Old Man was too softhearted. Now, get the irons off him, Mr. Kent. Don't be scared; I've got him covered."

"And me," whined the junior officer, "what if the bullet goes right through him? Why not leave the handcuffs on the bastard?"

"*I* have to account for ship's stores, mister, and those cuffs are on the inventory. Hurry up, now!"

Kent fumbled with the key, trying to keep himself out of the line of fire. The manacles dropped to the deck with a metallic rattle.

"Out, Falsen, *out!*" growled the chief officer, gesturing with his gun. Then, in tones of heavy irony, "Good hunting!"

Falsen stood ankle-deep in cold mud and, with upraised fists, cursed his late shipmates aboard *Epsilon Crucis*, cursed the boat that had brought him down to this dismal world, that was now lifting fast back towards the bubble of light and warmth that was the mother ship. Either Wilbrahim or Kent switched on a searchlight, trained it on him, and the harsh glare of it reflected from his eyes, making them glow like those of some wild animal. Then the lifecraft was hidden by the low cloud cover and only the fading clangor of its inertial drive told of its passing. Soon there was only the darkness and the falling rain, and the solitary figure clad in low shoes, shirt and shorts, dressed not for pioneering but for the control room of the intersteller ship from which he was forever banished.

Cursing, Falsen realized, would get him nowhere. With his right hand he brushed his wet, pale-blond hair away from his eyes and surveyed his surroundings. The rain was not heavy enough to impair visibility, although he was soon soaked and chilled. Enough light remained, once the castaway's eyes had become adjusted, for him to make out the horizon—a dim, featureless, deeper blackness against the blackness of the overcast sky. Level, unbroken by tree, hill or building, it was so straight that Falsen at first feared that he had been set down upon some tiny islet in the midst of a great, calm sea. (Wilbrahim would have been quite capable of doing just that.) Fighting down his fears he tried to remember all that he had ever read, in pilot books and navigating directions, about

Antares and its worlds. (He had never dreamed that such knowledge would ever be of vital importance to him.) He recollected vaguely that this planet's equatorial zone was encircled by a broad belt of almost level plain and swampland, and that only in low latitudes were temperatures endurable by Terran standards.

Once again he turned in a slow circle, eyes, ears and nose alert for any indication of life—of life, and warmth, and food. He heard nothing but the steady susurrus of the rain, smelled nothing but dampness and vegetable decay and . . . *and?* Smoke. Wood smoke, an elusive fragrance hinting at the presence of some form of intelligent life. He shook himself, then purposively started to trudge in the direction from which he judged that the faint aroma was drifting. The mud slopped over the tops of his shoes, making his feet èven colder. His saturated clothing clung clammily to his body but, as the exercise warmed him, trapped a moist heat. As he walked one hand explored his pockets, checking their contents. He had a large pocketknife of the type favored by the spacemen of his era; it incorporated a sharp blade, a screwdriver, a file, a tiny adjustable wrench, a corkscrew and a bottle opener. There was an "everlasting" pocket lighter, good for at least five more standard years. There was a sodden packet of cigarettes. Whatever he might find at the end of his walk, he was armed, after a fashion. He had a cutting tool or weapon. He had fire. He had, too, his physical strength and a considerable ability to look after himself in unarmed combat.

The smoke odor grew stronger and stronger, and with it another smell—a scent that promised even more than the warmth and dryness which he was now anticipating with increasing certainty. Yet it destroyed his hopes of food. He had fallen low—but not that low. Yet. He could see something ahead now, a hill that humped its not inconsiderable bulk well above the horizon, its outline softened by vegetable growth of some kind; bushes or low trees. The not unpleasant acridity of smoldering wood was strong now, but even his keen night vision could not discern the faintest flicker of firelight. Yet there must be, somewhere close now, a castaway like himself, somebody with the same needs and desires—or, he amended, similar needs and desires. For he was, by this time, quite certain that his fellow victim of harsh circumstance was a woman.

• • •

He walked cautiously, treading carefully to avoid snapping the twigs and thinner branches of the shrubs covering the relatively dry slope. The other, whoever she was, might be armed. And, armed or not, too sudden an awakening from sleep could make her dangerous. He climbed and circled the hill cautiously, following his nose carefully, stealthily, a mounting excitement in his veins. It was only now that he fully realised how dreadfully lonely he had been for most of his life. He savored the fragrance of the fire, of those other scents that most men would never have noticed. At last he could see a thin sliver of ruddy light; it had to be the mouth of a cave. It widened as he approached. And then he was at the entrance—it was little more than a fissure—and peering inside.

The fire burned low, casting a dull, crimson radiance over the clean sand floor, over the pile of small, broken branches a little to one side of it, over the neatly folded clothing and the huddle of blankets that covered . . . somebody. Walking slowly and softly, hardly breathing, Falsen entered the cave. He skirted the fire, made his way to the little pile of clothes.

Curious, he picked up the garments, one by one. They were a woman's, as he already knew, and they bore insignia similar to those on his own uniform. He looked at the epaulets on the shirt: black, with two narrow stripes of gold braid on a white backing. Purser or catering officer, he thought. But what was that stylized figure of an animal worked in gold thread above the rank stripes? *Surely not . . .* he thought incredulously. Then he almost laughed aloud. *Dog Star Line, of course.*

Meanwhile, he was cold. He stepped closer to the fire, stepped inadvertently on a dry twig. He turned again—fast this time, with no thought for caution. He saw the blankets tossed aside and the pale, naked figure of a woman leaped from her bed. Fortunately for him, his arms were longer than hers and he was able to catch and hold her before her clawed fingers reached his eyes. He grappled with her, caught her off balance and forced her down to the sandy floor. He felt the flesh of her shoulders crawl in his grasp, flinched from the animal hate that glared from her green eyes. He showed his teeth in a mirthless grin and growled, "Hold it! Hold it, you bitch! Dog doesn't eat dog!"

She seemed to understand, ceased to struggle.

He risked letting go of her, got to his feet and looked down at the woman. In the glow of the dying fire she appeared somehow unreal, her flesh gleaming with a shimmering insubstantiality. Yet she was solid enough, although slenderly built. He studied her features. She could almost have passed for his sister. Her nose was prominent, her chin much less so. Her parted lips were thin, although vividly red, and her big teeth shone whitely, the snarl at last softening to a hesitant smile. He looked at her body. Dark hair glistened under an upflung arm and sprouted in profusion from crotch to navel. Her breasts were small, and below the left one was a third, rudimentary nipple.

Yet she was beautiful, and others besides himself must have found her so. She had the animal grace, the savage vitality to arouse not a few men. He was becoming increasingly aroused himself.

She raised herself on one elbow, stared at him appraisingly.

She asked, her voice low and husky, almost a growl, "Who are you? I needn't ask *what* are you. Where do you come from?"

"My name is Falsen," he said. "Nicholas Falsen. I'm . . . no. I *was* second mate of the Commission's *Epsilon Crucis*. My shipmates decided that they didn't much care for my company. And so . . ."

"Why didn't they just kill you?" she asked, her interest caught.

"Some of them, most of them, wanted to do just that. But I'd saved the Old Man's life once." He laughed shortly. "And did *you* save any lives?"

She grinned back at him. "No. But I did make *my* captain's life a little less lonely. He's a sentimental slob. When it came to the crunch, he just couldn't bring himself to have me disposed of. So I was dumped here with enough stores to last me for about thirty standard weeks. I've been here for sixteen."

"You're Dog Star Line," he stated rather than asked.

"How did you . . . ? Oh, my uniform, of course. Yes. Dog Star Line. Purser, catering officer and maid-of-all-work aboard the good ship *Beagle*." But she was once again staring at him suspiciously. He saw her muscles tensing under the sleek skin. "I'm a light sleeper. I didn't hear you being landed— and you know as well as I do that even a small boat's inertial-drive unit makes enough racket to wake the dead."

"I was landed some distance from here," he said. "And downwind—not that there is much wind—on the other side of the hill from your cave entrance. Earth and rock and vegetation are quite good sonic insulation."

The suspicion faded from her face. "It figures," she said. "From the looks of you, you must have walked a long way—soaking wet and with mud up to your arse. But wouldn't it have been better to have stripped and carried your clothes?"

"I didn't know who, or what, I might find. I certainly wasn't expecting *you*."

"So you found me. And don't think that I'm not grateful. It's been damned lonely here."

"Since I *have* found you—what is your name?"

"Veerhausen. Linda Veerhausen. Now that we've been introduced, I'd better start making you comfortable. You're cold and wet and hungry. Get out of those stupid clothes and between the blankets. I'll get you something hot."

"I don't like to take your stores. . . ."

"Rubbish. I've hardly touched them. I've been living off the country. But this calls for a can of beef stew."

She went into a smaller cave that opened off the main one, and by the time that Falsen was stripped and between the blankets, still warm from her body heat, she was back, carrying the food container, thin smoke spiraling from the axial tube of chemicals that had heated its contents.

He was hungry—but for more than food. Although the smell of the savory stew tantalized his nostrils, so did the feral scent of her. He wanted her, *now*. He threw aside the blankets.

She dropped the can as he leapt at her. Its steaming contents, unheeded, soaked into the sand. She fell backward before his attack, sprawled in an attitude of abject surrender, arms and legs upraised and open.

Surrender?

Acceptance?

Or capture.

She clamped him to her, in her.

"You hairy bastard!" she whispered. Her sharp teeth nipped his ear. "You hairy bastard! I could *eat* you. . . . After those smooth-skinned frogs aboard the *Beagle* you're . . . You're real. Fuck me, damn you! Fuck me!"

Their coupling was brief, savage. There had been no foreplay; there was no afterplay. Limbs still entangled, they fell into a deep sleep, sprawled on the sand floor.

Outside, the steady whisper of the rain died and finally ceased.

CHAPTER 2

Falsen was awake with the dawn, snapping from sound sleep into instant awareness. He was alone. He threw the blankets to one side, walked on bare, silent feet to the cave entrance. Linda, standing on a little ledge overlooking the downward slope of the hill, sensed his coming, turned to greet him. A smile flickered briefly over her face.

"This is it," she said. "Your first morning on Antares VI. Or, since we seem to be a sort of Adam and Eve, shall we think up a nice name for this mudball?" She laughed. "It's better than *my* first morning. I didn't have company."

Low in the east a sullen, ruddy glow stained the gray clouds. It spread slowly, spread and lifted, suffusing all the overcast with dull crimson. And then there was a sun in the sky; all the pools and channels through the swamp glimmered like blood among the grayness of the vegetation.

"What's the program?" asked Falsen. "You're the oldest inhabitant."

"Breakfast," said the girl. "But we have to catch it first. Unless, that is, you'd sooner have something from the stores. . . ."

"Better keep the canned stuff for an emergency," he said. "But you're the catering officer."

"All right. We catch our breakfast. Look." She pointed. "See that pool? The one shaped like a horseshoe. . . . That's where I get my crayfish—they aren't crayfish, but I have to call them something. I'll show you."

"Do we go as we are?"

"You can dress if you like. But as we are is better for things like crayfish. If it were sheep, now . . ." She licked her red lips with a red tongue.

"Don't!" said Falsen sharply.

The girl ignored him.

"On my last long leave," she said, "I went to Earth. I already *knew* then, by the way. I spent a few weeks in the Scottish Highlands, one of those reserves that they have on Terra . . ."

"I know," interrupted Falsen. "I'm Terran."

"One morning," she went on, "a morning much like this . . . there were sheep." She smiled reminiscently. "I often wonder who, or what, that shepherd blamed."

"And yet, knowing the risk, you continued in space?"

"Why not? As a catering officer doubling as nurse, I had access to drugs. And I saw to it that there was a sudden increase in the mortality rate of the ship's cats. If it hadn't been for that passenger and her pampered Persian . . . And now . . ." she spat viciously, "*Crayfish!* There's more real meat on a cat!"

Together they made their way down the hillside, toward the pool. The spongy vegetation was soggy underfoot, still saturated with the night's rain. The rising of the sun had brought a steamy, uncomfortable warmth to the air and Falsen was thankful that he had not bothered to dress, that there was only his skin, hairy as it was, to get muddy, so that the discomfort was no worse.

They stopped at the horseshoe-shaped pond, and there Linda made a search of the vegetation along its bank. She selected, finally, a long tendril with an elongated, bright yellow berry at its end. Using her left hand, she lowered it gently into the water. Falsen saw that there were tiny fish in the pool, some gold in color, some silver. He *supposed* that they were fish . . . at least they filled the same ecological niche as fish did on other worlds. He supposed, too, that something with very weak eyesight might just possibly mistake the berry for one of the little creatures.

"The thing to do," explained Linda, "is to keep it moving, just so. And you need hands for this. . . . Now we're in business."

Carefully, so as not to disturb the water, she lowered herself to a prone position, still angling with her left hand, her right hand poised and ready. Falsen watched the pale-colored berry and saw the tiny fish dart up to investigate it. After only seconds they sheered off with a rather elaborate show of disinterest. Then, suddenly, they were gone, flashing away to the farthest recesses of the pond, while something big and gray scuttled over the muddy bottom. With scarcely a splash, Linda's free arm flashed down into the water, and then she rolled over onto her back, holding with both hands a thing that could have been an oversize, infuriated Terran spider. Uncertain what to do, Falsen stood by, more than a little sickened by the appearance of the thing that the girl had fished from the pond.

"Shall I . . . ?" he began doubtfully.

"No. All right. There!"

Something cracked loudly and sharply, and then the crustacean was rolling on the spongy vegetation, dead, a gray, hairy football in size and appearance.

"We cook him," said the girl. "I've tried them raw, but . . ."

The thing, Falsen admitted, wasn't bad eating. It would have been improved by salt, pepper and vinegar and a melted butter dressing, but it was much better than nothing. Then, after the meal, there was a cigarette from the pack that Linda had carefully dried when she dried his clothes. It was a shared cigarette, for, as Linda pointed out, she had not yet found any kind of vegetable growth whose dried leaves would serve as a tobacco substitute.

"But you will lose the desire," she said. "After all, it's not natural. I'm just having this one with you to be sociable."

"Then, let *me* finish it."

"No. It's funny, but with the smell of it the desire came back. After all, there's no reason why we shouldn't try to make the best of two worlds."

"The main problem right now," said Falsen, "is to make the best of one."

He got to his feet, walked to the cave entrance to survey the one planet that was left to them after all their years and light-years of interstellar travel. He stiffened suddenly.

"Linda!" he called. "Come here!"

"What is it, Nick?"

"Look! Do you see it?"

Away over the swamp, twenty kilometers distant, some-

thing was moving, something that reflected the crimson rays
of the sun. Were there birds on this world, wondered Falsen,
or flying reptiles, or giant flying insects? There was no reason
why there should not be. But, as it approached, he could see
no wings. A flying machine? But he would have heard an
inertial-drive unit in operation long before such a craft came
into sight.

Then he heard a faint humming sound, growing louder.

"An airship," said Linda. "Some people use them for
survey work. The Shaara, for example. . . ."

"Even the Shaara," said Falsen, "are supposed to come to
the aid of distressed spacemen. And I doubt if they'll know
about our family scandals. The Federation's not publicizing
our particular one! Quick! Get some damp wood on the fire!"

"But suppose they're human?"

"Even then, they mightn't know why we're here. We can
cook up some yarn about shipwreck."

As he talked he was tearing up armfuls of the brush growing outside the cave, throwing the damp branches onto the
fire. The dirty white smoke rose, a trickle at first and then
great, rolling billows pouring out of the cave mouth, flowing
down the hillside like a heavy liquid. Over the swamp the
airship rose slowly from the surface of the pool that it was
investigating, turned, made directly for the hill and the cave.

"Not Shaara," said Falsen, studying it. "It's not a blimp.
That thing has a skeleton of some kind inside its envelope. . . ."
He searched his memory. "Doralan . . . could be. But we'd
better get dressed."

"Why? This is better if we're going to . . ."

"We're not going to. Yet. We'll let them take us to their
ship. Hurry!"

CHAPTER 3

Falsen came out of the cave coughing and spluttering. The humming of the airship's motors was loud in the oppressively humid air. He looked up at the thing through watering eyes, was able to make out the big characters painted in black on the metallic-gray envelope, meaningless scrawls to him but indubitably Doralan.

And what were the Doralans doing here?

Running a survey, that was what.

Linda came out and stood beside him. Together they watched the airship as it nosed slowly down, losing altitude. A grapnel trailed from the control car, tangled in the partly exposed roots of a stout bush growing on the level ground at the base of the hill, caught and held. A winch motor throbbed, and gradually the great floating shape, a thick cigar with the control gondola below it and, further aft, two engine pods, was drawn downward until the skids beneath the aircraft were just touching the leathery foliage of the bushes. A short ladder extended from the cab, and three scarlet-cloaked, scarlet-hooded figures clambered nimbly to the ground.

Linda made a growling noise deep in her throat.

"Not now, you stupid bitch!" whispered Falsen. "Not now. You'd spoil everything."

"But they are so tempting," she whined. "Little Red Riding Hoods . . ."

". . . with lethal ironmongery trained on us from inside that ship."

"That shouldn't worry *us* much. Unless . . ."

13

In single file the Doralans marched up the rough path. Their scarlet, cowled cloaks were brave splashes of color against the somber, ruddy gray of sky and swampland. Within the hoods their faces were like those of very serious little girls, although their leader's countenance was somehow more mature than those of the others, broader, with wide, sensual lips. Their bodies—what little could be seen of them—seemed human enough in outline.

"But," whispered Linda, "they could be Terrans. I always thought that the Doralans were . . . different. . . ."

"They are," said Falsen quietly. "Just a case of parallel evolution on an Earth-type planet. Take 'em apart and they *are* different. But they're near enough to human for our purposes."

The leader of the Doralans, who wore gold stars on the collar of her cloak, addressed them. Her voice was thin and high, speaking accentless Standard English.

She said, "You are from Earth?"

"Yes," agreed Falsen.

"Why are you making smoke?"

"Because we are cast away on this world and we need help."

"I already suspected that. But why are you making smoke?"

"To attract your attention, of course."

"But in the course of our survey we were bound to have investigated what appears to be a geological anomaly, the only hill within kilometers. This call for help that was not seriously required has impeded our work. You are not injured. You do not seem to be dying of starvation."

Falsen said, "I'm sorry about that."

The officer glared at him, then turned to Linda.

"Lady," she said, "I will waste no more time in conversation with this inferior being. Tell the man to follow us to the airship. You are both to be taken to the Lady Mother." Linda looked bewilderedly at Falsen.

"The Doralans," he told her, "have a sort of matriarchal setup. The Lady Mother, I suppose, is the captain of their ship."

"You suppose correctly," the Doralan officer said. "And now let us waste no more time."

•　　•　　•

Falsen followed the women down the hill to the airship. He was surprised when the Doralan gestured him first up the ladder into the control car. But he was not allowed to stay there. He was jostled up another ladder into a sort of cargo hold, a compartment that was already half full of specimens—rocks, soil, samples of plant life and something that had once been an animal of some kind and that was very dead and beginning to stink.

He hoped that Linda, riding in comparative luxury, would not be tempted to do something foolish. He knew how it must be for her, sitting in close proximity to tender-fleshed, warm-blooded beings. She had been subsisting on a diet of canned foods with all the flavor and goodness cooked out of them, but superior to the so-called crayfish that were the only alternative.

He realized that the airship was under way, pitching gently as it drove through a slight turbulence. There was a dim electric light set in one of the bulkheads of his prison, and by its light he made an inspection of the specimens.

A rock is a rock is a rock . . . he thought. *And a jar of mud is a jar of mud.* The dead animal was more interesting. It was a huge worm, all of three meters long. There seemed to be no sense organs.

The stink, he decided, wasn't too bad, was no worse than some of the more exotic cheeses. He *knew*, somehow, that the meat would be quite edible, and he was suddenly very hungry. He considered shedding his clothing as a necessary preliminary to a satisfying feast, then dismissed the thought. That would be madness. What if the airship landed and the Doralans came in to discover him as he really was?

He compromised.

He pulled the knife from his pocket, opened the blade. The tough integument of the worm resisted the keen edge, then yielded suddenly. He cut a rough cube of rubbery flesh, brought it to his mouth and chewed.

Not bad, he thought, *not bad*. It was more like real meat than that crustacean had been. Not bad, but not overly good either. Nonetheless, he cut out another cube, and another.

But wouldn't questions be asked eventually? Wouldn't the scientist or specialist officer dissecting this specimen wonder about this too regularly shaped wound in the thing's body?

The airship lurched suddenly, dipped and shuddered. There was turbulence again, more severe this time. The pile of

geological samples shifted and rattled noisily, some pieces
falling onto and around the wormlike carcass. Falsen grinned.
He found a suitably sharp-edged piece of rock, used it to
enlarge the gap that he had made, placed it so that it looked
as though it had caused all the damage.

The ship steadied, droned on.

Falsen's senses registered the change in trim as it began its
descent. The loud humming of the main engines ceased, was
replaced by the quieter, higher note of winches. There were
female voices calling and replying to orders in a language that
was unknown to him but which he assumed to be one of the
Doralan tongues.

The hatch in the deck opened and Linda called, "You can
come out now!"

He clambered down into the control cab where Linda was
waiting for him, where a couple of scarlet-uniformed Doralan
women looked at him with dislike and curiosity. He stared
out through the wide windows. The terrain here was gently
rolling, drier than the swampland from which he and Linda
had been picked up but still with pools of water gleaming in
every depression. To the east was a range of high hills. And
there was the ship, a tall spire of gray metal. A Delta-class
liner, thought Falsen, but the lettering on her hull below the
control room was the Doralan sprawling scrawl. The big ship
had started her life as a unit of the Interstellar Transport
Commission's fleet; the Doralans had no yards of their own
and most of their tonnage was Earth-built, much of it
secondhand. Many of their space officers were Earth-trained.

"I am waiting for you!" called an irritated voice from the
ground.

"Coming, Carlin!" replied Linda.

She jumped down from the control car to where the Doralan
officer was standing. Falsen followed her.

"Come," ordered Carlin. "The Lady Mother is expecting
you."

They entered the ship through the after air lock, crowded
into an elevator cage, and were rapidly lifted through level
after level, finally stopping just abaft, or below, the control
room. They left the cage, walked along a short length of
alleyway terminating in a door. On this Carlin rapped sharply.
Somebody on the other side called out something, and the

door slid open. The furniture in the cabin beyond it was designed to suit the build of its present tenant, yet this was still the captain's dayroom of a Delta-class liner. Sitting behind the big desk was one of the small women who now owned and operated the ship, dressed, as were her crew, in uniform scarlet, in a high-necked tunic that left her smooth-skinned arms bare and displayed three gold stars on each side of the collar. Her hair was short-cut, glossy green with a silver streak. Her well-defined features were lined by experience and authority, yet the mouth was kindly. Sitting on the desk, a little to her right, was a huge ginger cat, a Persian. (And what was this brute doing aboard an alien ship?) The animal got to its feet as the Terrans entered, arched its back and spat viciously.

"Pondor!" said the Lady Mother reproachfully.

The cat replied in a mewling voice, and Falsen could almost have sworn that this reply was couched in words.

Imagination, he thought.

Carlin made her report to the captain. The Lady Mother heard her story, then spoke a few words of dismissal. To the castaways she said, in Standard English, "Please be seated."

"So you speak our language, Lady Mother," said Falsen.

He lowered himself to the built-in settee, this being the article of furniture best adaptable to his greater weight and bulk. Linda sat by his side.

"Yes," said the captain. "I speak your language. In my younger days I spent some time on Earth. I underwent my initial training in your Antarctic Academy. We have our own schools now, of course, but our spacewomen still avail themselves of your educational facilities. There is always so much that is new, and we are not innovators. We have heard, for example, that there is research being carried out in the field of faster-than-light communications so that ships will be able to talk to each other over the light-years. . . ."

"We haven't got it yet," said Falsen. *Fortunately*, he thought.

He felt a sudden, sharp pain in the calf of his left leg. He looked down. That big ginger cat had inflicted a row of deep scratches, was looking at the damage it had done with smug satisfaction. With an effort Falsen restrained himself from kicking out at the brute.

"Pondor," said the captain sternly, "that is no way to treat guests."

"They don't like me . . ." Was this animal talking, actually talking? wondered Falsen wildly. "They don't like me, and I don't like them."

"They are my guests."

"They are not *my* guests."

"Go. At once. *Go*."

"Oh, all right." As the arrogant beast, tail in air, sauntered out of the day cabin, they heard one word, uttered in a tone of great contempt, *"Females!"*

"What a . . . what a charming animal," said Linda faintly. "Do you have any more like him?"

"Yes."

"But . . . talking cats," said Falsen. "Are they native to your world, Lady Mother?"

"They are now. But the original stock was Terran, introduced by the first of your ships to visit us, long before we ventured into space ourselves. Since then there have been controlled mutations, breeding for intelligence. The trouble with Pondor is that somebody once told him that on your world, in some country called Egypt, cats were once worshipped as gods."

"A very long time ago," said Falsen.

"And now we will take refreshments," said the Lady Mother.

A stewardess had come in, a typical child-faced, chubby-legged Doralan woman, clad in a scarlet tunic which came down to mid-thigh. She was carrying a large tray on which were small spouted cups and plates of tiny cakes. She set this down on the desk, bowed to the captain and left.

At the Lady Mother's invitation Falsen and Linda each helped themselves to a cup and a plate of cakes. The tea was overly sweet and flavored with something like aniseed. The cakes had almost no flavor save that of sugar. Falsen sipped and nibbled, trying to hide his lack of enthusiasm.

The Lady Mother brought a box out of a drawer in her desk, set it on the surface. She pushed a switch on its side.

"You do not mind if I take a record?" she asked.

"This is your ship, Lady Mother," said Falsen.

"Then begin," said the Doralan captain.

• • •

"We are Nicholas Falsen and Linda Veerhausen," he started. "Second officer and purser/catering officer of the Commission's *Epsilon Crucis* . . ."

The Lady Mother interrupted him. "But surely that is a Dog Star Line uniform that Miss Veerhausen is wearing."

Linda was quick on the uptake. "I used to be with the Dog Star Line, Lady Mother," she said. "*Epsilon Crucis* was my first ship in the Commission's service. Their stores department was out of uniform trimmings, so I was wearing the old ones until I could get a proper set."

"I see. Go on, please, Mr. Falsen."

"We were bound," he said, "from Earth to Caribbea with general and refrigerated cargo. It was a quiet voyage until . . . until it happened. It was on my watch. Miss Veerhausen shouldn't have been in the control room with me, but she was. I'm glad that she was. It saved her life. . . ."

He took a sip of the now cold tea to gain time. Linda filled in for him.

She whispered, in a low voice, "It was horrible. Horrible."

"Yes," he said. "It was horrible. The secondary field of the instruments in control must have saved us, but the rest of the ship . . . have you ever seen what happens when a Mannschenn Drive unit runs wild?"

"No," said the Lady Mother. "But I've read about it."

So have I, thought Falsen. *I hope that you've read the same accounts that I have.* He said, "Everybody was dead, of course. They'd aged decades in microseconds. Except for the Mannschenn duty engineer. He'd been . . . everted. I'd cut the Drive, of course, as soon as the buzzer sounded, but it was too late. I don't think that I could have been any faster. . . ." He hoped that he was conveying the impression that a tardy response to the alarm was weighing heavily on his conscience. "And then, while we were investigating, hoping that we'd find somebody who wasn't dead, the Drive started up again by itself. I managed to stop it. Then it started again. I stopped it again. We couldn't tell how long it would stay stopped so . . . so we abandoned ship."

"You abandoned ship," echoed the Lady Mother, her voice shocked. "You abandoned a huge, expensive piece of highly advanced technology for which many worlds less wealthy than your own would have been grateful. I don't suppose you remember the elements of your trajectory . . ."

Falsen said that he did not.

The Lady Mother sighed. "Perhaps that is just as well," she said. "My orders are to carry out a thorough survey of this planet with a view to future colonization. But I must confess that I find the thought of a salvage operation tempting. Talking of salvage, where is your boat? Carlin told me that the two of you were in a cave and that there was no indication of how you got there."

Falsen made what he hoped was a regretful shrug. "Unless you've special mud-dredging gear," he said, "you'll never find her. The surface on which we landed seemed solid enough; it supported our weight even while we were carrying various bits and pieces to higher ground. We left the air-lock door open, of course, and the thing just filled and sank."

The Lady Mother sighed. "Mr. Falsen," she said, "I would not wish to be in your shoes when you return to Earth. Not only have you lost a ship, you have also lost a boat— and, if I may borrow one of your Terran sayings, lifeboats don't grow on trees. But any court of enquiry is a long time in the future. I expect to remain here at least two hundred days to complete my survey. Then I must return to Dorala to make my report. And then your own people will have to make arrangements to return you to Earth. I trust that you will not mind being separated so long from your own kind."

"*I* mind," mewed a voice from near deck level. Pondor, Falsen saw, had returned. "I mind their being here, aboard our ship. Find their boat for them, Lady. Tell them to go. They are not our people. They smell. They smell wrong."

"Rubbish, cat. If you'd spent all your life aboard an Earth ship, you would say that *I* smelled all wrong."

"*You* would never smell wrong, Lady. Make them go."

"When an animal tells me that I stink," said Falsen stiffly, "it's time that I went."

"Don't pay any attention to Pondor," said the Lady Mother, smiling. "He's jealous. He's used to being the center of attention, the only male aboard the ship. Just ignore him and he'll stalk out, all outraged dignity, and cuff his wives to restore his self-esteem."

"A charming animal," said Linda.

"If I thought that you really meant that," said Pondor, "I *might* like you."

"Just how intelligent are these cats?" asked Falsen while

Pondor glared at him. "They can talk—but they could be no more than a sort of mammalian version of the parrot."

"I really don't know," admitted the Lady Mother. "Of course, they couldn't compute a trajectory or build a ship. . . ."

"My people were gods once," said Pondor haughtily. "Gods don't build ships."

"Could you make a world, then?" asked Falsen nastily.

"I don't know. I've never tried."

The Doralan captain, to judge from her changing expressions, was not sure whether to be amused or annoyed, but when the cat jumped onto her lap she made no attempt to dislodge him. The stewardess came in to collect the tea things. The Lady Mother gave her orders in her own language.

Then, to Falsen and Linda with an apologetic smile, "I think that you'd better go now. Pondor does not approve of you. Prenta here will take you to the spare cabins that have been made ready for you. You will mess with my officers, some of whom speak English. I shall see you again."

"I hope that *I* don't," muttered the cat.

CHAPTER 4

The elevator cage was somewhere in the bowels of the ship, so, with an apologetic smile, the stewardess led them down the spiral staircase that encircled the axial shaft. It had been modified to suit the Doralans; its treads were too close together for easy negotiation by Falsen and Linda. The deck to which they were taken was just below the one on which the senior officers had their quarters. The cabins were small and the furnishings might have been designed for Terran children.

Falsen explored the one that was to be his. It did not take him long. There was a bunk, on which he would be able to sleep only if he curled up like a dog. (But as he almost invariably did this anyway, it would be no great hardship.) There was a little stool that folded back into the bulkhead when not in use. There were toilet facilities. Fortunately, the Doralans saw eye-to-eye with Terrans regarding the techniques for body-waste disposal, although the pedestal was both small and low. There was no depilatory dispenser in the shower cubicle, only one for liquid detergent. He pressed the button and ejected a few drops onto the palm of his hand, sniffed. *It reeks,* he thought, *like a whore's garret.* There was a hot-air blower for drying off.

He returned to the bedroom, sat down on the bunk. The door onto the alleyway was open and he could hear Linda talking to somebody in the next cabin. He considered getting up to join them, but then thought better of it. So far aboard this ship, the only person who had not regarded him as something that the cat brought in was the Lady Mother. To all the others he was just a member of a despised sex. The Doralans would talk freely to Linda; they would not do so to him.

He pulled out the pack of cigarettes. There were three left. He took one out and lit it, looked around for an ashtray. There was none, of course. And soon, he thought, there would be no more cigarettes. He shrugged. As a man he was a slave to the habit—but he wasn't always a man. To him, in his other form, nicotine was distasteful. He smoked slowly. When the ash was long he got up, went through to the toilet and shook it off into the bowl. He returned to the bunk, sat there, listening. Although his hearing was keen, he could make out only an occasional word.

Then Carlin came out into the alleyway. He recognized her voice as she called to Linda, "Our afternoon meal will be in about sixty of your minutes. I will call for you then."

Linda came into Falsen's cabin. She fumbled briefly with the unfamiliar door fastenings, then slid the panel shut. She sat down beside him on the bunk.

"Carlin was in a talkative mood," she said. "I think that she was trying to convert me to her way of thinking. She went on and on about this big ship of theirs, a crew of a hundred, and not a single male among them. Not counting, of course, Pondor. But he hardly ranks as crew."

"A hundred . . ." said Falsen thoughtfully.

"Yes. A hundred. And we are only two. But there's the value of surprise. And misdirection."

"We have to do it," said Falsen. "We have the right to survive—or to fight for survival. How we do it—that has to be worked out." He got up and paced up and down the narrow confines of the little cabin like a caged wild beast. "We have to take the ship. They won't have changed her controls much. And I'm a navigator. There are worlds out towards the Rim that won't be colonized for generations, if at all. There'll be no real expansion until there's some kind of FTL radio. . . ."

"What sort of worlds?" she asked dubiously. "Planets like this, which would be bad enough, or with atmospheres of chlorine or fluorine or something equally toxic?"

"Some of them. But there are *good* worlds, too. Planets with rivers and forests and animals equivalent to sheep and cattle and deer. . . ."

"And lions and tigers."

"We can compete."

"You're sure that there are such worlds?"

"Of course. The Federation has colonized a few already, within spitting distance of Earth. Such as *your* home planet, Austral. And get this straight: If we stay here the balloon is bound to go up, sooner or later. We have to get somewhere where there's no explaining to do. To anybody."

The girl was not listening. She was on her feet, tense, alert, staring at the door. Suddenly she strode to it, pulled it open, pounced with the same speed as she had shown during her capture of the crayfish. Swiftly and silently she backed into the room, the thing between her hands struggling viciously, trying to cry out, succeeding in spite of the pressure on its throat in emitting a strangled squeal.

"What . . .?" began Falsen.

"Shut the door!" she snapped. "Secure it, if possible."

He obeyed.

Then he saw what it was that she had. It was a cat—not Pondor but one of his mates. Like him, it was of Persian descent, but it was black. And the Lady Mother had implied that all the cats could talk.

"This *thing*," snarled Linda, "was spying."

"Can it understand English?"

"I don't know, but I'm taking no chances. I'll make sure that it won't talk!"

Claws drew angry furrows down her face as she lifted the cat to her mouth. There was a semiarticulate cry—then a silence broken by a horrid dripping sound. Blood ran down Linda's chin and the front of her shirt.

"What do we do with the body?" asked Falsen.

"It's *meat*, isn't it?"

"But . . . the bones and the fur . . ."

"There's only one way," she said. "Watch the door, will you? We don't want one of *them* bursting in in the middle of it."

While the body of the cat, its throat torn out, bled on the deck, she stripped. Falsen did not watch her change; nobody had ever seen him do so and he hoped that nobody ever would. He stood there, facing the door. From behind him, from deck level, he heard the tearing noises, the noisy slurping, the splintering and crunching of fragile bones to an assimilable sludge.

Then he felt her hand on his shoulder.

He turned around.

There was very little blood on her, only a few smears on her chin out of reach of her tongue, other smears on her small breasts. She looked . . . sated.

She said, "I enjoyed that, although I'm wondering if I'll be able to digest the fur."

Falsen noted that there were still a few black strands caught between her teeth.

He said, "You'd better get cleaned up. Use my shower. Wash your shirt at the same time; it will dry fast enough under the blower. I'll get the mess off the deck."

"What mess?" she asked.

He looked down. The hard, polished, composition surface was clean. He remembered those slurping noises.

He said, "You won't feel like having dinner, or whatever they call their afternoon meal."

"You'll just have to eat for two," she told him, grinning.

She had just finished dressing when there was a peremptory rapping on the door. Falsen opened it. Carlin stood there, resplendent in a form-fitting, gold-trimmed scarlet tunic that left most of her plump thighs exposed, and highly polished scarlet kneeboots. Her glossy green hair fell almost to her shoulders. She looked past Falsen at Linda.

She said, "You were not in your cabin."

"I was here," said Linda.

"So I see."

Were there regulations on this ship forbidding members of opposite sexes to be together behind a closed door? Falsen wondered. He knew very little about Doralan *mores*. Presumably, a matriarchal society had its own peculiar code of conduct. He grinned inwardly. If Carlin knew what they had been doing, she would have a real cause to be shocked.

"I am to take you to mess," said Carlin. "Both of you."

As she spoke, a pleasant sound issued from the concealed speakers of the public-address system, a crystalline tinkling.

"Come," said Carlin.

They followed her along the alleyway to the spiral staircase around the axial shaft. One deck down they came to a large room that was, to the humans, more alien than anything they had so far seen aboard this ship. There were low tables, some seating four, some six, with padded benches, the upholstery of which was glossy black. Every pillar was festooned with vividly green creepers bearing both scarlet flowers and glowing golden fruit. Huge pots between the tables contained plants not unlike organ-pipe cacti—but the Terran cactus bloomed rarely. All of these plants were encrusted with tiny scarlet blossoms.

The air was warm, carried a cloying scent.

Falsen had served in Delta-class liners, tried to remember what this compartment was like in such ships. The officers' smoking room, he recalled. A bar, a couple of dart boards, card tables and other tables with electronic games, a bookcase, a playmaster, magazine racks . . . definitely a masculine ambience. Although the Interstellar Transport Commission carried female officers, they were in the minority. Here *he* was in the minority—a minority of one.

Carlin led them to a table.

Doralans, already seated, stared at them curiously and, in Falsen's case, with some hostility. He felt big, gross, clumsy. He felt no better when he was off his feet and sitting on one of the benches, facing Linda and Carlin across the polished white surface of the table. He looked down at the cutlery—stainless steel it might have been—things that combined the functions of forks and spoons, one spoon that was just that and nothing more, one small knife.

There was a decanter of some dark wine and fragile, graceful tulip glasses.

Carlin poured—for herself, for Linda, for Falsen.

She raised her glass in salute—to Linda only.

Falsen sipped.

The wine was too sweet (of course) and, like the tea that he had drunk earlier, tasted of aniseed.

"You like our wine, Falsen?" asked Carlin, at last condescending to pay some attention to him.

"Yes and no," he replied. "I rather like the strong hint of aniseed."

"Aniseed? Oh, yes. It is one of *our* herbs, *dillum.* . . ."

The first course was served, a sort of fruit salad. Linda only toyed with hers. Carlin did not attack her portion with any great enthusiasm. Neither did Falsen, although he was hungry. While they were waiting for the bowls to be removed, he tried to make conversation.

"Lady Carlin," he began, hoping that this was the right form of address, "I trust that I am not bad mannered . . ."

"I have been on Earth," she said. "I am familiar with Terran manners."

"Aboard a ship," he persisted, "uniform is worn so that people know who does what. Those stars on your collar . . . what do they signify?"

"Badges of rank, of course."

"I'd already assumed that. And as your captain, your Lady Mother, wears three six-pointed stars on each side so you, with a couple of pairs, must be what we'd call, in our ships, the chief officer. . . ."

A stewardess removed the remains of the fruit salad, another one brought oval plates, each with a slab of some pallid flesh over which a green powder had been sprinkled.

Carlin picked up one of the fork-spoons. Linda and Falsen followed suit. Carlin seemed in no great hurry to attack her portion.

She said to Falsen, "No. Chief engineer. If you look closely you will see that each of *my* stars is actually a design of three interlocked wheels with points radiating from the rim."

She dug her implement into the pale flesh, breaking off a piece. She brought it to her mouth, chewed. Linda and Falsen did likewise.

Fish, he thought. *Or something like fish*.

Carlin still seemed to have no great interest in her food, so Falsen continued the conversation.

"We all have different ways of doing things—but it seems rather odd, to me, that an engineer should be in charge of a survey party, as you were when we were picked up."

"Why?" she asked. She grinned, and her face became almost attractive. "Oh, I know that as far as you Terrans are concerned the members of the spaceman branch are the Lord's anointed, just as members of the male sex are. With *us* seniority, regardless of branch or department, is taken into account when officers are required to be in charge of extravehicular activities. Tell me, Falsen, in what way is a master astronaut's certificate of competency superior to my chief engineer's qualifications when it comes to exploring the surface of an unknown world?''

Falsen admitted that he could not answer the question.

The plates, with their almost untouched contents, were taken away. A meat course followed. It was not steak, although it could have been. It had not been ruined by overcooking.

Carlin said, ''I hope that you do not mind. The stewardesses know that this is how I like my meat. I acquired the taste while I was on Earth, doing an engineering course at your Antarctic Academy. She must have assumed that you, being Earthpeople, would also like your meat rare and almost unseasoned.''

''What is it?'' asked Falsen, chewing happily.

''It is from our tissue-culture vats. The animal itself is not unlike the Terran horse. It is both a work animal and a food animal. Perhaps I should not have told you that. There is some odd prejudice, or culinary taboo regarding horseflesh among the English-speaking peoples on Earth. . . .''

''One that doesn't worry me,'' said Falsen.

''And you, Linda?'' asked Carlin.

''I . . . I'm just not very hungry. . . .''

And it's not a matter of taboo or prejudice, thought Falsen.

''Then pass me your plate,'' said Carlin.

The meal was terminated with thin crackers and a rubbery, strong-flavored cheese. Carlin and Falsen finished what Linda left.

CHAPTER 5

After the meal there was social activity.

Carlin took Linda and Falsen down to a recreation room which was common to all ranks. The compartment was dominated by a huge playmaster, of Terran design but modified, on the screen of which a ballet was being danced to high-pitched, wailing music. All the performers seemed to be female, although two of them were wearing huge codpieces. These, Falsen decided, were the clowns, the clumsy ones who tripped over their own feet, who were tripped and buffeted by the other dancers, those in women's costumes. It was all very funny to the Doralans, and Linda allowed herself an occasional chuckle. Falsen was not amused.

It was over at last and the huge screen faded into darkness.

Then a junior officer, with only one small star on each side of her tunic collar, seated herself at the console of a synthesizer while two crewwomen stood on either side of her, facing the audience. They sang while the officer played. The music was so excruciatingly painful that Falsen felt like squatting on his haunches, lifting his head and howling. It was like a cat fight.

At last the evening's entertainment was over. Falsen and Linda joined those helping themselves to wine and little cakes from a buffet table beside which room was made for them a little too pointedly. Did he stink? Falsen wondered. Surely any body odor that he might be emitting would be drowned by the waves of perfume that eddied from the Doralans. It was a cloying scent, one that both attracted and repelled.

Leave the aniseed component and take away the rest, he thought, *and . . .*

"I will take you to your cabins," said Carlin.

She led them back up to their accommodations, left them there.

"Goodnight," said Linda.

"I thought that you might be coming in with me," said Falsen.

"I want to be alone," she told him.

"We should talk things over. . . ."

"We will sort things out in our own minds first, and then we will compare notes."

He had to be content with that.

Inside his room he stripped and then curled up on the short bunk. He fell almost immediately into a dreamless sleep.

He awoke the next morning greatly refreshed. He did not need to be called. For him, when he was on a planetary surface, the first light of day was alarm clock enough, even when he was in a metal box with no outward-looking ports or windows. He threw back the thin blanket under which he had been sleeping, swung his feet to the deck.

Before he could stand up, his door opened. A junior officer stood there, staring with unconcealed disgust at his hairy nudity.

Her command of English was not as good as Carlin's, but it was adequate. "Mister, the Lady Mother you would see. At once." Then, as a hasty afterthought, "But first you will dress."

"Then, leave me to it," said Falsen. "Wait outside, please."

He made a hasty toilet. (Captains, he knew full well, did not like to be kept waiting.) He dressed. He regretted that he had not washed his uniform before retiring, but it was too late to worry about it now. He went out into the alleyway. The young Doralan was there, looking like a little girl beside Linda.

"What's all the flap about?" Falsen asked.

Linda replied while her companion tried to work out the meaning of the idiom. "It seems," she said, "that *something* attacked and killed the sentries outside the ship last night. Not only killed them but devoured parts of the bodies. . . ."

He looked at her suspiciously. She had wanted to be alone, hadn't she? But . . .

"Come," said the officer.

She escorted them to the elevator, up to the captain's day cabin. The Lady Mother was waiting for them, seated behind her big desk, on the surface of which sat Pondor. The animal spat a curse at them as they entered. Carlin was there, and two other officers of two-star grade.

"Miss Veerhausen," said the captain, "Mr. Falsen. Be seated, please." They lowered themselves to very low chairs. "I hope that you will be able to help us."

"In what way, Gracious Lady?" asked Falsen.

"The initial landing on this world was made by your Survey Service. Their reports were passed over to us by the Federation when it was agreed that we were free to colonize it. But in those reports there is no mention of dangerous animals. First surveys, I know, are often far too sketchy. But you have spent some time on this planet. You had no machines with you to scare away indigenous life forms, no bright lights at night. Did you see anything, hear anything?"

While Falsen hesitated, pondering his reply, Linda spoke up.

"Some nights," she said, "we heard something howling. And just once, early one morning, we saw something big and gray slinking away from outside our cave. After that we made sure that we kept our fire going. . . ."

The cat said, in his mewling voice, "I have explored all around the ship and I have not seen or smelled anything. Until this morning. And now the stink hangs heavy, even in here."

"That animal of yours has a strong imagination, Gracious Lady," said Carlin.

"Imagination or not," snapped the Lady Mother, "there was *something*. Something big and horridly vicious. I have seen the bodies. You have seen them, Lady Carlin. How they were mutilated. Partly eaten. . . ."

"Eaten. . . ." echoed Falsen.

"Yes, Mr. Falsen. Teeth must have been its main weapon, perhaps its only weapon. But the really frightening part of it is that it must have been immune to the fire of my people's lasers. We have checked the power cells; some of them were almost exhausted. Any normal animal would have been incinerated. Was this thing that you saw armored?''

"It seemed to have a scaly hide," said Linda.

The Doralan captain addressed Falsen. "I ask your advice," she said. "On Earth there are still large tracts of wild forest, of jungle, where men and women go to hunt, to kill large, dangerous beasts. We have nothing of that kind on Dorala. Our world was thoroughly tamed generations ago. The only surviving predators are no bigger than Pondor. We have no experience of the hunt. Perhaps you have.''

"I have," said Falsen. On one long leave he had been persuaded to take part in a tiger hunt in Bengal. His sympathies had been with the tiger.

"What do you advise?" asked the captain.

"What steps have you taken so far?" he inquired.

"I have sent the airship out to search the area. Should anything be sighted, I shall be informed at once.''

"That might help," said Falsen. Then, an idea germinating in his mind, "But the best way to track any kind of game is on foot. Aircraft just drive them to cover.''

"Would you be willing to lead a tracking party, Mr. Falsen?''

"Yes," he said.

"How big a team will you require?''

"Six," he said. "Preferably English-speakers. Armed, of course.''

"But what with, Mr. Falsen? The things seem to be immune to laser fire. Stunguns might be more effective . . .''

"Laser pistols *and* stunguns, perhaps," said Falsen. "And even a heavily armored beast has some weak points. The open mouth, the eyes, the soft skin at the joints of the armor . . .''

"You are the expert. I hope. Lady Carlin, please take Mr. Falsen and Miss Veerhausen down to the officers' mess so that they may break their fast before they leave the ship. And then assemble five suitable persons to accompany you and our . . . Terran experts.''

CHAPTER 6

Breakfast, in the almost deserted officers' mess, was an unsatisfying meal, a sweetish mush accompanied by aniseed-flavored tea. After it Linda and Falsen went to their quarters to discuss their course of action.

He said, "We'll try that range of hills. There are bound to be caves there. And where there are caves you might find . . . anything."

She laughed. "Yes," she said. "They found us in a cave, didn't they?"

He went to the door of his cabin, opened it, looked up and down the alleyway. There were no signs of life. He returned inside and shut the door.

He demanded, "What do *you* know?"

"Nothing," she said innocently.

"You slept alone last night," he said.

"So did you."

"I *slept*."

"You weren't the only one."

He said, "We must be careful. All right. We want this ship. We *need* this ship. As long as there are no engine breakdowns we can take her anywhere, just the two of us. But get this straight: I want to take her with the minimum of bloodshed. These people are human, even though they aren't our sort of human. They aren't animals, like that cat."

"Aren't they?"

"They're *people*," he insisted.

"There's somebody outside," she said.

33

It was Carlin. She was dressed for extravehicular activity, with a scarlet, hooded cloak over her tunic. The cloak fell open as she moved and revealed a shiny black belt with two shiny black holsters from which protruded the butts of weapons. She was carrying two other belts with holsters attached.

She said, "The guns you asked for."

She handed one belt to Linda, the other to Falsen.

Linda said, "These are no use to me. I can't use them. I was never trained."

"Just point at what you want to kill or stun and pull the trigger. The pistol with the red butt is the laser, the one with the black butt is the stungun."

Falsen buckled on his belt, then pulled the weapons out of their holsters and examined them. He held a reserve officer's commission in the Federation Survey Service and had taken small-arms training courses. Both laser pistol and stungun, he discovered, were of Terran manufacture, types with which he was familiar. He reholstered them. Linda disdainfully threw her belt onto Falsen's bunk, left it there.

"As you please," said Carlin coldly. "Come."

The man and the girl followed her into the alleyway, to the axial shaft and the elevator which carried them swiftly down to the after air lock. The Lady Mother was awaiting them there. At the bottom of the ramp were the other five members of the hunting party, timid-looking little girls in their scarlet cloaks and hoods. Two were junior officers with very small silver stars on their collars. The others, with no badges of rank, appeared to be enlisted women. There were other officers who, like the Doralan captain, were wearing only their tunics.

The Lady Mother asked, "What first, Mr. Falsen?"

"I'd like to examine the scene of the . . . killings," he said. He had almost referred to it as "the scene of the crime."

The Doralan captain stood aside so that they were first down the ramp. So the old rule held good even aboard this alien ship, Falsen thought. The commanding officer first aboard, last ashore. *Damn it*, he told himself, *these people are spacemen—or spacepersons. They're my breed of cat. It's all very well for Linda to think as she does, but she's only a tabby, not a real officer. . . .*

He stepped from the foot of the ramp onto the spongy,

mosslike ground cover, waited with Carlin and Linda for the Lady Mother to join them. She descended slowly and gracefully.

She said, "*They* came as far as this. Perhaps they wanted to get into the ship, but they must have been unwilling to set their paws onto the cold metal. But you can see where they rolled on the ground, the scuff marks and the smears of blood that must have rubbed off their bodies. *Doralan* blood, my surgeon assures me. Their victims' blood."

"Why do you say 'they'?" asked Falsen.

"There were at least two of them. There are, of course, the marks of teeth on the bodies of my people—and one of the things had smaller jaws than its mate, or mates." She walked slowly away from the ship. "Here," she said, "is where we found the bodies. They have been taken into the ship, of course, for autopsy, although the cause of death is obvious enough. As you see, there was considerable bleeding, also a struggle. Look where the . . . the . . . moss, would you call it? has been torn up."

Falsen looked around.

He said, "They must have attacked from that clump of shrubs. Have you looked there?"

"Of course."

A mewling voice broke into the conversation. Falsen looked down, saw that it came from Pondor. The big cat was addressing the Lady Mother in her own language. She replied to the animal briefly.

She said to the man, "He wants to know if anybody has seen Kristit—one of his two . . . wives." She smiled briefly and ruefully. "I am afraid that I was rather short with him."

"I feel sorry for Pondor," said Linda. "He must feel the loss as deeply as any of us would feel the loss of a mate."

"The *loss*?" asked Carlin sharply. "This is a big ship—or hadn't you noticed? A small animal, such as a cat, could be sleeping anywhere, out of sight."

"I just assumed," said Linda, "that whatever killed the sentries also killed the cat. After all, she'd have been little more than one mouthful, bones and all. . . ."

Falsen recalled the crunching sounds that he had heard when the body of Kristit was being disposed of.

Meanwhile, squatting on her haunches, Linda was examining the low shrubs, the clump of drab vegetation with its thin branches and broad, leathery leaves. She seemed almost to be sniffing the ground around the bushes.

She straightened up and pointed toward the low range of distant hills, crying, "They went that way!"

The Lady Mother asked, "How do you know?"

"See," said Linda, "how the tendrils of this mossy stuff have been disturbed. . . ."

Falsen looked, not really expecting to see anything. He did not. The Lady Mother looked, then said doubtfully that she *thought* that she saw the trail indicated by the girl. Carlin looked and remarked superciliously that, of course, Terrans were much closer to the animal than were Doralans. Falsen, lying, said that the trail was as easy to read as a tridi chart.

So they followed this doubtful trail, Linda in the lead, then Carlin and Falsen, then the other five members of the party. The Lady Mother, standing at the foot of the ramp, watched them go. She would still be there, thought Falsen, when they returned, anxious to learn that vengeance had overtaken the thing or things that had murdered her people.

But animals didn't murder. Not ordinary animals.

Overhead sailed the airship, its propellers throbbing.

"Tell that bloody thing to go away," Falsen said to Carlin. "If the things are lurking anywhere around, it will scare them off."

Carlin raised her left wrist—the one with the transceiver strapped to it—to her mouth, gave curt orders. The reply was faint but audible. The airship turned slowly, headed back toward the space vessel.

Linda was squatting again, was actually down on her hands and knees. She lifted her head and announced, "They traveled in a straight line. And fast."

"I don't know how you can tell all that," said Carlin in a tone of mock admiration.

The sun, a vague, ruddy ball of light in the thinly overcast sky, rose higher, drawing a steamy moisture, a stench of decay, from the shallow stagnant pools that filled every depression in the terrain. A diversion was caused by something that splashed loudly over to the left of the party. Three of the Doralans ran to investigate. There was a flash and an eruption of dirty steam as a laser pistol opened fire. But the target was only one of the crustaceans, a huge beast, its body almost a metre in diameter. It had been cooked as well as killed. Falsen called a halt for lunch.

With the exception of Carlin, the Doralans nibbled little sweet cakes that they brought out from their packs. The engineer helped Falsen and Linda dispose of the crayfish. The flesh was stringy but quite flavorsome.

After they had eaten, the party pressed on. The ground rose gradually, became drier. Even the air seemed drier. Here and there bare rock, veined with glittering seams, showed through the gray, spongy, mosslike growth. Once something small and lizardlike scurried from one stunted bush to another. Carlin fired her stungun at it, but missed.

"A pity," said Falsen. "It might be a small relation of the big things that did the killings."

"It might be," said the Doralan.

The party pressed on. Now and again they had to climb from ledge to rocky ledge. The Doralans, Falsen thought, had to be hot inside those cloaks of theirs. The faces of most of them were shiny with perspiration. Carlin's was not. She was sweating no more than were Linda and Falsen, in their light shorts and shirts.

Then—"There!" cried Linda. "They went in there!"

There was a narrow opening between two boulders, an opening that, by its very darkness, gave promise of depths beyond and below.

He said to Carlin, "You brought lights, I suppose?"

She said, "You're the self-appointed expert. You never said that we would need them."

He sighed. Then, "We shall just have to use the laser pistols," he said. "On low intensity."

Carlin said to Linda, "You should have brought yours, shouldn't you?" She scowled at Falsen, remarked cattily, "I seem to remember that you expressed surprise that I, a mere engineer, should be in charge of an exploring party. And now that you, a member of the Lord's Anointed, are in charge of one, you have given evidence of your lack of forethought."

"Call the ship," Falsen told her. "Tell the Lady Mother that we're going into a cave. Not all of us. Two of your people will wait outside so they can scream for help if we don't come out after a reasonable length of time. Unless, of course, your radios can punch their signals through tonnes of earth and rock.''

''As a matter of fact,'' she said, ''they can. In some respects our technology is superior to yours.''

She spoke briefly into her transceiver, listened to the acknowledgement. She said, her voice hostile, ''The Lady Mother impressed upon me that you are still in charge.''

''Then, come on,'' ordered Falsen. ''Follow me.''

He pulled his laser pistol from its holster, set it to wide beam and low intensity, pressed and locked the trigger. Even out here, in the diffuse sunlight, the radiance reflected from the rock was almost dazzling. He squeezed his body between the boulders. Where he could go the Doralans would have no trouble following, neither would Linda. There was a little more room inside the cave, but his body blocked the descending tunnel from the view of those behind him. There was a sparse covering of sand on the rocky floor. As he had done in Linda's cave, he wondered what the geological and meteorological past of this world could have been.

He called, ''You're right, Linda. They came this way.''

''Let me see!'' cried Carlin. Then, ''You clumsy male control-room ornament! Your big feet are obliterating the tracks!''

''It was something with claws,'' said Falsen.

The tunnel widened and took an upward turn. There was no more sand, only bare rock. Then it plunged downward again, steeply. Falsen kept in the lead, the beam of his laser pistol giving him ample warning of irregularities on the floor. It was not a straight way down. There were turnings, some of them almost at right angles. But still the direction was down, down.

The air, to Falsen's nostrils, smelled dry—dry and sterile. It was not the sterility of long-ago death but a sterility that had never known life. But he said nothing. Linda had led the party here, and all that he could do was play along with her. Some extra sense told him of the girl's mounting excitement, of the eager anticipation of a hunter with the kill almost within sight. *An extra sense?* Of that he was not quite sure. Perhaps it was only that his other senses were keen enough to appreciate her quickened breathing, the subtle change in her scent, just as the same senses brought him evidence of the fear—a

fear that was kept well down, well under control, but still
fear—of the Doralans.

But Carlin's distinctive odor was unchanged.

He turned, at last, the last corner.

His laser beam suddenly impinged upon something smooth
and gleaming, something that reflected the light like a huge
black mirror. Falsen hurried forward. There was sand here
again, and his feet destroyed the long, undisturbed smooth-
ness of the surface. (If there had been tracks they would have
been obliterated.) He directed his laser up, around. They had
come, he saw, into a huge cavern, a vast, subterranean hall
that was almost filled, at floor level, by the glassy waters of a
lake. Only here, where he had emerged from the tunnel, was
there any beach. Only directly opposite was there any other
way for anything to emerge from the water onto dry land;
there was a shelving rock ledge, the rim of it submerged. In
the gray but glittering rock wall beyond were the mouths of
two smaller caves or tunnels.

"They must have crossed the water," said Falsen.

"If you say so," said Carlin. "You've destroyed what
tracks there were."

"We shall have to cross," Linda said. "It looks deep."

"There are two tunnels there," said Carlin. "Which one?"

"The one to the right," murmured Linda. "Yes. That
one."

"Why?" demanded Carlin. "I'm beginning to wonder just
what special senses you people have got."

"Just what came with the lease," said Falsen.

"Nick," said Linda. "I'm going across. Carlin, I shall
want four of your people with me."

"You're not armed," Carlin told her.

"But your people are. I suppose that their weapons are
waterproof?"

"Of course they are!"

Then the Doralan officer snapped orders in her own language,
in a bad tempered voice.

CHAPTER 7

Four women—a junior officer and three of the enlisted people—
reluctantly removed their cloaks and their boots, even more
reluctantly pulled off their tunics and stepped out of their
brief underwear. It was not prudery that inhibited them,
Falsen sensed. It was just that they were scared, badly scared.

They stood there, shivering, in the harsh light of the lasers.
Their bodies were pale, fragile. They were almost breastless,
and at their pudenda was only a faint shadow of down. Carlin
gave another sharp order and they picked up their belts and
fastened them about their slender waists. The stunguns were,
of course, still in their holsters. They switched off and holstered
their laser pistols. Held by Carlin, Falsen and the other junior
officer, they would afford ample light for their passage across
the lake.

Linda stripped.

She looked far from fragile. Her breasts were not large by
Terran standards, but compared to the Doralans she was a
refugee from one of the cruder girlie magazines so popular
among spacemen. At the base of her belly was a veritable
dark-foliaged forest.

She said, "Come *on*."

She waded into the black water—to knee level, to thigh
level, then fell forward with a splash and began to swim. The
junior officer followed her, squealing at the first shock. She
turned a protesting face to Carlin, to Falsen. She whimpered,
in English, "It is *cold* . . ."

Carlin snarled something in her own language. The girl

replied briefly and then set off after Linda, moving sinuously and almost silently across the lake. The three enlisted women followed her.

Linda reached the far side. She waded up the shelving ledge to dry rock. She turned and stood there, her body whitely luminous in the laser glare against the dark cavern wall. The Doralans joined her, unholstered the weapons that served as torches. Linda turned again, dropped to her hands and knees, made an examination of the rock surface. She straightened up, made a beckoning gesture, set off for the tunnel mouth. The other women, their laser pistols switched on, followed her. The glare faded to a glow as they negotiated a curve, a corner. It died out.

Falsen said to Carlin, "I wonder what they'll find."

"Nothing!" snapped Carlin. "What is that expression you use? A wild-goose chase? That is what you have led us on."

"I am trying to help," said Falsen virtuously. "We have another saying that you may have heard. Don't look a gift horse in the mouth."

"Horses aren't the only animals with teeth," she said.

It was both what she said and the way she said it that disturbed Falsen. He was trying to think of a suitable reply when there was a sudden ruddy glare from the tunnel entrance. Somebody must be using a laser at full intensity. There was a crackling of rock shattering under the influence of extreme heat. There was screaming. The light died, the crackling noise ceased, but the screaming went on.

But not for long.

There was silence, briefly.

Then something was howling, a horrifying ululation that was not human, that echoed from the rocky walls, that seemed to be amplified rather than diminished with each reverberation.

The silence fell like a blow.

Falsen stripped, flinging his garments from him. He entered the water in a shallow dive, gasped as the icy chill of it shocked his skin. Something passed him, going like a torpedo. It was Carlin. Then the light from behind dimmed, flickered but did not go out, wavered up ahead and to both sides. The other Doralan, the junior officer, must be coming after them, he thought, swimming with the switched-on laser pistol in one hand.

Carlin reached the shelving ledge, stood up and waded

ashore, ran for the tunnel mouth, laser pistol in hand. Falsen
hit bottom, scrambled after her, the junior officer close behind.
Carlin vanished into the dark opening. Suddenly she screamed—
and it signified fury rather than fear. There was the reflected
glare of her weapon being used to kill rather than to illuminate.
She screamed again, viciously, and something was snarling.
Staggering backward, Carlin reappeared in the tunnel mouth.
There was a shower of molten rock and red-hot fragments as
the laser beam raked across the roof of it. She fell, blundering
into Falsen and the other Doralan, tripping them, dropping
her gun which, fortunately, was directed only at the rock wall
which glowed and splintered.

And there was something else bursting from the tunnel,
something huge and darkly gray and hairy, something whose
eyes gleamed green and evil in the reflected light. Its yellowish,
bloodstained teeth were suddenly at the throat of the junior
officer. She had no time even to scream.

Falsen fought the thing, pulling it off the body of its
victim. He got his fingers into the shaggy mane, his legs
around its body. Briefly they rolled on the hard, smooth rock;
and then it broke away, ran back into the tunnel. Falsen
followed, stepping on Carlin's supine body. He heard the
breath expelled from her lungs in a loud gasp. She would be
in no condition, he realized, to come after him.

Once he was round the corner just inside the entrance,
there was no light. Falsen found his way surefootedly, only
occasionally putting out a hand to steady himself against the
rock wall. The odor of freshly spilled blood was heavy in the
air, as was the acridity of scorched and fused rock. His bare
foot struck something hard and metallic. He picked it up. It
was a laser pistol dropped by one of the Doralans. Working
by feel, he made sure that the selector switch was on a safe
setting, then turned it on.

In the harsh glare he saw the bodies.

The crewwomen were dead. No close examination was
necessary; they were too close to being human, Falsen knew,
to live with their throats torn out. Linda was there. There was
blood on her face and her pale body. She blinked at the bright
light.

She said in a matter of fact voice, "It's you. Where's
Carlin?"

"She won't be following until she gets her breath back."

"So there's time . . ." she said.

"Yes. You must have been injured in the fight. . . ."

She laughed. "But I heal quick. Better put the light out, in case *she* comes. . . ."

He switched off the laser.

There was a little cry of pain from the girl, then, "Couldn't you have been gentler?"

"I could," said Falsen, his voice muffled, distorted, "but this has to look convincing. . . ."

He turned the light on again.

"She's coming now," said Linda.

Together they listened to the whisper of bare feet on the rocky floor. They saw Carlin round the bend in the tunnel. She was staggering slightly. She stared at the bodies of her women, whispered something in her own language. Then she looked at Linda.

She said, "You are wounded . . ."

Linda put a hand to the gaping wound on her left shoulder.

"It is only a scratch," she said valiantly.

"Only a scratch? It, whatever it is, nearly bit your arm off. Which way did it go?"

"Deeper into the tunnel," said Falsen. "Feel like following it?"

"No. We were lucky. We'd better stay that way. Can you walk, Linda? Can you swim?"

"With some help," she said.

And Carlin too had been injured, Falsen saw. There were scratch marks on her white belly, on one of her breasts. But unless they became infected, they were not serious.

She said, "Let's get out of here. It may come back. But first I must report to the ship." She spoke at some length into her wrist transceiver in her own language. Falsen could hear the questions and comments from the other end, recognized the Lady Mother's voice. Then Carlin told Linda and Falsen, "They are sending the airship for us, and a party to collect the . . . bodies. We will wait for them outside the cave."

The three of them, Carlin in the lead, Falsen supporting Linda, made their way through the tunnel, back to the shore of the subterranean lake. They waded out into the cold water, let their bodies fall forward and began to swim. Linda said that she would be able to manage by herself, but Falsen stayed by her side all the way across. On the other side they found a first-aid kit in one of the packs left with the clothing. Antiseptic was applied to the women's wounds, then syntheskin. The cloaks of those who would no longer need them were used as towels to dry off the bodies of the survivors.

After they had dressed they entered the passage back to the outside world.

When they emerged onto the hillside they found that the sun was not far from setting. A damp chill was in the air and a low mist was hanging over every pool and little lake. The airship was approaching, heading straight for them, the grapnels already dangling on their lines. It slowed down as it drew near, stopped when it was almost overhead, its momentum killed by reverse thrust.

Carlin caught one of the grapnels, wedged its prongs securely under a boulder. Falsen followed her example. Then the thing was winching itself down until the skids under the gondola were almost in contact with the ground. A ladder was thrown out and half a dozen Doralans clambered down. They were armed and were carrying portable lights. There were also long bundles that, thought Falsen, must be stretchers.

"You will wait here, both of you," Carlin snapped to Falsen when he made as though to enter the cave.

"You may need an extra gun," said Falsen.

"You are our guests," the Doralan officer said. "You have risked too much already and Linda has been injured. Wait here."

Then she and her party, one by one, negotiated the narrow entrance of the tunnel and vanished.

Falsen and Linda did not talk much while they waited for the reemergence of the Doralans. With the setting of the sun, the air became very cold and they decided that it would be warmer inside the ship. Falsen climbed the short ladder to the control cabin, found that the door at the top of it was firmly shut. He hammered at it with his fist. There was somebody inside the car, more than one person. He could hear conversation, the sound of voices that ceased briefly as he beat on the sliding panel, that resumed almost at once.

"Let me in!" he shouted. "Let me in!"

Faintly, through the thin metal, came the reply, "The Lady Carlin says not."

"It is cold out here," he called.

"The Lady Carlin said that you are to wait outside."

It was useless to argue.

Falsen dropped to the ground, rejoined Linda. They found a cranny between two tall rocks, huddled together. There was some protection from the thin breeze that had arisen, and they derived warmth from each other's bodies.

But it seemed a very long wait before Carlin and her party returned to the surface. There had been five bodies to carry and there were only three stretchers.

CHAPTER 8

Falsen said to Carlin, "I shall complain to the Lady Mother. She said that I was to be in charge of the hunting party. But you not only took over but forced Miss Veerhausen and myself to wait here, on the hillside, almost freezing to death. We were denied admittance into the airship, on *your* orders."

"There must have been some misunderstanding," Carlin said. "Some misinterpretation of what I told the pilot. As to the question of who is or is not in charge, *I* am. When I reported the killings to the Lady Mother she told me that I was, from that moment, fully responsible."

"For the killings?" asked Falsen nastily.

"No. For seeing that there are no *more* killings."

It made sense, Falsen admitted to himself. After all, he was the outsider, the alien. Not only was he a member of a different species but also of the wrong sex. The Lady Mother, familiar with Terran mores, had been prepared to overlook this. Her officers, none of whom had spent as much time on Earth as had their captain, were far less tolerant. Linda they would accept as a sister, but Falsen, a dominant male in his own culture, was a potential enemy.

"Can we go on board now?" asked Falsen.

"You may, but wait until the bodies and the equipment have been loaded."

Water ballast splashed down to the ground as the extra weight was taken aboard the ship. One by one the mutilated bodies, wrapped in their red cloaks, were passed up to the now open door, then the weapons and the portable lights. The

Doralans clambered up the ladder, followed by Linda who, in spite of her injured shoulder, managed without assistance. Falsen climbed after her. Carlin was last.

This time Falsen was allowed to stay in the control car, although the Doralans carefully avoided contact with him. He watched with interest as tugs on the tripping lines caused the arms of the grapnels to drop, releasing their hold on the soil. The airship lifted slowly, turned until the space vessel, brightly illuminated, a shining tower in the deepening dusk, came directly ahead, a glowing beacon in the milky sea that was the ground mist. The hum of the motors rose to a whine as speed was increased.

Accompanied by Linda and Falsen, Carlin reported at once to the Lady Mother who, with senior officers, listened to their stories.

When they had finished she said, "You said that you saw a beast slinking outside your cave, Linda, and that you thought that it had a scaly armor. But this thing that you fought today was, you tell me, hairy or furry. I find it hard to understand that it was not killed by laser fire. Heavy scales would afford some protection to their owner; a hairy skin would not."

Linda said, "Your people who were with me were using their laser pistols more as torches than as weapons. They were slow in switching from an illuminating to a lethal beam. Then their fire was wild. They *might* have hit the beast—but if they did it was nowhere vital."

"And you, Carlin?" asked Lady Mother. "*You* shot at it. Did you hit it?"

"I don't think so, Gracious Lady. It was on us before we were ready for it. It was fast. Very fast, and vicious."

"And hungry," said an officer who wore what looked like crossed swords on the collar of her tunic. "I have made a preliminary autopsy." (Those crossed swords, Falsen decided, had to be the Doralan equivalent of scalpels.) "A large portion of Dorilee's left buttock was missing. There were toothmarks around the wound. Marla's right breast was gone, exposing the ribs. . . ."

"So," said the Lady Mother at last, "it is obvious that there are dangerous predators on this planet. I find it hard to believe, Mr. Falsen, that your Survey Service did not know of the existence of such animals. But why were we not warned? After all, your government knew that Dorala planned a landing and an exploration. . . ."

"I'm only a humble second mate," Falsen said. "Government departments operate far above the level which I inhabit."

"Even captains," said the Lady Mother, "are told only what their employers, private shipowners or boards of admiralty think that they should know. I am inclined to believe that the fault lies not with your people but with mine. I know of instances . . . but no matter."

"I still think, Gracious Lady," said a sour-faced Doralan who seemed to be the spaceship's chief officer, "that this is an example of Terran perfidy."

"I know that you did not enjoy your training period at the Antarctic Academy on Earth, Prenta," said the captain mildly.

"I did not, Gracious Lady. But let us the facts examine. Earth ceded this planet to Dorala—and since when has Earth been in the habit of making gifts that are free and not with strings attached? In this there must, somewhere, be a catch." Obviously, much as she disliked Earth, she was proud of her command of Terran idiom.

"What do you mean, Prenta?" asked the Lady Mother.

"The presence of the Terrans on this world has not been explained properly. In the chain are weak links. How long was it, they have said, since they abandoned their ship? Many days. And yet, when we them found, Falsen had no beard— and we all know how disgustingly hairy Terran males are when they do not depilate their faces. But Falsen only now has begun to produce a facial growth."

"Prenta," said the captain, "you are being insulting. Miss Veerhausen and Mr. Falsen have risked their lives in our service. I myself have seen the wounds sustained by Miss Veerhausen. I am sure that Mr. Falsen will be able to explain why he is only now growing a beard."

"I can, Gracious Lady," said Falsen. "There was a tube of depilatory cream in the boat's stores. It was finished the day before you found us."

"So you see, Prenta, that there is an explanation. And if you wish, Mr. Falsen, my pharmacist will make up some depilatory for you."

"Thank you, Gracious Lady," said Falsen, rubbing a hand over his bristly cheeks.

"There are still unsolved mysteries," said Prenta sullenly.

"There is the odd vanishment of Kristit. Pondor is *your* pet; I am surprised that you are not more concerned about the melting into thin air of his mate."

"But there is no mystery, Prenta," said the captain. "Whatever it was that attacked our people and killed them, that also attacked Miss Veerhausen and Mr. Falsen, could have swallowed a cat in one gulp. But there *are* some mysteries. There are questions that *you* may be able to answer.

"Last night Canda and Weltin were among those killed. According to the watch list that you made up, they should have been on duty inside the ship."

"That is correct, Gracious Lady."

"Then, why were their bodies found outside?"

"The only thing that I can suggest, Gracious Lady, is that they became aware, as they should have been, of the commotion outside and rushed down the ramp to try to rescue their sisters."

"Without sounding the alarm?"

"That is a question, Lady Mother, to which I fear we never shall the answer know. All watchkeepers have written instructions, signed by yourself, to the effect that all hands must be roused at once at the first sign of anything suspicious. Canda and Weltin must have disregarded those instructions. Unfortunately, we cannot deal with them as they deserve."

"They have been punished," said the captain slowly, "with far greater severity than their offense deserved. But note this. As and from tonight, there will be no watches kept outside. The air-lock door will remain shut. You will see to it, Prenta, that searchlights are rigged to cover all the surrounding terrain, as well as infrared detectors and bio-sensitive radar scanners. It should be possible to keep an efficient lookout from the control room. And . . ." She looked around her day cabin. Then, "Pondor!" she called.

The big cat came in from the bedroom, glared at Falsen and Linda and—Falsen thought—at some of the Doralan officers.

"You want me, mistress?" he mewed.

"Yes. You are to cease being a passenger on this ship. You must help to ensure the safety of all aboard her. You, with your mate Tilsin, will prowl all night, through every alleyway, every compartment. It is possible that your senses might detect some danger beyond the range of our own."

"Then will you see to it, mistress, that saucers of food and drink are left out for us? It will be a long, hungry night. . . ."

You said it, cat, thought Falsen.

He asked, "And can *we* help, Gracious Lady?"

"Why not, Mr. Falsen? We are all in the same boat." She glanced quizzically at her chief officer as though to say, *You aren't the only one with a command of English idioms.* "Hold yourself in readiness, as we all must do. When—if—the balloon goes up, you must help us to shoot it down."

Prenta looked at the Lady Mother sourly. She did not like, thought Falsen, having a leaf taken from *her* book.

CHAPTER 9

As they left the Lady Mother's quarters Carlin said to Falsen and Linda, "Come with me. We will take supper and enjoy a talk in my cabin."

"This is an honor, Lady Carlin," said Falsen ironically.

"It is," she agreed. "But come."

They followed her to her accommodation, one deck down from the captain's quarters. She had a day cabin and a bedroom. The former was furnished with a low settee, a huge, overstuffed armchair and a coffee table. There was also a severe-looking desk with a hard, straight-backed chair—but as this seemed to be a social occasion, these were not to be used. There were holograms on the bulkheads, bright windows looking out on Dorala, on a city whose lofty towers were dwarfed by the tall trees growing among them, on a snowcapped mountain in silhouette against a clear, blue-green sky, on a cave village, every door of which was surrounded by an elaborate design carved out of the red rock of the cliff face.

"Be seated," said Carlin, waving them to the settee.

She went to a liquor cabinet, opened it, did things with glasses and bottles and ice cubes.

She said, handing each of them a moisture-bedewed tumbler, "You will like this. I acquired the taste when I did my Mannschenn course at your Antarctic Academy. It was, I believe, a traditional drink in one of your surface navies generations ago." She curled up in the big chair, looked at them over the rim of her own glass. "Down the hatch," she said.

Falsen sipped. It was pink gin—not his own favorite, but one that he did not actively dislike. Linda sipped, her face expressionless.

Suddenly Carlin asked, "What do you know about the Mannschenn Drive, Falsen?"

Before he could answer, one of the stewardesses came in, carrying a tray on which was a dish of sandwiches. They looked to be composed of more meat than bread, must have been constructed to Carlin's taste. And to his own, thought Falsen. And to Linda's.

The stewardess put the tray down on the coffee table and left.

Carlin picked up a sandwich, snapped at it rather than nibbled it.

She repeated, through a full mouth, "What do you know about the Mannschenn Drive, Falsen?"

"Not much," he said shortly. "I'm not an engineer."

"But you're a navigator. And I believe that in your space services engineering knowledge is one of the subjects required when you are qualifying for your Master Astronaut certificate."

Falsen nibbled a sandwich. It wasn't at all bad. Linda held one in her hand but had yet to bring it to her mouth. She wasn't hungry, thought the Earthman.

He swallowed the chewed meat, then said, "Yes, Lady Carlin. I got a pass in engineering knowledge as well as all the other subjects. I can tighten a nut or change a fuse with the best of them. But the Mannschenn Drive? It's best left severely alone by those who aren't qualified to tinker with it."

"I would just hate," said Carlin, "to let the control-room ornaments in this ship get their clumsy paws onto *my* drive."

She bolted a sandwich, washed it down with gin.

"More?" she asked, getting up to go to the liquor cabinet.

"No, thank you, Lady Carlin," said Falsen. "But I'll take another of these sandwiches."

"Go ahead. And you, Linda?"

"No, thank you."

Her glass, Falsen saw, was still almost full.

"So you're quite typical of your breed, Falsen," said

Carlin as she reseated herself. "All that the Drive is, as far as you're concerned, is a device that enables the ship to go astern in time, while going ahead in space, so that you get faster-than-light speeds by cheating, as it were."

"You can put it that way."

"But even you must have learned something when the Mannschenn Drive aboard your ship went out of control. Just what *did* happen?"

"What you, as a qualified Mannschenn Drive engineer, would expect." He hoped that his memories of what he had read of past disasters was accurate. "Some of the clocks were running backwards. Perspective was distorted and the colors of everything were . . . wrong. Why do you ask?"

"I'm naturally curious. After all, such a thing might happen to this ship. Especially with the Mark IV unit. I've heard that it's being taken out of your ships and being replaced by the Mark V as these become available. Would you know why?"

"I wouldn't," lied Falsen.

"Did *your* ship have a Mark IV?" asked Carlin.

"No," said Falsen. It was another lie.

"But as far as I can gather from your story, the temporal-precession field must have built up to a dangerous level. Was anybody . . . changed?"

"Some of the very unlucky ones were everted," Falsen told her. (That was something that he had never seen, only read about.) "And there was the onset of senility in seconds."

He was becoming increasingly uncomfortable and knew that Linda was, too. It was more than the psychological unease induced by Carlin's persistent questioning. (After all, it was only natural that a spaceperson should be curious about a disaster that had befallen somebody else's ship, should be anxious to work out ways and means to ensure that a like calamity should not occur on board her own.) It was the increasingly strong odor in the cabin that was making Falsen's hackles rise, that made him want to bare his teeth and snarl, that aroused the urge to attack, to kill. He glanced sideways at Linda. She was close to the snapping point; he could tell by the tenseness of the line of her jaw, by the overly taut skin over her cheekbones, by the subtle shifting of integument and muscle that he could feel through the thin shirt when he laid his hand lightly on her shoulder.

Down, boy, down! he thought to himself.

Down, you bitch, down! he thought at Linda.

He said, "You must excuse us, Lady Carlin. We are very tired after the day's exertions. And during our time in the cave, after our landing, we lost our tolerance to alcohol. . . ."

"As you please," Carlin said.

"Thank you for your hospitality," said Falsen, getting to his feet.

"The pleasure was mine," said Carlin with obvious insincerity.

She did not get up to see them out of her cabin.

Outside in the alleyway, the door shut behind them, Linda said, "Phew! I couldn't have stood it any longer in there. That woman *stinks*!"

"There are a few of them aboard this ship with strong body odor," said Falsen.

"And I *hate* gin," Linda went on. "But why was she curious, so very, very curious, about our . . . disaster?"

"Other people's disasters are always interesting."

"She'd have found the truth even more interesting."

"If she'd believe it," Falsen said. "But these people don't have any frontiers of the dark in their cosmos."

"I wonder why we should be the only ones?"

"Some sort of mutation, I suppose. One that never spread but which has persisted for centuries. A recessive gene, perhaps . . ."

They had walked, by this time, to the door of the elevator. The lighted cage stood there, waiting. Even though their cabins were only one deck down, they would be able to save themselves a walk down that rather awkward—to Earthly legs—spiral staircase.

CHAPTER 10

Pundoora, originally *Delta Puppis*, was an old ship and had reached the age where things, lacking proper attention, were always breaking down. The Doralans seemed unable to find the petty officers and skilled senior enlisted people without whose dedicated services a vessel, at least insofar as minor machinery was concerned, could not function at maximum efficiency.

When the ship had been taken over, the elevator control-panel buttons had not been changed, although the Doralan numeral equivalents had been painted beside them. Falsen and Linda wanted to get to Level 4. Falsen pressed the button. The cage began its descent. 4 flashed on the indicator board, but the elevator did not stop. 4 . . . 5 . . . 6 . . . 7 . . . 8 . . . 9 . . . Then, at the tenth level, it pulled up with a jerk. Falsen jabbed Number 4 button. Nothing happened. Linda tried—and the door opened.

They were in territory unknown to them. This, thought Falsen, was a chance to explore with a valid excuse ready-made if they were accosted by a Doralan patrol: The elevator had brought them down here against their wishes and would not take them back up to where they belonged; they were trying to find their way back to their own quarters.

They stepped out into a narrow annular alleyway from which radial passages opened. The lighting was dim, barely adequate. Linda wrinkled her nose. *"Cats!"* she said disgustedly.

"Or cat," corrected Falsen. "There's only one tom aboard

this ship. Pondor. He must have been here recently. Perhaps he's here now." He called, in what he hoped was a "Come, pretty pussy" sort of voice, "Pondor! Here, Pondor!"

"He'll never come to you," said the girl.

"Just as well for him," Falsen said. "If he did, I'd wring his bloody neck."

They walked slowly and carefully through one of the radial passages. They came into what was obviously a big storeroom. There were tiers of shelves, stacked with crates, cases and drums. Most of the deck was occupied by stacks of larger packages. There were huge compressed gas cylinders clamped along one bulkhead, some white, some blue, some red. Reserve oxygen? Helium for the scout airship? Fire-fighting CO_2? There were smells: alien spices, something that could have been tar, an unidentifiable chemical acridity.

And cat.

Pondor, thought Falsen, must have gone to great pains to mark out his territory. But why should he have done so? He was the only tomcat aboard the ship.

He voiced his thoughts to Linda.

"But who," she asked, "could hope to fathom the feline mind, such as it is? Who would want to?"

"Something moved!" snapped Falsen suddenly. "Look!"

"The storekeeper," suggested Linda. "Or whatever her title is aboard this ship."

Falsen did not hear. He was attacking a rather untidy stack of packages like a terrier at a rat hole. He put all his strength into pushing a huge bale to one side. He squirmed into the aperture thus uncovered. There was something at the end of the dark tunnel, something that squealed, that struck out with ineffectual claws. Falsen avoided the feeble blows, got his hands on the thing. It seemed to be human. He grabbed its ankles, backed out, dragging it with him.

"One less," said Linda viciously. "Have you killed her yet?"

Falsen laughed. *"Her?"* He pointed down to where the Doralan's red tunic had been pulled up above the hips. *"Her?"*

Linda stared. The brief undergarment at the top of the thighs could not hide the telltale bulge.

"A . . . stowaway," she said at last. "A male stowaway."

"One who was stowed away," Falsen told her. "But by whom?" He stirred the supine, sprawling form with his foot.

"Who brought you aboard, fellow?" he asked. "Who's your owner?"

The little Doralan moaned and stirred, opened his eyes, stared in terror up at the Earthman. He was an unprepossessing specimen, almost chinless, bat-eared, his limbs spindly. But he was well-endowed where, presumably, it mattered most. To somebody.

But who?

Falsen repeated his question, slowly.

The Doralan made a head-shaking gesture. It was plain that he did not understand, did not know English. But why should he? He would not have been sent, at great expense to the Doralan taxpayer, to enroll for any kind of astronautical course at the Antarctic Space Academy.

"I'll make the little swine talk!" snarled Linda, raising her own foot.

If the Doralan did not understand the words, he understood the tone in which they were uttered. He squealed shrilly, rolled over and then, almost on all fours, before he could be stopped, scuttled to a far corner of the storeroom. He melted into a three tier stack of big bales.

Falsen and Linda ran after him, found the fissure into which he had squeezed. It was too narrow to admit either of them. Given time and the use of a stowbot they could have uncovered the new hiding place.

"I'd like to know," said Linda at last, "just who it is who's brought her boyfriend along for the trip . . . Carlin, perhaps. Did I tell you that she lent me the Doralan version of a vibrator? If she's not needing it, that figures. Or the saintly Lady Mother, who seems to have made quite an impression on you . . ."

Linda must have sensed, thought Falsen, his growing feeling for the Doralan captain. There was no sexuality in it. There never could be. But with Carlin? *She* exuded sexuality, and she would not be fussy where she took her pleasures. Any member of whatever species would do for her, as long as he was male. That little rat he had flushed out of hiding might well be hers. It was just as well, thought the man, that she had a stud of her own race along. To become involved with her could seriously interfere with his and Linda's plans.

"Let's get out of here," he said, "before somebody starts wondering where we are."

"Shall we report what we found?" she asked. "Will you tell the Lady Mother?"

"No," he said. "We don't know what toes, of how many persons, we might be treading on. We must remain on friendly terms with these people until . . ."

"Until we steal their ship," she laughed.

They made their way back to the axial shaft. The elevator cage was no longer there. Perhaps the malfunction had been discovered and corrected. Falsen pressed the call button. After not too long a delay the cage came up from one of the sternward levels. Then, obedient this time to Falsen's command, it carried them to Number 4 Deck.

A junior officer was awaiting them there. She said very correctly, making it plain that she was addressing Falsen only, "The Lady Mother presents her compliments, sir, and requests that you join her in the control room."

CHAPTER 11

The big ship's control room was bright, although the only internal illumination came from screens and instrument dials. Through the big viewports beat a steadily shifting reflected glare as the big searchlights swept the terrain surrounding the vessel. Falsen stared out. The almost featureless plain looked, in the harsh brilliance, as though it were covered with fresh snow, and every pool of water glittered like ice.

"It is very quiet," said the Lady Mother.

The Doralan captain was sitting in her chair, a small, frail figure, forlorn somehow and lonely. Beyond her a junior officer was peering into a hooded screen—bio-sensitive radar, guessed Falsen.

"It is very quiet, Mr. Falsen," repeated the Doralan.

"It is, Gracious Lady," agreed the Earthman.

But, to his ears, it was not. There was the murmur of machinery. There was the soft breathing of the sleepers throughout the ship. (In spite of all that had happened, of all that might happen yet, people still had to have their rest.) And was Linda sleeping? he wondered. He did not trust her. She was too impatient, too . . . ruthless? Yes, ruthless.

Something was padding almost silently up the companion-way into the control room. Instinct made Falsen stiffen—and reason told him to relax. It was only Pondor. The animal stalked over the deck, spat at Falsen in passing, went to the Lady Mother and rubbed against her legs.

"Well, cat," she asked, "is all well?"

"I have a name," mewed Pondor. "I wish that you would

use it.'' He condescended to allow the Lady Mother to tickle his ears. Then, ''All is quiet,'' he said. ''I left Tilsin making her rounds of the lower decks.''

The presence of the cat was making Falsen nervous; he started to pace up and down, four steps one way, four steps the other. Carlin came in, made a report to the Lady Mother in her own language. Then she fell in beside Falsen, tried to match her stride to his, attempted to make conversation. Falsen answered in monosyllables. He thought, *Was it your boyfriend we found, I wonder? Is this why you're trying to be nice to me?*

''It is too quiet. . . .'' whispered the Lady Mother.

Falsen stopped his nervous pacing, stood still with every sense alert. He did not join the Doralans at the viewports in their scanning of every inch of the terrain with their high-powered binoculars. But . . . *There is something wrong*, he thought. *Linda? Is she up to something?* Out of the corner of his eye he saw a little light flashing on an otherwise dark console. He knew what it signified; the control room layout had not been changed. He thought, *The silly bitch! What the hell is she playing at?*

The sudden clangor of alarms struck like a blow, *was* a blow to the auditory senses. The Doralans fell back from the viewports. A pair of binoculars dropped to the deck with a clatter. The Lady Mother gripped Falsen's arm, pointed with her other hand to the flashing light and cried, ''Look! The after air-lock door is open!''

Already the ship was in an uproar. Falsen could visualize the way that it must be—full illumination flashing on in every compartment, every alleyway, the crew boiling out through the open doors of cabins and dormitories, some in night attire or naked, some half-dressed but with every woman among them armed. Somebody, somewhere, was firing at something; to him the distinctive hiss and crackle was audible above the general tumult. Yet it could not be far away, must be only a few decks down from the control room on one of the accommodation levels.

The stupid bitch! he thought. *The stupid, vicious bitch!*

He ran from the control room. He was not sure what he would do, could do, but he had to see what was happening. He used the spiral staircase; at a time like this it would be too easy to be trapped in the elevator cage. There seemed to be

Doralans everywhere, milling about, getting in his way. He pushed through them, knocking some of them down. The air was thick with the smell of fear and, as he approached the deck where his own cabin was situated, of blood.

Somebody was running with him, keeping close beside him. It was Carlin. Her cat face was almost smiling, her cat's eyes alight with excitement. She was not frightened. He almost liked her.

Almost.

He cursed her as, accidentally or by intent, she tripped him. When he scrambled to his feet the chase had surged past and over him and the staircase was deserted. But it was only a few steps to the deck where whatever it was had been happening.

He heard the babble of frightened voices that, after a few seconds, was stilled by the clear, authoritative commands of the Lady Mother. He approached slowly, fully alert, ready to fight or to run as dictated by circumstance.

Carlin was waiting for him.

She said, "Come quickly. She is hurt. She is asking for you."

The crowd of Doralans parted to let Falsen through. He was shocked at what he saw. There were bodies on the deck, which was slippery with blood. It was the manner of their killing which horrified him; the eyes clawed out, the disembowelment. What beast could have been responsible? He forced himself to ignore them, walked to where Linda was sprawled naked and bleeding against the door of her cabin with the Lady Mother and the ship's surgeon bending over her. He tripped over something, half stumbled. He looked down. It was a cat, or what was left of a cat. It could not be Pondor, so it must be Tilsin, his mate. Something had torn the animal's head from its body.

"Nick . . ." whispered Linda, looking up at him.

Her face was very pale beneath the blood that streaked it, especially around the mouth. *Her* blood? Falsen wondered. There was more blood on her shoulders and down the front of her body. Falsen stared at the deep gashes on her belly and wondered how, and by what, they had been inflicted. Not by herself; that was obvious.

"*She* did it!" screamed Pondor suddenly.

Was the animal telepathic? wondered Falsen.

"*She* did it! *She* killed Tilsin!"

Squalling, he launched himself at the wounded girl, his claws reaching for her eyes. But the Lady Mother caught him in mid-flight, held him at arm's length while his scrabbling hind feet tried to rend her wrists. Then she threw him from her. There was a dull thud as he hit the bulkhead. He fell to the deck, then got unsteadily to his feet. He glared wildly at his mistress.

"She did it," he mewed. "I know she did it! Kill her. Kill her!"

"Take him away," the captain said to one of her officers, "and shut him up somewhere until he comes to his senses." Then, to the surgeon, "How is she, Magadja?"

"She has lost some blood, but her injuries are only superficial." She was speaking in English for Linda's and Falsen's benefit. Falsen appreciated the courtesy. The woman deftly cleaned the wounds, sprayed them over with syntheskin, then said, "Mr. Falsen, you are stronger than we are. Will you move her into her cabin?"

"I can move myself," Linda whispered, "with some assistance. . . ."

Falsen helped her to her feet, supported her into the compartment. She flopped, but not ungracefully, onto the bunk. He caught her limp hand in his. He could feel her fear, knew that something had frightened her very badly.

He said, "Don't worry. You're safe now."

He wished that he were able to believe what he had just told her.

"Miss Veerhausen," the Lady Mother said, "I am sorry to be obliged to question you before you have recovered from your ordeal. But you appear to be the only survivor of this . . . massacre. For the safety of all of us, I must know what happened."

Falsen felt Linda's hand go tense in his.

She said haltingly, "I . . . I was going to sleep. Then I had the . . . feeling that something was wrong. Very wrong. There was a strange odor in the air. I got up from my bunk and went out into the alleyway. And . . . and *it* attacked me."

"*It?*" asked the captain. "What was . . . *it*?"

"I . . . I don't know. It had teeth and claws. It was like an animal that we have on Earth called the tiger. . . ."

"A tiger?" echoed the Doralan. "I have seen a tiger. In a zoo. But a tiger? Here?"

"*Like* a tiger, I said. But it seemed to run on its hind legs only. . . ."

"Was there more than one?"

"Yes. I saw others while I was fighting it off."

"Do you know who opened the air-lock door, Miss Veerhausen?"

Linda stared up at the captain.

"How could I know?" she asked.

"Somebody must know," the Lady Mother said. "Or somebody did know—before she died."

Carlin came into the room.

"Gracious Lady," she said, "I have been down to the after air lock. There is blood on the ramp, and more blood on the moss at the foot of it. I followed the trail as far as I could before it petered out. . . ."

"I will see for myself," the captain said.

Falsen and Linda were left by themselves.

CHAPTER 12

"What *did* happen?" demanded Falsen.

He stood there, looking down at her as she sprawled on the bunk. He stared at her wounds, red and glistening beneath the transparent syntheskin. Only a little deeper, he thought, and the viscera would have been exposed. They might, they just might have been self-inflicted, but . . . He looked at that other wound on her shoulder, the one that she had received in the cave. It was healing fast, but it was still visible.

"What *did* happen?" he repeated.

"What I told the Lady Mother," she muttered sulkily. "Oh, I did leave something out. I killed Tilsin. The sound of her padding up and down outside was driving me crazy. Those cats hate us, you know. . . ."

"There's only one of them left," said Falsen. "Pondor. But go on."

"I . . . changed, then went outside to deal with Tilsin. It was lucky that I was ready, because I'd just killed her when that . . . *thing* jumped me. I was able to fight it off . . ."

"And was it really as you described it?" he persisted. "A sort of cross between a kangaroo and a tiger? That's even more fantastic than the big, gray, armor-plated beast that you told the captain about. You weren't treating her to another fairy tale, were you?"

"I was not!" she snapped.

"But where did it come from?"

"How should I know? It must be something native to this world."

64

"The Survey Service," he said, "made a thorough exploration . . ."

"And you're Survey Service Reserve, aren't you? You believe everything you read in Survey Service reports. Well, Lieutenant Falsen, SSR, I'm not and I don't."

He laughed without humor. "I'll be frank. I don't always myself. I was involved in an exploration project during my last training cruise. It wasn't a very pleasant planet—it was rather similar to this in many respects. As a navigator I was on the cartography team. We did a thorough job, but the other specialists seemed to spend most of the time in their pneumatic tents, watching their portable playmasters, playing cards and getting drunk. But their reports!" He held his hands apart. "Books this thick!"

"So your precious Survey Service missed a large, very dangerous animal on this world. After what you've just told me, that figures. But I was alone here for a long time. I never saw anything like what I saw tonight. I was never attacked—until now."

"You must smell wrong and taste wrong. Obviously the Doralans smell and taste right."

"Do they? But how did those things get into the ship?"

"Some fool opened the air-lock door," said Falsen. "Whenever there's something that should not be done, there's always some idiot around to do it."

But how, he wondered, had the predators gotten up to the accommodation decks so quickly? The interval between the coming on of the tell-tale light and the attack had been a very short one. Could such oddly constructed beasts as Linda described have negotiated the spiral staircase from the stern to an upper level so quickly? Yet they must have. To suppose that they had used the elevator would have been the ultimate absurdity.

However they had done it—in a series of bounds, perhaps? —they were deadly dangerous, to Linda and himself as well as to the Doralans. He looked again at the ugly wounds on her belly, still glaringly apparent despite the bio-adhesive. He looked at that other one on her shoulder. He remembered how her face was scratched when she killed that first eavesdropping cat—and how, when she had gone down to the messhall with him, the skin of her cheeks had been unblemished.

He said, "We must help the Doralans."

She said, "We help ourselves. Only ourselves."

"We must help the Doralans," he repeated, "until such time as this mess is cleaned up."

She grinned at him derisively. "Sweet on the Lady Mother, are you? Oedipus Falsen. . . . Oh, I suppose that one myth is as good as another. Or is it Catface Carlin you're lusting after? Don't let *me* stop you—as long as you remember to whom you really belong."

"Yes," he admitted. "We're two of a kind. The only two of our kind on this planet. But don't forget that the Doralans are . . . human."

"Human?" she scoffed. "And would it make any difference if they really were?"

While they were talking, the ship subsided slowly into as nearly a silent state as she would, while in commission, ever attain. Soon the only sounds, apart from the perpetual mutterings and whisperings of life-support machinery, were those being made by the cleaning-up party in the alleyway, the unfortunates whose task it was to mop up the blood and remove the spilled guts. Somebody vomited noisily. Linda laughed. She was not squeamish, Falsen thought. But neither was he.

She said, "I think you'd better stay with me for what's left of the night."

"It will be as well," he said.

He took off his shirt.

She told him, "There is no need for that. I'm not in the mood. I'm wounded—or hadn't you noticed? Besides, this bed is too narrow."

He stepped out of his shorts, his shoes.

He said, "It is as well to be prepared. If you hadn't been, you would have been badly hampered. You'd be in a worse state than you are now. Or dead."

"Old age," she remarked, "doesn't set in all that fast."

"There are more ways of dying than of old age."

"But not here. Not on this world, aboard this ship."

He shrugged. He stood there naked, listening intently.

He said, "They're finished outside now."

"Not the mess but the waste," she quipped.

He ignored this, went on, "If the Lady Mother wanted us, she'd have sent for us by now. I imagine that, the way things are, she doesn't want any outsiders getting underfoot."

"Not even you?"

"Not even me."

He curled up on the deck like a dog, was scarcely aware when Linda extinguished the light over her bunk before going to sleep herself.

CHAPTER 13

The next morning they were called to a conference by the Lady Mother. For their benefit the proceedings were conducted in English, although it was obvious that this courtesy to them did not please most of the Doralan officers. While the discussions were under way, reports were coming in from both the airship and the scouting helicopters, the latter machines being flimsy contraptions each carrying only two persons and with a very limited range. Only the dirigible was capable of lifting electronic detection devices of all kinds, including bio-sensitive radar and other equipment with which it was possible to chart subterranean features.

A large screen had been set up in the captain's day cabin, and in it was displayed a map of the terrain over which the airship was flying. By it was a speaker from which issued the voice of one of those aboard the dirigible. She was speaking in her own language, but a Doralan officer was acting both as interpreter and expounder.

This woman, Falsen noted, was a specialist officer of some kind. The marks of rank and department on the high collar of her scarlet tunic were not the usual stars but pairs of compasses or dividers. A cartographer, he thought. Or a geographer.

She said, scowling at the Terrans as she spoke, "This . . . picture nothing will mean to you. . . ."

How true, thought Falsen. The screen was like an abstract painting, glowing blotches of green and red, blue and yellow, darker patches of brown and near-black, shifting slowly from right to left as the airship proceeded on its mission.

With the tip of her pointer, the cartographer indicated a big patch of blue over which was a stippling of brown dots.

"This is the . . . pond," she said, raising her voice so that she could be heard over the shrill gabble from the speaker. "No. *Lake.* The lake in the . . . cave. Where *our* people were killed. . . ."

"And where the Lady Linda was injured," said the captain mildly.

The cartographer scowled, went on, "And yet the bio-sensitive radar life does not show in the cave. There is no sci . . . sci . . . ?"

"Scintillation," supplied Falsen helpfully.

"What you say," she snapped. "But. But look. You see the blue line. . . ."

There was a sharply defined edge to the azure patch that represented the subterranean lake, but from it extended a line of the same color, almost straight at first, then meandering. The other patterns on the screen swung and shifted as the airship's pilot attempted to follow this road to . . .

Where?

Or what.

"Still," said the specialist, "there is no life. No scintillation." As she produced the final word triumphantly, she glared at Falsen.

"But," said the Lady Mother, "we *know* that whatever made the first attack on the watchkeepers outside the ship came from the cave . . ." *But you don't* know, thought Falsen. *You only suppose.* "And we *know* that there was something in the cave that killed people. And we *know* that last night's attackers, killers, headed back to the cave. . . ."

"That is so, Lady Mother," agreed Carlin.

"Now," the captain went on, "we may suppose that the beasts are . . . amphibious, capable of swimming underwater for long distances. Lady Linda, did you get the idea that the thing which attacked you last night was so capable?"

"It . . . it was all very confused, Gracious Lady," said Linda. "But on Earth practically every land animal can swim if it has to."

"It is so on Dorala," said the captain. She returned her attention to the screen. "Look! Another lake, in another cavern."

"No, Gracious Lady," said the cartographer. "Yes, it is a lake—but not under the ground."

"But there is life in the lake," the Lady Mother said.

Yes, there was life. There were bright points of electric scintillation moving through the deeper blue that indicated water. Two of these, a large one and a smaller, merged, became one. Something must have eaten something.

"We must mount an expedition," the captain said. "We must wipe those things out."

An officer, another specialist with golden flowers on her tunic collar, protested. Falsen did not know what she was saying, but the exchange of words was heated. After a sharp order from the captain she repeated herself in English.

"Gracious Lady, as your ecologist I must object. We must not tamper with the natural order of things on this world."

"It is the natural order of things," said the captain, "that the stronger kill the weaker. The . . . things were stronger than my people when it caught them unprepared. When we are prepared we shall be the stronger. Besides, do not forget that it was *my* people who were killed. By my oath of high office I am bound to exact vengeance. I have the means at my disposal to turn that lake into a glowing, radioactive crater."

"Gracious Lady, you would not. You must not."

"Lady Dimilin, *I* give the orders aboard this ship."

Orders, thought Falsen, might be legally correct but morally wrong and, although he was coming both to like and respect the Lady Mother, he sympathized with the stand that the ecologist was making. He recalled the histories of one or two Earth-colonized planets where the conservationists had been shouted down. The flame trees on Austral, the water dragons on Cruxhaven, the first destroyed because their pollen caused some distress to certain asthmatics—among whom were the governor and his wife—the second wiped out because they made an occasional meal from the herds of Terran cattle grazing on the river banks. When the flame trees were all gone, the musk moths changed their feeding habits and their larvae wiped out crop after crop of honey fruit, one of Austral's major exports. When the water dragons were almost extinct, the barbed-wire weed got out of control, choking many navigable river channels. The water dragons had been mainly herbivorous, eating meat only now and then.

He wondered if, at some time in the future, an alien conservationist would rush to the protection of Linda and himself, trying to have them classed as members of a protected species. . . .

The Lady Dimilin used these very words.

"Gracious Lady, it is not only you who have authority. I was enjoined by the Council to, at my discretion, declare any life forms discovered on this world members of protected species."

"But you are not the captain, Lady Dimilin." She turned to the Terrans. "Mr. Falsen, Miss Veerhausen, how is it in your ships?"

"In both the Survey Service and the Merchant Service the captain is the captain. He makes the decisions. Of course, in serious cases his officers may lay complaints against him. . . ."

"And what happens then?"

"If the allegations are really serious there will be a court of enquiry."

"A risk that I should be prepared to take. That I *am* prepared to take. Our general regulations are modeled very closely on yours."

Dimilin made herself heard again.

"Gracious Lady, you spoke of your oath of high office. But my understanding of it is that it empowers you to take punitive action only against intelligent beings. How can you *punish* an animal that does only what its instincts make it do? An animal that, in all probability, plays an important part in the ecology of this planet."

The Lady Mother sighed.

"Very well," she said at last. "We will evaluate the reports received from the air-reconnaissance parties. And then, Lady Dimilin, we will endeavor to obtain a specimen predator for you to dissect, evaluate and do to what you will." She turned to the officer standing by the radar display. "Lady Kurrajong, while we have been . . . arguing have you heard anything of importance?"

"Only this, Gracious Lady. The Lady Pansir insists that there are living beings of some kind in the lake. Of that we are already aware. There is the scintillation. Many are small, but some are large. The water is . . . murky."

"And nothing has come up to breathe?" asked Falsen. "Those things last night, and the other times, have to be air breathers."

"On your world, perhaps, they would have to be," said the ecologist. "But on *our* planet we have animals that can exist, and function, either in air or in water. With . . . gills? Is that the word? *And* lungs."

"Large animals?" Falsen asked.

"The *dolisen* is. It is a herbivore that comes out of the rivers when the *flaren* trees bear their fruit. It is then that the females give birth. If, for some reason, the *dolisen* became extinct there would be no more *flaren* trees. The droppings of the animals are essential to fertilize the plants. And should the *flaren* trees be . . . exterminated, there would be no more *dolisen*. The fruit, chewed and . . . and . . ."

"Regurgitated," supplied Falsen.

"What you say. The chewed fruit is what the *dolisen* young live on until they are old enough to follow the adults back to the water, where they live on weeds." She turned to the captain. "So you see, Lady Mother, how important it is that we do not remove as much as one link from the chain of life on this world."

"The *dolisen*," said the captain, "do not kill and eat people. But if it is possible, you will have your specimens before I take strong action."

CHAPTER 14

Finally the airship returned and was moored close by the space vessel. It would not lift off again until the following morning; its next expedition could, possibly, occupy all the daylight hours.

Linda and Falsen were left to their own devices for most of what remained of the day, while the Lady Mother conferred with her senior officers and her specialists. For much of the time they stayed in Linda's cabin, discussing in low voices how best they could make this menace from outside the ship, this attack by indigenous predators, work in with their own plans. The girl said that if *they*, whatever *they* were, killed off all the Doralans, it would be so much the better. Falsen found it hard to agree with her. He knew that his was a chauvinistic attitude; as far as he was concerned, it was *wrong* that a mindless carnivore should kill and eat a thinking being. He was the sort of man, Linda sneered, who would risk his own life to save his worst enemy from a shark and then, only minutes later, find some excuse to slip a knife between that person's ribs.

Falsen did not agree. "When you've saved somebody's life," he said, "you have an obligation to them."

"You might," she told him. "I wouldn't."

They took their late afternoon meal in the officers' mess, ignored by those Doralans who were eating there. They toyed with a succession of dishes that were pretty to look at but insipid in flavor and utterly unsatisfying. They visited the big common room but, although nothing was said, it was obvious that their presence was unwelcome. Some sort of funeral service—or was it more of a wake?—was in progress. There was dismal, wailing music from the snythesizer. There were, Falsen thought, eulogies to the dead spacewomen being delivered by an officer wearing a somber gray uniform instead of the usual scarlet.

It was a relief when a messenger found them and told them that the Lady Mother required their presence.

The Doralan captain was in her day cabin. Sour-faced Prenta was there, and Carlin, and the ecologist and the cartographer. Pondor was there. He was hating them, Falsen knew. He was not only hating the Terrans. He was sitting on the deck at his mistress's feet, glaring at all the others with baleful yellow eyes.

"Mr. Falsen," said the Lady Mother, "do you wish to volunteer to accompany tomorrow's expedition? It has been suggested that you, representing Earth, should be among those present."

"I volunteer, Gracious Lady," Falsen said.

"And so do I," said Linda.

"But, Lady Linda, you were injured last night."

"I heal quickly, Gracious Lady," said the girl. "As you say, I was injured. I want to get back at whatever did it."

"Let her come if she wants to," said Carlin.

"Very well," the Doralan captain said. She turned to the Terrans. "The Lady Carlin will be in charge of the hunting party. The Lady Dimilin"—the ecologist inclined her head as her name was mentioned—"will accompany. In an advisory capacity. She, in spite of everything that has happened, is anxious that there shall be no needless killing. Of predators, that is. . . ." She allowed herself a tight smile. "The plan of campaign is that the airship shall lift off shortly after dawn and proceed to the lake where the sightings were made. A depth bomb will be used either to kill or to stun one of the larger animals. The body will be brought back here for proper examination."

"It sounds simple," said Falsen.

"It will be simple," said Carlin.

You hope, thought Falsen.

"Those of you who will be going out tomorrow," the Lady Mother said, "had better get a good night's sleep. I do not think that you will be disturbed. The ship is sealed, and every air-lock door has been secured by spot welding. Armed sentries are patroling every deck. . . .''

"It is not enough," mewed Pondor.

"What do you know about it, cat?" asked the captain amusedly. "What would you do about it if you were in my shoes?"

"I do not know," admitted the animal reluctantly. "But be careful. Be very careful."

"I don't think that we shall be troubled tonight," said Carlin confidently.

CHAPTER 15

It was a quiet night.

Linda and Falsen slept together on the deck of her cabin. They made love first—although love might not be the right word to use to describe their short and brutal coupling, little more than an explosive release of tensions.

Early in the morning they were awakened by a junior officer. The little Doralan looked down in horrified disgust at their naked bodies, the fleshy tangle of bare limbs.

She whispered, "The morning meal is waiting for you. You will, please, to hurry."

She left them hastily.

Falsen went to his own quarters to make his toilet. He showered, depilated using the cream that had been prepared for him by the ship's chemist. It worked, although it was too highly scented. He put on his uniform, which he had washed the previous night before joining Linda. He thought, as he dressed, that the maintaining of appearances was something of a bore. If—when—he and Linda were by themselves, alone together, there would be no need to bother with clothing.

He joined Linda in the alleyway outside their cabins. Together they went down to the officers' mess. Carlin beckoned them to her table. They sat down to a meal of some sweet mush and aniseed-flavored tea. It filled their bellies but did not satisfy. At other tables the airship pilot, the ecologist and officers who were either just coming off watch or going on watch were eating hastily.

"Come," said Carlin, rising from her seat.

She led the way to the axial shaft, the waiting elevator cage. They dropped down through compartment after compartment to the stern of the ship, to the after air lock. The air in the chamber still bore acrid traces of the burning away of the spot welding that had secured the door. The air outside, at the head of the ramp, was chilly and dank, smelled of soggy corruption. The probing searchlights, mounted high on the towering hull, were still sweeping the plain, the harsh glare reflected by stagnant pools and the occasional outcropping of pallid rock. At its short mooring mast, like an elongated skeletal pyramid, rode the airship, a huge, silvery wind sock that swung lazily this way and that as the light, uncertain airs backed and veered.

Apart from the floodlights and the searchlights, the morning was still dark, although low in the east was a somehow ominous band of crimson against which black hills showed in silhouette.

The Lady Mother was waiting for them at the foot of the ramp, cloaked and cowled against the chill. Pondor was with her, his eyes glowing greenly.

She said formally, "Lady Carlin. Lady Linda. Mr. Falsen. The airship is ready. The crew and the hunters have boarded, are awaiting you and the Ladies Dimilin and Pansir."

Pansir? wondered Falsen. *That must be the pilot*, he thought.

The two women named hurried past, their cloaks streaming out behind them in the breeze. With the dawn the wind seemed to be rising; the crimson glow to the east was brighter now, higher in the otherwise drab sky.

"Good hunting," said the Lady Mother. Coming from her, the words sounded odd.

"We shall do our best, Gracious Lady," said Carlin.

There was a sudden spatter of cold rain.

"Get on board," said the Doralan captain. "Mr. Falsen and Miss Veerhausen have no cloaks."

"A little rain will not hurt them," said Carlin.

"Get on board, I say!"

The Lady Mother's voice was sharp.

"Very well, Gracious Lady."

Carlin led the way over the spongy moss to where a ladder

hung from the control car, the end of it just brushing the surface of the ground. She was first up it. Linda was next, moving with considerably less agility. Falsen was last. Nobody offered to help him up through the door into the cabin.

It was a bumpy flight. The ship creaked and complained as pockets of turbulence twisted her frame, lifted her and as suddenly pulled her down. Bracing himself on the after bulkhead of the control car—there was no seat for him—Falsen watched how the ship was handled. The pilot sat behind a steering wheel, looking some of the time out through a forward window that a wiper was trying, without much success, to keep clear of streaming rain, and more often down at a dimly glowing compass card. To her right sat another woman, an enlisted woman or petty officer, staring at an altimeter dial. She, too, had a wheel, mounted with its axis at right angles to the fore and aft line of the ship. The altitude coxswain, thought Falsen, remembering the course that he had taken on the history of aviation during his studies at the Academy. He tried to recall what he had read about such matters as aerodynamic lift, the regulation of the altitude of a dirigible without valving gas or dumping ballast.

He looked out through a side window. There was very little to see; the rainfall was so heavy that the spray generated by its impact covered the ground like a mist. Now and again there was the violet glare of nearby lightning, diffused by precipitation but still dazzling, accompanied by detonations of thunder that were loud above the steady drumming of huge raindrops on the envelope overhead.

He said to Carlin, who had a chair close to where he was standing, "This is not an ideal day for a hunting trip. Your meteorologists must have goofed."

"We *had* a meteorologist," she replied, "but she is dead. Not that it would have made much difference. Meteorology is an art rather than a science—and on a new world, a strange world, it is an art that would take many years to learn."

But the wind seemed to have dropped, he thought. There was almost no turbulence and pilot and altitude coxswain were less tense, were no longer having to fight their controls. And the rain was easing. No longer was the ground beneath the airship obscured by spray. Ahead, the overcast was thinning and the ruddy sun was breaking through, a red ball little more than a blotch of lurid luminosity in the less luminous cloud cover.

It's a fine day after all, he thought. *Let's go out and shoot something*.

CHAPTER 16

They reached the lake, an almost perfect oval of dark water rimmed by low, black hills. As they flew over it the rain started again, a steady downpour that pocked what had briefly been a mirrorlike surface. It wasn't going to be such a fine day after all, thought Falsen, but there would still be something to shoot.

The bio-sensitive radar indicated that the water was teeming with life. A cloud of tiny green sparks drifted slowly across the screen and then, suddenly, a much larger blotch of luminescence was among them. The little points of light scattered, their numbers diminished. It, whatever *it* was, was feeding, was feeding well. Yet nothing was visible from the control car. Even if the water had not been murky, the torrential rain would have reduced the possibility of subsurface sightings.

Carlin snapped orders in her own language. The airship pilot replied briefly.

Carlin said to Linda and Falsen, "A party will be set down on the northern shore. I would like you to be among them."

"In this rain?" he demanded.

"There are spare cloaks. Small, perhaps, but they will keep the upper parts of you dry."

A crewwoman found two of the scarlet, hooded garments, handed them to the Terrans. Falsen shrugged into his. He could not fasten it in front, and its hem came to upper-thigh level. But it would be better than nothing.

The dirigible lost altitude, driving down at a shallow angle.

Pumps throbbed as expanding ballonets compressed helium cells, reducing buoyancy. The airship passed over the northern shore at a height of about fifty meters, stopped, her momentum killed by reverse pitch. There was almost no wind and she drifted very slowly over the soggy surface. The engines started again, the four screws swiveling on their outriggers to push her down. There was a soft jar as the skids under the gondola made contact.

"Out!" ordered Carlin.

A sliding door at the after end of the control car was opened. Carlin jumped out and down, her cloak billowing behind her, landed with an audible squelch. Black mud spattered her chubby bare legs. Falsen followed her, then Linda, then six more Doralans. They stood there, sheltered from the rain by the huge but flimsy hull above them. Then the airscrews swiveled again in their mountings and the dirigible lifted, headed back out over the lake.

The downpour was not cold, luckily. Neither was the ooze that filled his low shoes, that soaked his ankles. The air was filled with the sweet-sour scent of rotting vegetation.

They stood there, Terrans and Doralans, staring out over the expanse of dark water. The scene was dreary, the low, dark hills in the near distance half obscured by the drifting veils of gray rain, the miserable, stunted trees and shrubs, all of which looked like the barely living survivors of some forest fire. But there could never be a forest fire on this world. Everything was always too damp to burn.

Carlin said, pointing, "There is something there!"

The waters were disturbed by more than the heavy rain; concentric ripples were spreading out from a central point. The Doralans twittered among themselves in their own language, their little-girl voices. Carlin spoke into her wrist transceiver. Falsen could hear, faintly, the pilot's reply.

Over the lake the airship, a great, silver cigar, dull-gleaming through the murk, was moving slowly. It was almost over the center of the disturbance when a small, dark object dropped from the car, plunged down into the water. It hit the surface with a small splash and vanished. Almost immediately there was a yellow subaqueous effulgence and a pillar of spray that climbed high before collapsing around itself. There was a muffled boom. A muddy wave surged inland, washing around the calves of the beach party before it subsided.

The explosion had done no good at all to whatever it was that had briefly broken surface. Falsen had a confused impression of long tentacles—*tentacles?*—flailing in a death flurry, of something big and gray and glistening, lashing out madly at the enemy that had dealt it a mortal blow. Even these first glimpses told him that it was nothing at all like the predatory beast that Linda had described. Then it was still. It floated there, almost submerged. It could have been no more than a big, slimy log.

Carlin snapped orders.

Reluctantly two of her people removed their scarlet cloaks, dropped them to the wet ground, shed their tunics and their brief underwear. They buckled belts about their slim waists, above their surprisingly full hips and buttocks. Among the gear landed from the ship were grappling irons and coils of light line. The women each attached grappling irons to their belts. They walked slowly, with an obvious lack of enthusiasm, to the waterline while others paid out the line behind them. Falsen felt very sorry for them as he watched the trembling of their pale, naked bodies. Carlin snarled at them and they quickened their pace. They waded out into the lake.

"Do you have to do it this way?" Falsen asked Carlin.

"How else? Besides, they are safe enough." She gestured with the laser pistol that she had pulled from its holster. "I'm a good shot. If anything attacks them I'll get it before it touches them."

"*If*," said Falsen, "you can see it in time. Apart from reflection, refraction and this blasted rain, that water is muddy."

She shrugged, then said, "They are keeping a lookout from the airship too, you know. They have their instruments."

The two Doralans were swimming now, moving sinuously out into the murky lake, making very little disturbance. Their bodies shimmered pallidly just below the surface. Line from the two coils was running out quite rapidly. The swimmers were getting close to the barely floating hulk. Then one of them was treading water while she detached the three-pronged grapnel from her belt. Briefly her body lifted clear of the surface as she plunged the barbed points into the gray flesh. Her companion stayed close to render assistance if it should be needed—or if it were possible to give it. Carlin already had her pistol aimed at where the head of the animal should be, might be. *But she is only guessing,* thought Falsen.

Yet there was no movement, save for that imparted by the grapnel, of the inert mass. The second swimmer plunged her iron home, and then the two of them were striking out for the beach, making far faster progress than they had done on their outward passage. They stumbled ashore, their hairless bodies dripping and glistening, their mouths open as they gasped for breath.

Carlin ignored them. She holstered her pistol and barked orders at the other members of her crew. They tailed on to the lines, two of them to each. Hand over hand they dragged the big, floating body into the shallows. It grounded at last. They dropped the lines and, joined by the swimmers, waded out. They had to go just over knee-deep. Then they were rolling the thing up on to the muddy beach.

There were no tentacles. Falsen's first impression, gained when the thing had been threshing in its death flurry, had been erroneous. There was a big, barrellike body tapering to a long tail at one end and to a long . . . tail? neck? at the other. There were no limbs or fins or easily discernible sense organs.

The Terrans and Doralans stood around, looking at it.

It could only be, thought Falsen, some sort of giant leech, capable of ingesting—and excreting?—from either end. Each "neck" terminated in a puckered orifice.

"Obviously," said Carlin, "this . . . *thing* is quite incapable of clawing or biting."

She did not sound surprised.

"But it could give you a nasty suck," said Falsen facetiously.

Carlin glared at him.

"But what does it eat?" asked Linda. "Its prey must be something big."

"Not necessarily," Falsen told her. "There used to be whales, enormous brutes, in Earth's seas that fed on tiny crustaceans."

"We will leave such discussions," said Carlin coldly, "to those best qualified to engage in them. No doubt the Lady Dimilin will be able to inform us." She spoke into her wrist transceiver, received replies from the airship. She said, "There's nothing at all showing now on the bio-sensitive radar. The explosion must have scared everything into the underwater caves and tunnels. So, I think that we should return to the ship. I do not like this weather."

Neither do I, thought Falsen. *Unlike seamen and airmen,*

spacemen are not meteorologists—but some sense, some instinct was making him increasingly uneasy.

The airship drifted in, losing altitude. There was no wind to interfere with the maneuvers. This time grapnels were dropped, their spade-tipped arms taking a firm grip on the soft soil. The ship was winched down until the skids under the car touched the mossy, spongy ground. Abaft the car a hatch opened in the envelope, and through this a big wire net was lowered. Falsen and Linda helped the crewwomen to roll the carcass of the giant leech onto it, getting gray slime all over themselves. Carlin just stood there, watching. A winch hummed and the net was lifted into the cargo compartment. The hatch closed.

They boarded the airship, Carlin last of all after inspecting the grapnels to make sure that they would come free with the first jerk. She exchanged words with the pilot, who seemed to be objecting to something.

She said, "You will go aft into the passenger space with the others. The Lady Pansir says that you . . . stink."

She was right, Falsen admitted. That slime did smell, although he himself did not consider the odor all that offensive. But he did not argue. He followed Linda up the short ladder to the main keel. They made their way aft to a cabin, the walls of which were bulging gas cells. They sat at one end of it, on the deck, while the six slime-besmeared Doralans sat at the other, looking at them with ill-concealed dislike.

Faintly, from outside, came the splashing of dumped water ballast. When the motors started, the drumming of the rain on the envelope was no longer audible. The ship was lifting, swaying gently.

And then, suddenly, it was as though she had run into something at full speed—or something had run into her, from the starboard beam, pushing her over, wrenching and shaking her.

And she was lifting, lifting fast, going up like an archaic rocket.

CHAPTER 17

Falsen reacted instinctively. This was an emergency; his place was in the control room. He jumped to his feet, but a violent lurch threw him against the wall, the side of one of the gas cells. He rebounded, fell over Linda who was still seated.

She looked up at him, her eyes wide in her pale, terrified face.

"Nick! What's happening?"

"I'm going to find out."

He scrambled up, steadied himself against the resilient skin of a cell. He could hear the Doralans screaming softly, a low, eerie keening. There were other noises—the groaning of tortured metal, sharp twangs as, somewhere inside the structure of the airship, wires parted. A shrill alarm bell was sounding somewhere aft. The lights flickered, went out. They came on again, but with greatly reduced intensity.

Falsen stumbled forward along the keel catwalk which was tilted up at a sharp angle, was bucking under his feet. He ducked just in time to avoid a broken strut that swung viciously at his head like a club wielded by a giant. Abruptly there was a shift of the airship's attitude, and he found himself running downhill towards the nose, caught a guide wire to stop himself.

The ship leveled, although she was still rolling from side to side. He completed his journey in a staggering run, reached the hatch over the enclosed ladder down to the control car. He clambered down to the gondola, was momentarily blinded as lightning flared all around the airship, the harsh, blue glare beating in through the big windows like a physical blow.

Then he could see again through smarting eyes.

The pilot, Pansir, was wrestling with her wheel, endeavoring to keep the ship on course. On the starboard side the altitude coxswain, assisted by Carlin, was engaged in an even harder struggle to maintain an even keel. Two other Doralans were working feverishly at the transceiver, had its casing open and were removing what looked like burned-out components. The Lady Dimilin was huddled in a chair, looking both thoroughly terrified and quite useless.

He looked out through a window into a hell of swirling, ruddily luminous vapor masses, toppling pinnacles, yawning chasms, writhing dragon shapes that fought and merged, that fissioned into the semblance of a gailoping squadron of demon cavalry, charging the ship with upraised sabers. There was more lightning, but distant. Through a deep rift before it closed Falsen could see the ground. It was close, too close, with jagged white outcroppings.

The pilot screamed an order.

Carlin and the altitude coxswain strained at their wheel, turning it slowly and jerkily clockwise. The airship's nose lifted, only slightly at first, then steeply. There was a clatter from the vicinity of the transceiver as replacement printed circuit trays were spilled to the deck. From somewhere aft came a sharp crack, loud, like the report of a gun.

The ship . . . *groaned*.

Falsen could feel the weight on her, like a giant hand trying to press her down onto the waiting rocks. She groaned, but there was fight left in her. She clawed her way upwards with an odd pitching motion, yawing from port to starboard, starboard to port. Huge hailstones hurtled at her, scarring the tough transparency of the control-car windows.

The huge hand was lifted, and briefly, very briefly, there was a feeling of relief in the control car, a diminishment of the acrid scent of fear. And then the ship was grabbed, grabbed and wrenched, tossed upwards. Again Carlin and the altitude coxswain were wrestling with their wheel, trying to bring the ship's nose down.

Lightning flared again, close but not dazzling; the windows were thickly coated with ice.

But the pilot knew her job. She would bring the ship

through, juggling buoyancy and ballast. And, thought Falsen, there would be plenty to jettison should the need arise. Equipment, weapons, the carcass of that huge beast from the lake. He would be able to help in such work, would no longer be a passenger, a mere looker-on. His Terran strength would be useful.

Something nudged his shoulder.

Linda, he thought. She must have followed him.

But he *knew* that it was not Linda.

The stink was sour in his nostrils, the touch through his thin shirt was cold and clammy. He cried out as he pulled away from the strong suction, heard a patch tear from the back of his shirt.

Like the trunk of a Terran elephant, like a gray, questing, sightless worm the *thing* slid over his shoulder. It was gashed in several places, oozing a stinking, green-yellow ichor. Dimilin saw it coming at her and screamed, tried to scramble out of the chair in which she had been cowering. The puckered orifice at the end of the neck fastened on her at the base of her throat. Again she screamed.

Falsen caught hold of the slimy trunk, tried to pull it away from the struggling Doralan. It squirmed in his grasp and undulations ran along its length. From the end of it, where the sucker had attached to the ecologist's throat, came a horrid sucking noise, a loud slurping.

Still Falsen struggled, although he knew that it was too late to save the Doralan woman. The undulations became more violent, a whipping motion. He lost his grip on the ichor slippery hide, was flung forward and to starboard, knocking Carlin and the coxswain away from the altitude control wheel. They had been fighting to slow the ship's rate of descent, battling downdraft and the weight of accumulated ice. With their hands no longer gripping its spokes, the wheel spun uselessly. To those in the control car it was like being in the cage of a too rapidly descending elevator.

Carlin had her laser pistol out, was firing at the giant leech. The slashing beam missed at first, took out the port after window of the car. Cold air gusted in, bringing with it a flurry of sleet. The pilot was screaming something, orders that only the coxswain heeded. She got to her feet from where Falsen had knocked her, staggered to the wheel and took hold of it. The two radio technicians were scrabbling on the deck, trying to save the transceiver components from being trampled on.

Suddenly there was the stink of burning meat. Carlin had hit something organic. Falsen couldn't see what it was; he had joined the coxswain in her struggle to get the ship's nose up. Together they strained at the wheel, trying to force the spokes clockwise. It gave suddenly, too suddenly. Terran and Doralan fell sideways to the deck, the woman on top of Falsen.

He felt the control car hit, heard the rending of metal. He rolled from under the body of the coxswain, tried to get to his feet, just as the airship rebounded from the surface, lurching wildly. He was flung to port, straight for the gap where the window had been, fell through it. It was a drop of only about two meters and he fell into a deep drift of slushy snow. He lay there, dazed, while the crippled airship passed over him, rising at first and then falling again. He thought that it would clear the rounded peak towards which it was heading, but it did not. The gondola hit, its skids jamming on something. But it was not the skids that broke away; it was the ladder into the hull and its enclosing tube.

The ship was turning as she rose, the screws on their outriggers still revolving. Her skin was torn in several places, and from the rents protruded the broken ends of girders. Her rudder was only a metal skeleton from which streamed tatters of fabric.

But she was making headway against the screaming wind, flying as steadily as though the pilot's hands were still at her controls. She was lifting as she flew, would pass directly over the snow-filled hollow in which Falsen was crouched.

A hatch was open in her belly. From it something dropped, a pale object that seemed to be struggling during its descent, that extended arms in a swimming motion. Its fall occupied only seconds, but it seemed to Falsen to last for a very long time; he knew what this piece of jetsam was.

It fell only two metres from where he was standing, thigh-deep in the wet snow.

Then Linda was struggling to her feet, was wading through the drift towards him. She was naked and her skin was blue with cold, but she seemed to be uninjured. She fell into his arms, pressed herself against him.

She whispered, "So you got out too . . . you would, just as I did. . . ."

He said nothing, just held her tightly.

She went on, "So we're back where we started, only worse off. We must be the only survivors. . . ."

He said, "There will be others. The control car is over on that hill."

Slowly they ploughed their way out of the drift and walked toward the gondola, the icy wind on their backs.

CHAPTER 18

The control car had suffered remarkably little damage.

The window burned out by Carlin's laser fire had been covered with a scarlet cloak; as it was on the lee side, the makeshift repair was effective enough. The drained body of the unfortunate Dimilin had been carried outside and laid among the rocks to await burial. Linda was wearing the dead ecologist's tunic and cloak; they were both too short for her and the tunic was too tight, but they were better than nothing. Of the giant leech there was no trace save for a few smears of yellowish ichor; the thick part of its body must have been jammed in the hatch in the airship's keel; so, with the breaking away of the gondola, it had been borne aloft with the derelict.

Working in glum silence, the two radio technicians were trying to put the transceiver together again. The pilot sat slumped in her seat, staring at the now useless controls. She had been sobbing hysterically until Carlin slapped her face sharply. An occasional despondent sniffle still escaped from her. Carlin was still standing, in spite of all that had befallen, very much mistress of herself and of the circumstances. Linda and Falsen sat on the deck, looking up at her.

"So, the thing was not dead," said Carlin slowly. "Dimilin should have made sure that it was before it was brought on board. What happened in the passenger space, Linda?"

"We were all frightened," said the Terran, "when its sucker came snaking in, feeling about . . ." She managed a small laugh. "We were all frightened before then, of course.

I don't know what the others were thinking, but I thought that the ship was breaking up. . . . Well, the sucker fastened onto one of the women and . . . *sucked*. It was over in seconds. The others just huddled there, terrified. I was the only one who tried to fight it. . . .''

"So you tried to fight it," murmured Carlin. "Did you have a weapon of any kind, a knife . . . ?"

"What is this?" Falsen demanded. "A court of enquiry? Can't you see that she's badly shaken? Give her a chance to recover."

"We are all badly shaken, Mr. Falsen. But I think that we should try to sort things out while memories are still fresh." She returned her attention to Linda. "So you fought it. Did you have a knife?"

"No," Linda said at last.

"No? But the thing, or the part of the thing that got in here, had been wounded. It was gashed, bleeding. . . ."

"I was lucky," said Falsen, "that I was not in the same state when I came in here. There were all sorts of sharp ends of broken metal and plastic flying around inside the ship."

"I am not questioning you, Mr. Falsen," Carlin said coldly. "So you fought it, Linda, without weapons. And then it just gave up the struggle and ran away from you, to find easier prey elsewhere. Odd . . . very odd."

"It had killed all the others first," Linda told her. "Two by sucking their blood, the others while it was thrashing about."

"All right. We know that it can kill and that it can deliver very hard blows. So you frightened it off, all by yourself. And then what did you do?"

"I tried to get forward to the control car, to warn you all. But it was blocking up the alleyway. I tried to find some other way to get to you. There was an open hatch; it must have blown open. I looked down and out. I could see the control car, a long way down, stuck on the top of the hill. And I saw Nick, standing in what looked like a snowdrift. So I . . . jumped."

"So you jumped. Have you any idea how high the ship was when you jumped?"

"No . . ."

"Well, I have. I saw it all. The ship must have been all of

a thousand *verslag*—that's about five hundred of your meters—off the ground.''

"I think that you're overestimating, Carlin," said Falsen.

"I bow to the superior judgment of a navigator," she sneered. "But, all the same, it was a long drop."

"You should be congratulating her," flared Falsen, "not interrogating her as though she's some sort of criminal."

"It is I, Mr. Falsen, who will have to submit a written report on this business. I must endeavor to find out just what did happen. But, as Mr. Falsen feels that I should, I do congratulate you, Linda. Most people, falling as you did, would have been smashed to a bloody pulp."

"The snow was deep," Falsen said. "And there could have been some freak updraft."

Carlin laughed, "Yes, we've had our fill of freak updrafts. And downdrafts. But there's another thing that puzzles me, Linda. Why were you naked when you jumped out?"

"I . . . I was fighting the thing . . . my uniform . . . torn . . ."

"As you can see," Falsen told Carlin, "it took a patch out of the back of *my* shirt."

She said coldly, "I am trying to get the Lady Linda's story, Mr. Falsen. I shall get it faster if you do not persist in trying to tell it for her. I am still puzzled by her nudity when she abandoned the airship."

"My clothing," said Linda, "was in the creature's way when it tried to get its sucker on to my skin."

"Then why," asked Carlin, "didn't it suck you dry, as it did with Dimilin?"

"I . . . I don't know. It . . . it sort of lost interest."

"Perhaps it didn't care for the flavor of Terrans. It didn't fasten on to Falsen either, although it could have. But, Linda, surely it didn't pull your shoes off?"

"I kicked them off myself, Carlin. The deck was slippery underfoot and the ship was lurching. After I'd fallen a couple of times I thought that I'd get along better with bare feet."

"All right. You're here. You're alive. So is Pansir. So are Dorral and Lur. So is Falsen. So am I. I think that I'm speaking for all of us when I say that I want to stay that way. We don't know how long it will be before we're picked up. My guess is that the Lady Mother will lift ship and come looking for us. The helicopters are too small for a rescue operation and their range is very short. There are the parts for

assembling another airship in the stores—a smaller craft than
the one we have lost, and nonrigid—but putting the thing
together will take time. There is another problem . . ." She
spoke in her own language to the radio technicians, listened
to their reply. "Yes," she went on to Linda and Falsen,
"there is another problem. Dorral and Lur think that the
transceiver is back in working order. But the power cell was
broken when we crashed. There will be other power cells,
hopefully intact, in the airship. But *where* is the airship?"

To that rhetorical question there was no answer.

Carlin continued, "It may be down not far from here.
There may be survivors. And there will be the emergency
rations and, too, the power cells. . . ."

Falsen looked out through a window. The wind had risen
again, was bringing with it huge wet flakes of snow.

He said, "We can't make a search in this weather."

"Of course not," agreed Carlin. "We shall have to wait
until it clears. Sunset is not far off. Perhaps tomorrow it will
be better. So, we sleep. The warmth from our bodies will
keep away the worst of the chill. . . ."

It was, Falsen realised, quite stuffy in the control car.
Probably the snow piling up on the weather side was acting as
insulation.

"And we should not be squeamish," Carlin continued.
"We must keep our strength up. We will eat before we rest."

Of the other Doralans only Pansir understood Standard
English. She expostulated in that language, "What do you
say, Lady Carlin? What is it you mean? There is no food in
the car."

"There is outside," Carlin said.

And there is precedent, thought Falsen, *ample precedent.*
But usually survivors of a wreck waited until they were
starving before doing the obvious thing.

"Carlin!" cried the pilot. "Surely you do not intend . . ."

"What else, Pansir?" She squatted down by the radiowomen's tool box, took out from it a short knife, tested the
edge of it on her thumb. Carrying it, she went to the sliding
door on the lee side of the car. Falsen helped her open it; the
panel had been slightly warped by the crash. He looked out
after her into the swirling whiteness. After she had taken no
more than three steps he lost sight of her. He wondered how
she would find that white corpse among the snow-covered

rocks and if, after having found the body and done what she had to do, she would be able to find her way back to the gondola.

He turned, called to the others, "I'd better go with her."

Pansir looked at him with loathing.

The icy wind eddied about him, seeming to assault him from all directions at once as backdrafts were engendered by the large boulders and by the control car. Yet this was advantageous; his abnormally keen sense of smell was able to pick up both Carlin's distinctive scent and the odor of dead flesh.

When he found her she was stooped over the body of the ecologist, was working busily with her knife at the right hip joint. There was very little blood.

She turned, looked around and up. She did not seem pleased to see him.

"What do *you* want?" she demanded.

"I thought that you might need help."

"I don't." Then, grudgingly, "Since you are here you might as well lend a hand. Get hold of her leg just above the knee and twist. . . ."

Falsen did as he was told. The skin of the corpse was cold and wet and he had to take a very firm grip to prevent his hands from slipping. He assumed—rightly, as it happened—that Doralan skeletal structure was similar to that of Terran humans, that at the hip there would be a ball-and-socket joint. He twisted, first one way and then the other. It seemed to him that Dimilin was resisting this brutal violation of her body. But that could not possibly be. She was dead, very dead, drained of all vital fluids.

He looked down at Carlin, who was hacking away with the inadequate little knife, sawing through gristle and tendon. The exposed flesh was almost as pale as the peeled-back skin, as the white-gleaming bone. In the swirling gray pallor of the snowstorm the only touch of color was Carlin's scarlet cloak, although its brightness was fast becoming dimmed by the adherence of the huge wet flakes.

He wrenched viciously, felt something tear. He twisted the other way and tugged. Something gave. He went over backward, still clutching the severed limb in both hands. There was enough snow on the rocks behind him to cushion his fall.

Carlin was standing over him. She stooped, extending a hand. He thought that she was about to help him to his feet but he was wrong. She snatched the severed limb from his relaxed grip. She turned, the grisly trophy clutched to her, vanished into a snow flurry. Falsen scrambled erect, set off after her. He could not see for more than a foot ahead of him. He felt the beginnings of panic. He might well miss the control car and wander into the storm. He deliberately let his mind go blank, allowed instinct to take over.

He was almost surprised when he stumbled into the metal side of the car. He felt his way along it until he found the sliding door. When he had it open only a crack, the smell of roasting meat assailed his nostrils. Carlin had set the naked, severed limb on the deck, had set her laser pistol to low intensity and was playing the wide beam over the . . . meat. Linda was watching, the pointed tip of her pink tongue playing over her lips. Pansir was making a major production of not watching. The radiowomen were trying not to watch but could not refrain from ever more frequent and lengthy glances.

Carlin switched off her laser. The meat was little more than warmed through.

She said, "All right. We have food. Who wants some?"

"I do," said Linda.

"Then, help yourself. Here's the knife."

Linda took the blade, carved a thick strip from the thigh. Pansir was watching, her face contorted with horror. Dorral and Lur looked on in shocked silence. Linda handed the knife back to Carlin and with her other hand brought the meat to her mouth. She chewed hungrily.

"Falsen?" asked Carlin.

"I may as well," he said. "Thank you for letting us have first go. Or is this just an attempt to blacken us in the eyes of your fellow Doralans?"

"Are you hungry or aren't you?" she demanded.

"I am," he admitted.

He accepted the knife, hacked off a large portion of the almost bloodless flesh. It was too dry, he thought. That leech had taken the best of it. While he was eating he watched Carlin, who was slicing the calf muscle away from the bone. She offered this portion first to the pilot, who screamed and averted her face. She held it out to the radiowomen. He could not understand what they were saying, but he could guess. Their expressions were not hard to read.

"When they are really hungry," said Carlin, "they will eat." She bit into the flesh that she was holding, continued talking through a full mouth. "But why wait until you are weakened by starvation before doing the logical thing?"

You cold-blooded bitch! thought Falsen. It was one thing for Linda and himself to make a meal from the dead body of the ecologist. In their case it was not really cannibalism. But Carlin should not have been putting on such a show of gustatory enjoyment. Perhaps it was intended to persuade her fellow Doralans what she was doing was neither wrong—which, of course, it was not—nor revolting.

Linda had another portion of almost-raw ecologist. Falsen had his second helping, as did Carlin. By this time it was almost dark in the wrecked control car. Pansir suggested that Carlin use her laser pistol as a torch. Carlin said that the charge must be conserved in case the device should be required as a weapon.

Falsen and Linda huddled together for warmth. Pansir, Dorral and Lur huddled together, whimpering softly. Falsen realised that, in spite of the circumstances, he would sleep well. (After all, he had a full belly.) In his arms Linda was already snoring softly. But surely there was rather too much of her, too many legs, too many arms. . . .

Carlin had joined them, was bedding down with them.

Presumably, her shipmates would have none of her.

CHAPTER 19

Falsen was awakened by the light streaming through the control-car windows. They were clear of their coating of caked snow and ice, afforded a view of a rocky landscape with only a few fast-diminishing patches of white in crevices and hollows. The sky was almost clear, the overcast high and thin.

He disentangled himself from Carlin and Linda, who protested sleepily. The three other Doralans, he saw, were already awake, were staring at him with hostility. They must have spent a miserable night, tormented by hunger. But had they? Surely there had been much more meat on Dimilin's leg when he had retired.

And so what?

He went to the sliding door, pulled it open. The air outside was quite mild. He found a pool of melted snow among the rocks, drank from cupped hands. In a hollow out of sight from the wrecked cab he relieved himself. He was hungry then, went in search of the dead ecologist's remains. He found the body—what was left of it. It looked to be no more than a bag of loose skin over dry bones. He stirred it with his foot. Something moved. He stamped, in sudden revulsion. From the hole in the skin where the leg had been removed emerged something long and gray, many-legged, that vanished into a crevice between two boulders.

That was breakfast, that was, he thought.

"We should have kept her in the car," said Carlin.

"We didn't," he said, turning to look at her.

"We didn't," she agreed. "And so we're hungry. Linda and I had what was left of Dimilin's leg. It wasn't much. The others had been at it during the night. They denied it, of course, but . . ."

"But you and Linda had something," he complained. His belly complained too.

"More gristle than meat," she said.

"But *something*. . . ."

"You're the mighty hunter, aren't you? There are animals of some kind around here. Go and catch something."

I'd like to catch you, he thought. *That's a pleasure yet to come. But not here, not now. Not until we're out of this mess.*

He stood there, turning slowly until he was facing the wind, the light, steady breeze that was blowing from the south. He could smell the usual scents—brackish water, rotting vegetation. And, faintly, faintly, something more. A metallic tang and meat not too long dead, still perfectly edible.

"Are you coming with me?" he asked. "You've a pistol. We might need it."

"Of course," she said.

"And Linda . . ."

"I left her in charge, in the car. Pansir's quite useless, and the other two are only erks. I told her to make sure that none of them wandered off and got lost."

"All right, then. Let's get going."

He led the way, downhill, following his nose. The going was not too hard, the moss-covered ground smooth enough, although slippery between the boulders. The previous day's snowfall was now almost vanished; around the surviving drifts a funguslike growth, fleshy yellow balls atop slender stems, was sprouting. Already the spheres were swelling, almost visibly, and some of them, disturbed by the eddies generated by their passage, burst, emitting gray clouds of airborne spores.

They came to the bottom of the valley, waded across a shallow, icy-cold stream. Falsen had lost the scent but thought that if he carried on in a straight line, up to the crest of the ridge, he would find it again. It was heavy going uphill, and the diffused light of the planet's primary was surprisingly warm. His shirt was damp with perspiration, but he did not pause for a rest, telling himself that he would do so when he got to the crest. Behind him he heard Carlin's animallike panting.

He arrived at the top of the ridge.

There was no need for him to rely any longer upon his sense of smell. Downhill, no more than three kilometers distant, was the wreck of the airship—a tangle of frames and longerons poking up through torn silvery fabric. It did not look like anything that had ever flown; it could have been a huge circus tent demolished by a tornado.

"Come on," he said, starting down the boulder-strewn slope.

They made good time without any pauses for rest. Carlin, Falsen had to admit grudgingly, was as surefooted as he was—more so, perhaps. He could see how it was that she, although an engineer, had been placed in charge of the spaceship's exploration parties. She could adapt, could revert to the primitive without mental or physical strain.

The smell of meat was becoming stronger. Falsen stumbled over the first of the corpses, a crewwoman who had either jumped or fallen from the airship before the final crash. The cause of death was obvious—legs broken and the skull shattered on a rock. Falsen was tempted. He was hungry.

And Carlin?

She looked at the broken body, then at him.

She said—regretfully?—"There are emergency provisions aboard the airship. . . ."

She did not mention the possibility of there being survivors of the wreck. But there were no survivors, Falsen knew. The only smell carried by the light breeze from the tangle of metal and fabric was that of death.

They pushed on.

There were two more Doralan bodies, broken by their falls as the first had been. There was what they decided must be the remains of the giant leech. Its swollen body had burst on impact, spattering rocks and moss with blood—its own and that of its victims, still undigested.

There was the wreck itself.

They found a rent in the fabric long enough and wide enough to admit them. Carlin used her laser pistol, set for wide beam and low intensity, as a torch. She seemed to know where she was going. To Falsen the interior of the crashed airship was no more than a sort of maze, a tangle of tunnels whose walls were loose fabric from which protruded sharp points and edges of metal and plastic as a hazard to the unwary. Soon his shirt was ripped in several places and one leg of his shorts was shredded. Although she had the light and was in the lead, Carlin fared little better.

She said, her voice a high-pitched twitter, "We're almost there. . . ."

"Where is 'there'?" asked Falsen squeakily.

Was he losing his voice? he wondered. Was he suffering from a sudden attack of laryngitis?

"The galley," replied Carlin, her voice so high as to be almost inaudible. She laughed shrilly. "The atmosphere in here must be almost pure helium. But it won't kill us."

"I hope," said Falsen in a disconcerting soprano.

The noise of tearing fabric was normal enough as Carlin enlarged a rent. And then she and Falsen were standing in a little compartment where there was a recognizable microwave oven and a large urn for tea-making. There were cupboards, one of which Carlin opened, taking from a shelf two cylindrical containers with rip-off tops. She handed one to Falsen. The contents of the cans heated automatically once they were broached. About all that could be said in favor of the thin, sweetish mush was that it was hot.

Carlin threw the empty container into a bin. She handed her laser pistol to Falsen.

"Hold this," she ordered, "while I disconnect the power cells from the appliances. It's less trouble to carry them back to the car than to unship the radio and bring it here."

That made sense, he thought.

Later, as he struggled up the hillside away from the wreck, burdened with a sack improvised from envelope fabric in which were not only the power cells but cans of food, he decided that, whoever was being saved trouble, it was not himself.

CHAPTER 20

They heard the spaceship long before they saw her, the distant, irritable mutter of her inertial drive drifting in through the almost still air, seeming to come from all directions at once. She had been maintaining a listening watch, it seemed, and had replied as soon as Carlin made her call on the now operable transceiver. Now she was homing on the signal from the wrecked control car. The mutter increased in intensity, became a grumble, a snarl beating down through the ruddy overcast. Standing outside the car with Linda and Pansir, Falsen stared upwards. He saw her at last, a silvery spindle dim through the cloud veil and then dropping clear of the vaporous ceiling. Her descent was rapid at first and then it slowed, slowed and stopped. She was hanging about a kilometer above the castaways. Suddenly, with the application of lateral thrust, the beat of the mighty engines rose to a crescendo. She moved slowly away, proceeding toward the main wreckage of the dirigible.

Carlin came out of the car.

She said bad-temperedly, "*She* says that she can't land here."

"Did you expect her to?" he asked.

"Why not?" Carlin made a sweeping gesture. "There are patches of ground that are big enough, clear of rocks . . ."

"But none of them level," Falsen told her. "*I* wouldn't try it."

She snorted, went back inside the car.

"A typical engineer," said Falsen to Linda. "Knows more

about navigation and shiphandling than any captain. But if I were in the Lady Mother's shoes, I'd do just what she's doing now. Find a nice level site in the big valley, near the airship, and set down there."

The spaceship dipped from sight beyond the further ridge. The cacophony of the drive was muffled by the intervening tonnes of rock and soil, then ceased. She was down.

Carlin came out of the car again.

"She is sending helicopters for us," she announced. She walked to where the pitiful remains of Dimilin were sprawled among the boulders. The skeleton was complete now, although the bones of one leg were bare, not covered by wrinkled skin. She stooped, caught hold of the thin integument, tugged, ripped. Ribs were exposed, and pelvis, and the bones of a clawlike hand. She said, "If we had known that her body would be so . . . mauled by scavenging animals, we would have kept her inside the car." She looked sternly at Pansir and the two Terrans. "Remember now, all of you. There was no cannibalism. I've had words with Lur and Dorral, put the fear of Birrick into them. They won't talk. They know that I know that they had a nibble of Dimilin's leg during the night. As *you* did, Pansir. The Lady Mother is easily shocked. We don't want her to know what we've been eating." She laughed harshly. "It's just as well that we brought those cans back from the airship. The empties are evidence that we haven't been eating what we shouldn't."

Falsen felt argumentative. He asked, "But why bother to lie? It has always been held—in Terran law, anyhow—that in certain circumstances cannibalism is justifiable."

She sneered, "And in your case, of course, it wasn't really cannibalism, was it?"

How much does she know? Falsen asked himself.

The helicopters came, five of them, flying in line astern. They were flimsy machines, little more than open frameworks surmounted by whirling rotors. They circled the control car before they landed, looking for clear patches among the rocky outcroppings. They set down on the bare slope on which Carlin had thought that the Lady Mother would be able to land the spaceship. The pilots remained in their aircraft.

Carlin led the way to the waiting helicopters. Falsen looked at the one that was supposed to carry him and said, "I'd rather walk."

"Do not be foolish," Carlin told him. "Get in."

Falsen sighed and insinuated his body into the tangle of structural members behind the pilot's seat. *She,* he noted enviously, was sitting in relative comfort on a proper chair, protected by a curved windscreen. He had to make do with an affair of flimsy-seeming straps, like a hammock in miniature, that barely accommodated his buttocks. There were looped straps through which, he thought, he was supposed to insert his arms. There was a horizontal spar on which to rest his feet.

He looked around. Linda was seated. The uniform that she had taken from the dead Dimilin had split in several places as she had made the necessary contortions to get into the too-small seat; the hem of the short tunic had ridden up almost to waist level. She looked like a near-naked slave girl imprisoned in a metal cage.

Carlin was seated, as were Lur and Dorral. The radiowomen looked scared.

Overhead the rotors began to spin, the blades blurring to transparency. The helicopters sprang into the air. There was no canopy to block the downdraft over the passenger seats, but there was an arrangement of vanes which quite effectively deflected it.

Carlin's aircraft in the lead, the helicopters rapidly flew across the col, passed over the ridge beyond which was the wide valley. There was the spaceship, a dull-gleaming tower not far from the untidy tangle of spars and fabric that was the wreckage of the dirigible. Looking at it, Falsen was reminded of something that he had once seen during a leave on Earth, a holiday that he had spent mainly in the bush. He had come upon the body of a bird—how it had died or been killed he never knew. It had been swarming with ants, many of which were carrying fragments of flesh back to their city.

So it was with the airship.

Like ants, the scarlet-uniformed spacewomen were all over her. Cutting torches were flaring, shearing through frames and longerons. Salvageable equipment was being carried out from the wreck. Envelope fabric was not being slashed haphazardly but cut away in neat rectangles and rolled up tidily and loaded onto little powered trolleys to be carried to the spaceship. From an open cargo port in her side a boom was extended, with a hoisting tackle. As Falsen watched, a roll of fabric was lifted and then swung inboard.

The helicopters came in for a landing.

While Falsen was disentangling himself, a junior officer came from the spaceship, talked briefly to Carlin. Carlin gave orders in her own language to Lur and Dorral, then said, "The Lady Mother wishes to see us."

The five survivors walked to the spaceship, climbed the ramp to the after air lock. The elevator cage was waiting for them. They were carried swiftly upwards to the captain's quarters.

The Lady Mother was waiting for them, sitting behind her big desk. She rose as they entered her day cabin—Carlin in the lead, then Pansir, then Falsen and Linda and, finally, the two petty officers. She motioned them to chairs and resumed her own seat. A stewardess came in with a big tray, poured cups of the inevitable aniseed tea.

A tremulous smile lightened the Lady Mother's careworn face. She said, "I must congratulate you on your survival." She repeated this in her own language for the benefit of the monolingual radiowomen. The smile faded. "But there were many who did not survive," she said.

"They died well," said Falsen tritely.

(Some of them, he thought, most surely had. Some, terrified, had gone screaming into the darkness.)

"They died," said Carlin bluntly. "Others have died. It may well be that more will die."

"Lady Carlin," snapped the Lady Mother, "that was unnecessary."

"Please accept my apologies, Gracious Lady," said the engineer insincerely.

"I accept," said the captain at last. "And now, while the dreadful events are still fresh in your memories, I wish to hear your stories. All that you say is, of course, being recorded. Do you have any objections Mr. Falsen? Miss Veerhausen?"

"No," said Falsen, and "No," said Linda.

"Very well. Perhaps, Lady Pansir, you will make your report first. I am sure that you are anxious to supervize the . . . taking apart of your airship and the bringing of the control car from where it was dropped. Would you mind using Standard English so that our guests will understand what is being said?''

Slowly, at times searching for words, the airship pilot told her story. It was a straightforward account of what had happened. There was only one omission, the dismemberment and eating of Dimilin's corpse. Then she was dismissed and hurried from the day cabin, no doubt anxious to save what she could from the wreck.

Lur and Dorral did little more than answer the Lady Mother's questions and then were allowed to go.

''And now, Lady Carlin?'' asked the Lady Mother.

''There is very little that I can add, Gracious Lady. My opinion is that the airship would not have been lost if the . . . leech had not intruded into the control car at a crucial moment. Until then the Lady Pansir was in complete control.''

''Mr. Falsen?''

''I'm a spaceman, not an airshipman, Gracious Lady. But I was impressed by Pansir's competence.''

''Miss Veerhausen?''

''That *thing* should never have been brought aboard the airship, Gracious Lady.''

''So . . .'' The Doralan captain toyed with her empty teacup. ''So . . . so the Lady Dimilin seems to be to blame for the disaster. But this is a strange world, with strange animals. We have to learn as we go along—too often the hard way. Lady Carlin, will you make a personal inspection of the inertial drive? It seemed to me that during our flight here from the first landing place it was not behaving as well as it should.

''Mr. Falsen and Miss Veerhausen, as you were among those aboard the airship, it will be fitting if you attend the funeral rites for those who lost their lives. The ceremony will take place just after sunset.

''Tomorrow morning we lift ship and return to our original base.''

''Why not stay here, Gracious Lady?'' asked Falsen. ''This is as good a location from which to explore, to carry out surveys, as any.''

''It is not, Mr. Falsen. There is *something* infesting the neighborhood of the first landing site, something that lurks in the caves and the lakes, something that has already killed too many of my people. If this world is to be made suitable for colonization, that something must be identified and brought under control—or exterminated.''

Yes, there was something, Falsen thought.

There was the thing that *he* knew about, that would be there no matter where the spaceship landed on this planet's surface.

But there was something else.

CHAPTER 21

They stood there among the ship's senior officers, their uniforms in bedraggled contrast to the gold and scarlet of the
Doralans. (Linda's discarded clothing had been found in the
wrecked dirigible and returned to her.) The spacewomen were
drawn up with military precision in a hollow square, in the
center of which, on a slab of some dull metal, were disposed
the bodies of those who had died in the airship disaster. They
had been arranged with what decorum was possible, the more
dreadful wounds concealed, limbs straightened.

The Lady Mother came out from the spaceship. She was
wearing a somber gray uniform, not her usual scarlet. In her
arms she was carrying what looked like a bundle of cloth, its
colors, even in the fast-dimming light, bright, almost garish.
As she approached the metal slab she shook this out, threw
the ends of it from her, released it so that it settled over the
bodies, covering them.

It was a silken flag, a banner of glowing crimson upon
which was a design of interlocked triangles in gold and silver.
The flag of Dorala, Falsen wondered, or of one of the major
nations of that world? The ensign of the Doralan space service?
Yes, that was it. He recalled having seen a chart displaying
the colors of the various spacefaring powers.

The Lady Mother made a minor adjustment to the folds of
the flag, pulling it slightly to cover one protruding foot. She
stood there briefly, her head bowed, then walked slowly to
the group of senior officers. She did not join them, although a

space was made for her, but took position a little ahead of the rank.

She spoke, her voice high and clear. Eulogy or prayer? Falsen did not know, but even though the valediction was said in a language strange to him, he sensed the poetry of it, the measured cadences. She paused, and there was a response from the Doralans. She spoke again, paused again. Again there came the murmured response.

Suddenly her voice was sharper, crackling with authority. Under her gray cloak was a belted side arm. She drew it from its holster with a sweeping gesture. As one, her crew followed suit. She brought her hand down, aimed at the flag-covered slab. The spacewomen did likewise.

She fired, as did the others.

The almost invisible beams impinged upon the pyre. Banner and bodies flared, and it seemed that the corpses writhed in the midst of their smoky combustion. But it was all over in seconds, and on the incandescent surface of the slab, blue-white dimming to red, was no more than gray ash and a few fragments that could have been charred twigs. The smell of incinerated flesh was sweet and heavy in the damp air.

Linda sneezed loudly.

The Lady Mother reholstered her pistol. The other Doralans put away their weapons. The senior officers made way for the Captain as she walked slowly back to the ship, to the ramp, to the open air-lock door. The crew members broke ranks. Some of them brought a metal container, a cylinder with a screw top, from the foot of the gangway, set it down by the pyre. One put an experimental finger to the surface of the metal slab, no longer glowing, and withdrew it hastily.

Her voice very matter of fact Carlin said, "They will have to get the ashes into the urn as soon as possible in case any wind should spring up during the night. *She* has decided that the remains are to be taken back to Dorala and scattered in the atmosphere."

"Are there any further ceremonies here and now?" asked Falsen.

"There will be the . . . wake. You have already attended one. I do not think that you should do so again; the last time that you did so it was felt, by many, that an outsider should not have been present."

"I can understand that," said Falsen. "After all, as far as you people are concerned, Linda and I are the aliens."

"*You* are," said Carlin. "Linda isn't. It's a matter of sex rather than of race. And your world should be represented at the ceremonies. By the Lady Linda."

"Must I?" asked the girl.

"Yes," Falsen told her.

"Yes," said Carlin firmly.

CHAPTER 22

Falsen sat in his cabin, hunched up on the short, narrow bunk. He supposed that he might as well try to get some sleep; there was nothing to do to occupy himself, nothing to read. Presumably Linda would look in on him when the wake was over, but he did not know how long it would be. He was beginning to undress when he heard the tapping on his door.

"Come in!" he called.

It was Carlin.

"Is the wake over?" he asked.

"No. It will go on for hours. I've just finished checking the inertial drive; there was nothing wrong with it that a spanner couldn't fix. And now I'm going to have a drink. Or two. And I don't like drinking alone."

"I've nothing here," said Falsen.

"I didn't think that you would. But I have plenty in my cabin."

Should he? Falsen wondered. Then, *Why not?*

Nonetheless, a little later, he was feeling uneasy.

This was the first time that he had been really alone with one of the Doralans. He was neither xenophobe nor male chauvinist, but this alien female was inducing in him a strong feeling of disquiet. His skin prickled as his body hairs, confined by his clothing, tried to stand erect.

Carlin smiled smugly. Her broad face with its pug nose and wide, thick lips could have been that of some predatory

animal toying, sharp-clawed, with a helpless, terrified prey.
Her very big, very deep blue eyes regarded him.

She said throatily, "You Terries have a saying that I have
heard and rather like. 'This is Liberty Hall; you can spit on
the mat and call the cat a bastard.' "

Falsen managed a laugh. "If he were here I'd do just
that."

She laughed too. "You don't like Pondor any more than he
likes you. Both you and he have made it obvious."

"I've rather gained the impression," he said, "that he
doesn't like you much either."

"He doesn't like anybody except the Lady Mother. And
himself, of course. But be seated, Mr. Falsen."

"Thank you, Lady Carlin."

There was only one chair in the cabin and she had taken the
divan. He did not think that she wished him to sit by her. He
lowered himself on to the too-soft cushion. His buttocks sank
deeply into it. It seemed that the padded arms were about to
fold inwards and imprison him in a firm embrace. *Imagination,*
he told himself sharply; nonetheless, this piece of furniture,
constructed to the requirements of Doralan rather than Terran
anatomy, had readjusted its contours under his weight almost
as though it were a living thing.

There was what seemed to be a very long silence.

She broke it.

"The cat got your tongue?" she asked, then laughed.
"You have so many sayings about cats in your language."

" 'A cat may look at a king,' for example," said Falsen.

And he, no king, was looking at a cat. No, not quite a cat
. . . her legs, exposed by her short uniform tunic and folded
under her, were too plump, although tapering to daintily slim
ankles. Yet the feet were . . . pudgy. She had kicked off her
sandals and he could see her short toes, each tipped by a
pointed, scarlet enameled nail.

Paws.

And claws.

"Shall we take refreshment, Mr. Falsen?" she asked.

A nice saucer of milk? he wondered wildly.

She slid off the divan. Her legs, despite their plumpness,
were very long in proportion to her torso. She looked down at
him trapped in the chair.

She said, "I could offer you a choice of our own wines—but we both like gin, don't we? Pink gin . . ."

"Pink gin would be fine," he said.

She padded to the large cabinet set against one of the bulkheads of her cabin, her feet silent on the thick carpet. The door opened as she uttered a short, musical word in her own language; a shelf, with a little recessed sink, slid out. She stooped to get bottles from the lower compartment. The hem of her tunic rode up. She was wearing nothing under it. Her rump was large, firm, poised enticingly above the smooth fullness of her bare thighs. More than just a hint of pink gleamed moistly at the conjunction of the twin dusky moons.

She straightened, busied herself mixing the drinks. She did so in the classical although rather wasteful manner, shaking bitters into the chilled glasses, swirling the aromatic fluid to coat the inner surfaces, throwing out the surplus into the sink. She poured gin with a generous hand, added tetrahedrons of ice.

She handed him one tumbler, then returned to her seat on the divan, raising her own glass in salutation as soon as she was settled.

"Here's looking at you," she said.

"I've been looking at you," said Falsen. Somehow it seemed expected of him.

She laughed. "I suppose that you must have been. In our ships we are so used to an all-female environment that it never occurred to me that I might be offending male susceptibilities. . . ."

All-female environment? thought Falsen. *What about the male stowaway in the storeroom?*

He said, "My susceptibilities weren't offended."

"I am glad about that. After all, you are a guest."

"Yes."

"You do not look very comfortable in that chair. And your clothes look tight."

"I'm all right," said Falsen.

He gulped his drink. It was good, although there was a subtly alien quality to it. There should not have been; even though distracted by the display of female flesh, he had seen familiar labels on both bottles, the gin and the bitters. The ice, perhaps? Could it make any difference if it came in three-sided pyramids rather than cubes?

She stated definitely, "You are *not* comfortable."

She tossed down the remains of her drink, dropped the tumbler carelessly to the deck. She slid sinuously off the divan, displaying her hairless pudenda as she did so. She approached him slowly, slinking almost, her plump, short-fingered hands extended. He put down his own glass, unfinished, as she came to him. He was acutely conscious of the scent of her, too acrid to be altogether pleasant, alien yet disturbingly familiar. He knew that she wanted him (she had been making that obvious enough) and knew that he wanted her. He tried to get up, but that damned chair was reluctant to let go of him. Then she had taken his hands in hers and was pulling, lifting. She was amazingly strong.

They stood pressed together, body to body. He could feel the taut nipples of her almost nonexistent breasts through her clothing and his. He walked her backward to the bed. Her foot came down on the glass that she had dropped; it did not break but rolled under her sole. She fell backward on to the divan, pulling him with her. They were kissing, her tongue busy in his open mouth. Somehow her tunic was off, a splash of gold-trimmed scarlet on the black carpet. He felt her hands busy with his own clothing, and his slate gray shorts and shirt joined her more colorful uniform on the deck.

At first he was awkward. But this, he soon realized, was not her first experience of interspecies sexual congress. (She must have done more at the Antarctic Academy than acquire a taste for Terran liquor.) She fondled him expertly, and her little capable hands guided him into the voracious depths of her, the hot moistness, the unfamiliar, soft-yet-firm internal protuberances that clutched and held.

He wondered what the sound was, the vibration that was transmitted from her body to his, then knew that she was purring with pleasure.

Abruptly, explosively, it was over. She erupted beneath him as her claws scored his back. She subsided as he collapsed upon her, yet, consciously or unconsciously, she was reluctant to let go of him. Her hands roved over his body and she whispered (as Linda had done that first time), "You hairy bastard!" Then, "Oh, the *feel* of you!"

Almost automatically his hands were caressing her. Her skin was not as smooth as he had expected that it would be; from groin almost to breasts he could feel stubble. So she was not as hairless as he had thought the Doralans to be. But so what? After all, he had been supplied with depilatory cream from the ship's stores; if there had been no demand for it, it would not have been available for his use. (But hadn't he been told that it had been made up especially for him?)

At last he rolled off her. There was barely room for both of them, side by side, on the divan.

She raised herself on her elbow, looked down at him. A satisfied smile curved her full mouth.

She murmured, "We must do this again some time, Falsen. Admit it, I'm better than that bitch of yours."

But she was not. With her there could never be the very real togetherness that he shared—sometimes—with Linda. After all, he and the Terran girl were the same breed. This Carlin would always be an alien.

"We can do things together, Falsen," she whispered.

"We've just proved that," he said.

But had he grasped her real meaning?

What *was* her real meaning?

"Don't go yet," she cajoled as he made a move to slide off the bed.

"I must, Carlin. The wake or the service or whatever you call it will be over soon and Linda will be looking for me. I must shower, and . . ."

"You mean that I stink?" She was amused rather than furious. "You mean that your Dog Star Line bitch will smell the scent of me on you?"

"Frankly, yes."

"You're odorous yourself, Falsen. But *I* don't mind."

He broke away from her, not without reluctance, swung his feet to the deck. He picked up his shirt, shrugged into it. He put on his shorts. He stooped to kiss her.

He said, deliberately flippant, "Thanks for the party, Lady Carlin."

She said, "I'll see you again, Falsen," Then, as he turned to go, "We're compatible. I had to be sure of that. You need me—and I just might need you. . . ."

Aren't the fancy boys that you've got stashed away in the storerooms good enough for you? he thought.

"When the balloon goes up . . ." she murmured.

And what the hell do you mean by that? he asked himself as he let himself out into the alleyway.

• • •

Later he was asked by Linda, "How did you get those scratches on your back?"

Hadn't they faded yet?

"That bloody Pondor," he lied. "He attacked me."

She picked up his shirt from the deck of his cabin.

"No blood," she said. "No rips apart from the patch that the leech took out. Odd . . ."

"I wasn't wearing it at the time," he told her. "I went down to the gymnasium to get some exercise while the rest of you were at the wake."

"Oh. You should complain to the Lady Mother—you seem to be rather a pet of hers. She should keep that beast under proper control."

Which beast? he wondered.

CHAPTER 23

It was good to be back in the control room of a spaceship under way, thought Falsen, even though he was only a guest and the flight a suborbital one. Before lift-off the Lady Mother had sent a junior officer to invite him up to Control for the short journey back to the original landing site. He had accepted gladly. He wanted to see how the vessel handled and if any modifications had been made to the instrumentation since her transfer from Terran to Doralan registry.

He sat in one of the spare seats, looking around. The Lady Mother was in her chair and the sour-faced Prenta was in hers, the copilot's position, ready to take over should, for any reason, the captain suddenly become incapable of handling the ship. There was an officer at the radar-altimeter, but the radio-telephone transceiver was unmanned; on a world with no Aerospace Control there was nobody to talk to.

Green ready lights glowed on panels, indicating that the ship was sealed, all air-lock doors securely closed. Looking out through a convenient viewport, Falsen saw that nothing of the wrecked dirigible remained on the ground outside. All its components, including the control car, were now neatly stowed in the spaceship's holds. Perhaps the thing could be repaired and reassembled, perhaps not, but all that material would be reused.

Carlin's voice sounded from an intercom speaker. Somehow Falsen could not imagine her in gloves and overalls, queen of her engine room. But that was where she was. She was no pussycat but a skilled astronautical engineer.

A buzzer sounded and the ship trembled as the inertial drive shook itself into life. Inside the ship, thanks to the insulation, its operation was almost silent, but the arhythmic vibration transmitted through every structural member, through the shell plating. A loose fitting somewhere began to rattle. Falsen saw the Lady Mother frown, heard her say something in a sharp voice to her chief officer.

The spaceship lifted slowly at first, then with increasing rapidity. On the master altimeter display figures appeared, flickering into and out of existence at regular intervals. Falsen did not know, of course, what the actual readings were. In a Terran ship they would have been meters at first and then kilometers. There would probably be a table of equivalents within the literature in the vessel's technical library.

Outside the viewports the ground was dropping away. This was a good place to be leaving, thought Falsen. It was a pity that the destination had little, if anything, more to offer. There would only be the swampy terrain with the outcroppings of rock, and that cave and the lake.

If I were the Lady Mother, he thought, I'd scrape up what fissionable material I could from the ship's power reserves and make a bomb and drop it in that lake, and then get the hell off this dreary mudball. He wondered if such a course of action had occurred to her. In the Federation Survey Service there were handbooks giving instructions on how to make explosive devices from whatever was at hand. Quite possibly the Doralans carried such useful instructions in their exploring vessels.

The cloud ceiling was low.

Nothing could be seen now through the viewports but swirling, formless, masses of crimson vapor. The vibration of the drive became stronger as lateral thrust was applied, as the ship's trajectory became a parabola.

Falsen realized that the Lady Mother was speaking to him.

"I said, Mr. Falsen, that I could have made this flight at a relatively low altitude, but I am indulging myself. I want to get out of the atmosphere of this planet, if only briefly. I want to see the sun, unobscured by mist and cloud. I want to see the stars."

"It's your ship, Gracious Lady." *And I don't sound very gracious,* he thought ruefully. He forced a smile. "I shall be pleased to see the stars again myself."

"I thought that you would be, Mr. Falsen." She smiled herself. "Even though the Lady Prenta thinks that I am wasting both time and fuel."

Overhead the mist was thinning and, to one side, the glare from rising Antares was almost dazzling. Viewports polarized, cutting the light down to a tolerable level. Overhead the sky was black, studded with bright, multicolored jewels that were the stars, some great and some small. Recognizable even at this distance, one of the other planets, a gas giant of the Antares system, glowed as a tiny globe. The primary itself, the obscuring clouds now far below and astern, was a sphere, a ruddy furnace, one limb ragged with great prominences. Away from it the ship's shadow, a long black spindle, was cast onto the writhing surface of the eternal cloud.

The Lady Mother sighed.

"I wish I could stay up here. But we must come in for our landing."

"It seems a pity," said Falsen.

This woman is a real spacer, he thought. *Just as I am. The trouble is that it's not all that I am. . . .*

The officer by the radar altimeter turned to the controls of another panel close by that instrument. Something was beeping faintly.

The captain said, "I left visual and radio beacons at the original site. The radio beacon, at least, is functioning."

All Survey Service SOP, thought Falsen. The space ship was dropping now, on the descending leg of the great arc. Ruddy, swirling tendrils of mist rose about the control-room viewports, shutting out the stars, dimming the great red sun. The cloud was thicker again, an oppressive crimson glare that seemed almost solid.

A tiny, pulsing spark appeared at the very edge of the stern view-screen, began to creep, almost imperceptibly at first, towards its center—the radio beacon, guiding them in. Guiding them in, Falsen thought, to whatever it was that awaited them. He grew increasingly uneasy. He knew that there were things that he, that he and Linda, would have to do if they were to survive, make a fresh start elsewhere in the universe. He hoped—but Linda, he knew, did not share his scruples— that he would be able to take the ship without further bloodshed. But it was not this act of piracy that was bothering him. There was some much more immediate danger, to everybody, to Linda and to himself and to the Doralans.

He shifted uneasily in his seat.

The Lady Mother noticed and said, "I thought that you were enjoying the ride, Mr. Falsen."

"I was." He corrected himself. "I mean, I am."

The inertial drive sounded healthy enough, and Carlin, he hoped, would keep it that way. The Lady Mother's competence was not in doubt; apart from what he had seen of her shiphandling, he knew that, on any world, only outstanding officers are selected for the command of exploratory expeditions to strange worlds.

The beacon spark had not reached the center of the screen when the ship broke through the cloud ceiling into the relatively clear air below. Looking out through a viewport, Falsen could see the sullenly glimmering lake—it looked like blood—set in its ring of low black hills. He wondered briefly just what lurked in that body of water besides the giant leeches. But soon, he hoped, he and Linda would not have to worry about that, although it could be of some concern to those marooned. It was a pity that they would have to be left here—but their predicament would not be as desperate as that of the Terrans had been. Sooner or later a ship would be sent from Dorala to find out what had happened, to pick up the survivors.

The vibration of the drive diminished as the ship dropped faster and faster, almost vertically now. As a merchant spaceman, Falsen did not approve of the approach although, during his training cruises in the Survey Service, he had seen the technique used often enough. An almost free drop, with the captain watching the diminishing radar-altimeter figures intently; and then, at what seemed to be the last second, slamming on the vertical thrust, bringing the vessel to a shuddering halt.

He had been bold enough to express his disapproval once to Captain Bannerman. The Old Man laughed harshly and said, "You merchant spacemen are all the same, treating your ships as though they're made of glass. Don't forget, Lieutenant Falsen, Federation Survey Service Reserve, that although this is called the Survey Service, it's really a fighting navy. Earth's fighting navy. If you're ever in command of a warship, you may find out that there are times when you have to get downstairs in a hurry—just as there are times when you have to get upstairs in a hurry. And when, for your sins, you're captain of a mere transport or survey ship proper, you keep in practice just as I'm doing now. So keep your eyes glued to the radar-altimeter screen, and if I haven't put the brakes on by the time it reads fifty meters, either give me a nudge or pray to all the Odd Gods of the Galaxy. Or do both.''

Falsen smiled at the memory.

He looked at the succession of figures showing at the bottom of the stern view-screen, then at the same flickering numerals on the radar-altimeter display. Possibly the young officer at the altimeter had been told, by her captain, what Bannerman had told him. She was beginning to look worried. So was Prenta, in her copilot's chair. He wished that he knew which of the luminous squiggles corresponded to fifty meters.

He looked at the Lady Mother.

One hand was poised over the control console before her and she was watching the screen intently. The hand descended, not hurriedly, to the small thrust-adjustment wheel, turned it firmly clockwise. The vibration of the drive rose to bone-shaking, teeth-rattling intensity—then stopped. Throughout the ship alarm bells were sounding.

The drive started again—but too late, much too late.

Had this not been an old ship, her structure weakened by age, she might still have made her landing without disaster. Had each of the three great vanes of her landing gear struck soil of uniform consistency, all might yet have been well. But two of the vanes sank into mossy loam; the third struck a boulder only centimeters below the soft surface. Fatigued metal twisted, snapped. The ship heeled over, a toppling tower. There would still have been time to get up and clear, had the inertial drive not cut out again for the last time, had a feed line from the water tanks to the auxiliary reaction drive not fractured with the first shock. The brief blast from the venturis arrested downward motion but did nothing to stop the topple.

Strapped in his chair, Falsen watched the far horizon swing up, up, until all that he could see through the viewport was the gray, marshy soil rising up, faster and faster, to hit him, to smash him.

Carlin . . . he thought. *If she'd done a proper overhaul on her engines instead of cavorting with me* . . .

He would survive, he knew. And so would Linda. But what of the others?

What of the ship?

She hit, with a bone-shaking thud. Had it not been for the softness of the terrain, things would have been very much worse.

He squirmed out of the retaining strap, let himself drop. He landed on all fours on the transparency of a viewport, through which he could see black mud and white wriggling things, some crushed but still twitching. He came erect, looked up. The Lady Mother was directly above him, staring down at him. Her face was colorless, but she was alive.

"Unsnap your belt!" he called. "I'll catch you!"

She understood, released herself. She dropped heavily, clumsily, but he broke her fall, even though he was knocked over backward. The pair of them sprawled, recovering their wind, while Prenta and the junior officer managed to get out of their seats unaided.

The chief officer glared at him.

She said, "I have heard of the men you call, in your ships, Jonahs. You are one. First *your* spaceship. Then the dirigible. Now *this* . . ."

The Lady Mother was recovering.

She rolled off Falsen, got shakily to her feet.

She snapped, "Lady Prenta, do not be absurd. There are no such beings as Jonahs. I am ashamed that a guest has been subjected to the ordeals suffered by Mr. Falsen during his time with us."

"And is he the only one who has been suffering, Gracious Lady? We all have had more than our fair share of ordeals!"

"Enough, enough. I shall wait here, with Mr. Falsen, while you and the Lady Tamsin make an inspection. No doubt all department heads will have their hands full, so I shall rely upon you for the damage reports."

Prenta and Tamsin scrambled up to the hatch in what had been the deck but was now a vertical bulkhead. Beyond the circular aperture there were the sounds of a brief scuffle and Prenta's voice cursing angrily. Something, thought Falsen, must have gotten in her way.

That something was Pondor.

His green eyes glared down from the opening.

He spat, "What have you done? What have you *done*? You have broken my ship!"

Then he was gone.

Lady Mother sat down again, leaned against Falsen. He could feel her trembling. And if she *knew*, he wondered, if she knew what he was and what his intentions were, would she regard him as such a tower of strength? Would she not hate him as Pondor did, and more than one of the ship's crew?

CHAPTER 24

He should find out what had happened to Linda, Falsen thought. But she would be all right. Like him, she was hard to kill, and any injuries she had sustained would soon heal. The Lady Mother needed him more than Linda did at this time. He could not leave her alone.

"Mr. Falsen," she said softly, "you are an experienced spaceman. What did I do wrong? I must know. . . ."

"Your landing approach," he told her, "was according to the text books . . ." *The Survey Service text books,* he thought, *but not the spacemanship manuals, harping on the theme of Safety First, preferred by the Merchant Service.* "But perhaps you put rather too much trust in the ship's machinery, the inertial drive especially." *And the person who was supposed to maintain it in proper working order . . .*

There was silence for a while, broken by the buzzing of a telephone. Falsen got up, made his way carefully over the smooth, curved surface of the viewport to the vertical deck, climbed it by using chairs and instrument pedestals as hand and footholds. As soon as he got to the command chair the instrument fell silent.

He remained where he was for a little while, waiting for the telephone to buzz again. While he was in this central position he looked up and down and around at the various displays. There were more red lights than white or green, but he could see almost at a glance that the ship was still sealed, that life-support systems were operational. Air circulation was being maintained, so there must still be power—but was it from the hydrogen-fusion generator or the emergency-battery banks? How were things on the farm deck, where the tanks of algae extracted carbon dioxide from the atmosphere, releasing oxygen? And the inertial drive? That was O.U. bloody T., as was the emergency reaction drive.

"Come down again, please, Mr. Falsen," called the Lady Mother. "Ignore the telephones. If anybody wants me, they know where to find me."

He dropped back down to where she was sitting.

He said, "According to the indicators, things don't look too bad. I'm assuming, of course, that the layout hasn't been changed since this was a Terran ship. I can't read Doralan."

"Panegan," she corrected him. "Dorala is the world, Panegar is the nation. On Dorala we have more than one language."

"Oh."

"But Panegar is the major spacefaring nation," she told him. "But why am I babbling about inessentials? The safety of my ship, my people, my people especially, should be my main concern. How many have been hurt? Or killed? Too many have been killed already."

"If they were at landing stations," said Falsen, "strapped into their bunks or chairs, they should have come through, just as we did."

"There is always somebody," said the Lady Mother, "who will disregard safety regulations. . . ."

And some, thought Falsen, who would not have been able to observe such rules. Those stowaways (somehow he was sure that there was more than one of them) in the storerooms . . . surely they were crushed in a cascade of bales, drums and the Odd Gods of the Galaxy alone knew what when the ship toppled. He felt sorry for them.

"Here is Prenta back," said the captain.

The chief officer dropped into the control room through the open hatch. Her uniform was torn and dirtied, and there was a blood-oozing abrasion on her right knee. She started to make a report in her own language.

"In English, please," said the Lady Mother.

"Very well, Gracious Lady. To begin with, the ship is still sealed. The after air lock is buried in mud, but we shall be able to get out through a cargo port—after we have cleared away the mess of stores and equipment that block the way to it. The . . .''

"Lady Prenta, at the moment I am more concerned with the people than the ship. What of casualties?"

"Very few, Gracious Lady, and none serious. We were lucky." She could not resist adding, "For a change."

"I wish a report, Lady Prenta, not humorous comments."

"Very well, Gracious Lady. There is surprisingly little structural damage. The fusion generator is still functional and supplying power. The farm deck is a shambles, but it will be possible to salvage algae and other plant life. The contents of the tissue-culture vats, however, must be regarded as a loss. I have talked with Lady Carlin, and she assures me that she will be able to repair the inertial drive. I suggested that lateral thrust be used to lift the ship, but she told me that too little thrust is developed laterally to raise such tonnage from the surface. I went aft to try to discover why the reaction drive failed to function. There is nothing wrong with the mini-reactor that I could see, but feed pipes to the chamber are fractured. The automatic sealing must have functioned, however. The reaction-mass tank is still almost full . . .''

"The least of my worries," said the Lady Mother. "Water is one commodity of which there is no shortage on this world. And now, Lady Prenta, as soon as you have recovered your breath, will you organize a working party to clear one of the cargo ports so that we can get out of the ship? I wish to make an exterior inspection."

"Very well," Prenta said. "I shall report back to you as soon as the cargo port is cleared."

"How is Linda?" asked Falsen. "Did you see her?"

"Yes. She is all right. Jonahs never come to any harm themselves, do they?"

She scrambled up to the hatch in the control-room deck, wriggled through it and was gone.

CHAPTER 25

Somebody had had the sense to run the elevator cage as far aft as it would go, to its sternmost terminus just above (when the ship was in her normal attitude) the reactor room. It was possible, therefore, to get to one end of the ship from the other by walking through the axial shaft. The spiral staircase encircling the outside of this normally vertical tunnel would have been impassable to anybody but a trained gymnast.

After he had helped the Lady Mother up to the access hatch in the control-room deck, Falsen accompanied her along the inside of the shaft. Although it was possible to walk without stooping, the going was not easy; the metal lining was so smooth as to be slippery underfoot. Some of the dim inspection lights were out, probably broken by the shock of the ship's fall. Ahead, however, there was a much brighter illumination streaming in through the open door to the storeroom.

They came to this opening and found that a light ladder had been lowered through it. The captain went up first, closely followed by Falsen. Prenta was waiting for them, looking very tired but, at the same time, pleased with herself. She and her gang had done well—although, Falsen thought, gravity must have done most of the work. Had the cargo port not been directly overhead, the task of clearing a way to it would have been almost impossible, would have been impossible without the aid of a team of stowbots and experienced operators. The contents of the storeroom had fallen, fortuitously, to either side of the axial shaft. It was as though, Falsen thought, he and the Doralans were standing at the bottom of a trench, one with outward sloping sides. But the sides were not of earth but of crates and bales and drums. There had been breakages, leakages. The air was heavy with chemical odors and the aromatic acridity of alien spices.

Yet nothing, nobody, had died in here, Falsen knew as he inhaled the conflicting scents. There was no smell of death. Nonetheless it was in this compartment that he and Linda had found the stowaway, where probably there had been other Doralan males hidden. Either those beings had been elsewhere— but where?—when the ship had crashed or they had been very lucky.

Or proof against all normal and most abnormal hazards.

Another folding ladder had been extended and set up to reach the rim of the cargo port. Crewwomen were already up on the hull; some of them were peering down over the rim of the aperture.

"Come with me, Lady Prenta," said the Lady Mother. "And you, Mr. Falsen."

She climbed nimbly to the opening in the hull. Now that she was *doing* something, Falsen thought, she had shaken off her stunned apathy. Prenta went up after her. Falsen brought up the rear. He pulled himself up onto the curved plating, looked around. It was strange, uncanny almost, to see a spaceship in such a position, half-submerged in mud, an enormously long metal cylinder, tapered at each end, extended at full length in a trench—a grave?—of her own digging. Aft, two of the great vanes were exposed, each sixty degrees from the vertical. The third one had to be buried.

The Lady Mother made her way cautiously down the curved metal surface, slippery in the drizzling rain, to where another ladder had been set up, the foot of it on the ground. Prenta was even more cautious, went down backward on her hands and knees. Falsen swallowed his pride and followed suit. Walking around on the outside of a ship in space, with the vessel in free-fall, was one thing. Here, with the tug of gravity threatening a nasty fall, it was another.

He reached the ladder, got his feet onto a rung, his hands onto another well above it. He clambered down rapidly, stepped onto mossy ground outside the ridge of displaced soil. The Lady Mother and Prenta were walking slowly aft. He set off after them.

When they got to the stern they could see the cause of the

disaster. That brief, ineffectual blast of the emergency reaction drive had blown a pit of its own into the soggy surface, a trench lined with baked clay in which the broken vane, the exposed metal of the fractures still bright, not yet dulled by the damp air, was visible in its entirety.

"It can be repaired," said the Lady Mother at last. "We have power for the flame cutters and welders. If necessary we shall have to . . . cannibalize? Is that the correct expression, Mr. Falsen? There are bulkheads in the ship not essential to her structural integrity, required only for the making of airtight compartments."

"It is possible," said Prenta doubtfully.

"Why so pessimistic, Lady Prenta? We still have the ship, almost undamaged save for this vane. I have talked to the Lady Carlin; she assures me that she will soon have the inertial drive in working order. Even the Mannschenn Drive has survived, although it will require recalibration before the ship is ready for a deep-space voyage."

"Have you not forgotten one thing, Gracious Lady?"

"And what is that, Lady Prenta?"

"Before we can lift off this world the ship must be restored to an upright position."

The captain's face lost its animation, clouded.

"That," she admitted, "is indeed a problem, but not an insuperable one. There must be a way. Let us regard it as an interesting exercise in spacemanship. What is your opinion, Mr. Falsen?"

Falsen was remembering how he, among others, had been confronted with just such a problem. It had been during his last training cruise in the Federation Survey Service during which he, together with several others, reservists and regulars, was supposed to achieve promotion from lieutenant junior grade to lieutenant. Aboard the ship, an obsolete cruiser, were officers who were both instructors and examiners. There had been the elderly, crusty Commander Blivens whose specialty was spacemanship. It was rumored that Blivens had actually served in rockets, but he wasn't really that old. It was rumored that he had first gone to space in the Ehrenhaft Drive ships, the gaussjammers. This was possible.

Falsen recalled a lecture given shortly prior to the spacemanship orals. The young officers were seated in rows in the compartment used as a lecture hall, with old Blivens strutting back and forth on the platform to one side of it, three steps one way, three steps the other. Suddenly he ceased his circumscribed perambulation, stood and faced his audience.

He barked, "I suppose you're wondering why I always walk when I'm talking. I'll tell you. It's because it's a luxury. When I started my career, it was free-fall all the way, all the time. You young gentlemen take luxuries for granted these days—but there'll be times, in the Survey Service especially, when you'll find that you'll have to make do without 'em.

"Now, here's a problem. You're in command of a ship—I suppose some of you will get that far—and you've made a botched landing. That happens to the best of us. You've toppled. Your ship has crashed onto her side. You want to get her up onto her vanes again so that you can lift off once you've buried your dead and made your repairs." He laughed harshly. "I can just hear what you're thinking, you young gentlemen out of the Merchant Service especially. 'What's all the fuss about?' you're asking yourselves. 'Just weld towing lugs onto the stem, if they're not there already, and hook on a tug, or some other heavy lift vessel, and up you come.' Your only real worry will be writing the report on the original accident, trying to convince the Admiral or the Astronautical Superintendent or the Managing Director that the Odd Gods of the Galaxy had it in for you personally.

"But it's a hypothetical Survey Service ship that you're captain of, gentlemen. It's not at some commercial spaceport with all mod cons, including tugs, where you've made a disgusting exhibition of yourself. Furthermore, it's not at a Survey Service base with every conceivable facility on tap. You've made a landing on some planet, newly discovered, maybe inhabited by intelligent beings and maybe not, but with no modern technology save what you've brought down with you. You've made a landing and made a balls of it. There's no other ship with you and it will be *years* before your radio signals, informing the nearest base of your whereabouts, get there.

"If your ship had a mixed crew, you might think, 'What does it matter? We'll just stay here and start a colony.' But you don't have a mixed crew. You want to get home to your everloving wives and children. Oh, perhaps *you* don't, but most of your officers and men do.

"So, gentlemen, just *how* do you get your ship ready for lift-off? I'll be generous; I'll let you have all the power you want. Your hydrogen-fusion plant is still churning out the kilowatts. None of the ship's machinery, in fact, has been badly damaged.

"And now I'll carry on with my stroll while you exercise your tiny minds."

It was Falsen who was first to come up with an answer. He suggested that the inertial drive be used, with maximum lateral thrust, to lift the ship bodily and then to turn her through one hundred and eighty degrees.

"That would work, Mr. Falsen," said Commander Blivens, "*if* an inertial-drive unit were capable of exerting maximum thrust in all directions. Unfortunately it is not. Don't ask me why not. I am not an engineer. There are some matters that must remain eternal mysteries even to me."

There was a further period of silence. Some officers busied themselves with pens, paper and pocket calculators. Then two of them—Falsen remembered their names, Li Po and Abdul Fahmi—formed a committee of two and conducted a low-voiced conversation.

Finally Li Po raised his hand.

"Yes, Mr. Li?" said Blivens.

"Sir, am I correct in the assumption that the ship carries tools—spades, mattocks, picks and the like?"

"The original purpose of your landing, Mr. Li, was to explore, not to start a market garden."

"Then, sir, am I allowed to order my artificers to fabricate such implements from materials at hand?"

"You're the captain, Mr. Li. You give what orders you please. Whether or not your crew will obey them is another matter."

"Then, sir, I have my tools manufactured to my design by my engine-room crew. I have also had baskets constructed, small ones that may be carried on the head. My intention will be to excavate a pit at the stern, under the stern of the spacecraft. Some men will be digging, others will be removing the soil with the baskets. The ship will eventually slide into the pit, stern-first, coming to rest at such a small angle from the vertical that a lift-off will be practicable."

"Very ingenious, Mr. Li. But how large is your crew? How many men were employed to build the Great Wall of China?

How long did it take? And what is the nature of the soil in which you will be digging your pit? Is there bedrock, and, if so, how far down?'' He grinned, and his craggy face was almost pleasant. "But you made a good try, Mr. Li, which is more than can be said to the other young gentlemen.''

"Mr. Fahmi, do you have a contribution to make?''

"Yes, Commander, sir. Like Mr. Li I intend to use manpower, although in a different way. Also I shall make use of mechanical power. My engineers should be able to make jacks as well as the picks and shovels and all the rest of it. My hole, which I shall dig, will also be under the ship's stern. The first of the jacks will raise the bows as far as possible. The hole will be filled, and more earth brought in to support the stem. Another jack will raise it some more. And so on. At the finish, one side of the ship will be supported by an artificial hill . . .''

"It could work, Mr. Fahmi, if you were a pharaoh—not a mere space captain—with unlimited labor to build your pyramid. But you—and Mr. Li—have a big ship to raise and only a small crew, a crew, moreover, with only a limited life span.

"But there is a way in which the joy can be done in a short time and without crippling physical effort. It *was* done, once, by a certain Captain Dalgety. You may have heard of him. He called himself a privateer, flying under the flag of the Duchy of Waldegren, but he was really a pirate. Some time ago he wrote his memoirs. I read the book, in which, among other stories, is the one about how he got off a world called Tahlehn, one with no technology and no spaceport facilities, upon which he had made a clumsy landing. I have urged that this account be included in the Survey Service manuals of spacemanship, but my Lords Commissioner of the Admiralty feel strongly that the Survey Service holds a monopoly on spacemanship and that anything done by a pirate, a Waldegrenese pirate at that, is not worth bothering with.

"But this is what Dalgety did. . . .''

"So this is where you are!'' somebody was saying. "I was worried about you. . . .''

It was Linda.

He looked at her. She had come through the wreck without a scratch.

She said, glumly, ''We shall never get off this world.''

"We shall," said the Lady Mother, but without conviction. "If the worst comes to the worst, when we do not return to Dorala at the appointed time, another expedition will be sent to rescue us."

"And when will that be, Gracious Lady?" asked Prenta sharply. "How many of us will still be alive? If our run of bad luck continues, there will be nobody, except these Jonahs!"

"That will do, Lady Prenta!" said the captain sharply. "Mr. Falsen, I am your senior in both age and rank—but I believe that your actual space experience exceeds mine. Also, you are the heir to a long tradition of spacefaring. I am not. . . ."

"As well ask Pondor for advice," Prenta muttered.

The Lady Mother ignored her.

"Mr. Falsen, you seemed to be deep in cogitation. Do you have any ideas?"

"I think I do," he said. Then, "I do."

CHAPTER 26

The ship was battened down for the night, the cargo port sealed tightly against predators. There were those who had urged that some sort of encampment be set up outside the fallen hull. Fabric from the wrecked dirigible's envelope could be used to contrive shelters, they argued, protected by an electrified wire fence. Sentries, with orders to shoot on sight, could be mounted. But the Lady Mother had been adamant. Only inside the metal shell, she insisted, would there be safety during the hours of darkness.

Safety there might be; great discomfort there certainly was. Most of the cabins were uninhabitable, and the normal toilet facilities unusable. Some furniture, strongly secured to decks and bulkheads, had remained in position, but what use was a chair or table at ninety degrees from its normal stance? Other things had broken away from their moorings, fallen and been broken. The only food available was from the stock of emergency rations; the spoiled contents of tissue-culture vats and hydroponic tanks had been taken outside just before dark and incinerated by laser fire lest the raw meat attract carnivores.

The public rooms were now dormitories, with mattresses spread over the curved surface of the inner hull. Airtight hatches, normally closed at all times, had been opened to allow progress between compartments without having to use the axial shaft which now, of course, was an overhead conduit.

The dull sun was long since down, but not everybody was sleeping or trying to sleep. In a space that had been a minor storeroom from which the contents had been removed, Falsen

133

sat with the Lady Mother, Carlin, Prenta and two of Carlin's senior assistants. He wished most sincerely that this meeting were taking place outside the ship; he found it hard to think clearly in these conditions. The air, despite the efforts of the chemical purifiers, was stale, carried the taint of unwashed bodies and of body wastes. (The improvised latrines had to be close to overflowing; perhaps at least one of them had already done so.)

They disposed themselves on cushions that tended to slide down the curvature of the smooth hull lining; Falsen, Prenta and the captain on one side, Carlin and her assistant engineers on the other. Between them was a transparent scale model of the ship, a beautiful toy—but more than a toy. It was standing upright on its vanes until Pondor, who had slunk in unnoticed, batted it with a forepaw. It fell with a muted clatter.

"Get out of here!" screamed the Lady Mother.

"I only did what *you* did," replied the cat insolently.

"Get *out*!"

"All right."

The animal sauntered away, jumped through an open hatch in the bulkhead/deck.

One of the engineers reached out to restore the model to its original position. Falsen put a hand out to stop her.

"Leave it," he said. "This is the way that the ship herself is now"—he rose to a squatting position—"on her side, with the access hatch to the inertial-drive room, the hatch that is used, sometimes, during major overhauls in port, *down*, buried in the mud. . . ."

"We are already aware of that," said Carlin sharply.

Falsen ignored this, went on studying the model. Through the transparent skin he could see the tube that was the axial shaft and, on its underside, like the nest of a solitary wasp plastered against a very straight twig, the cylinder that represented the inertial-drive room. Here the transverse decks, both ahead and astern of it, were very thick, as they needed to be to take the thrust; and the walls of the tube, too, were thicker than elsewhere.

"We shall have to cut through the shaft," said Falsen, "to get the inertial-drive unit up and out."

"The shaft is the ship's backbone," said the Lady Mother. "The main component of her structural strength."

"Not the *main* component, gracious Lady, but one of the

two main components. The other one is the hull itself. The hull, thanks to the nature of the ground on which it fell, is supported evenly along its length. In any case, I do not think that it should be necessary actually to sever the shaft. Just an opening, big enough to allow passage of the largest components of the drive, in what is now its lower wall, and a similar one in the upper wall. I assume that the engine-room equipment in this ship is as it was when she was a Terran vessel. . . ."

"Better," said Carlin.

"Good. Then, in that case you will have what we call mini-innies—small versatile units that can be used for lifting, fetching and carrying, their control boxes at the ends of long leads."

"Ours," said Carlin, "are radio-controlled."

"Better. Well, we have to do some more cutting and burning, through bulkheads that are in the way and through the shell plating itself. Piece by piece, the inertial-drive unit will have to be taken out of the ship and then reassembled on the ground. We shall need a long—a very long—umbilical cable to feed power into it, also a platform of some sort rigged on top of it with a control panel. Then we shall have our tug. Are the towing lugs still in place at the bows of the ship, or have they been removed?"

"They are still there," said Prenta.

"Any towing wires in your stores?"

"We do have a reel of something heavy. It came with the ship. There's a certificate somewhere in my office to cover it. If I can find it. But surely, Mr. Falsen, the finest wire rope in the universe would not be able to support the weight of a ship? A big ship."

"The weight of the ship will be supported by this planet. At no time will she be clear of the ground."

Prenta was stubborn. "Couldn't we," she asked, "dig a sort of pit under the bows? Get the reassembled drive unit down into it and then secure it to the stem and *push* the ship upright?"

"Such a pit," said Falsen, "would fill with water in as much time as it would take to dig it. Besides, the way that I propose has already been used. It worked."

"It's a *big* job," complained Prenta.

"Of course it's a big job," the Lady Mother told her. "But

it has to be done if we're to get back to Dorala under our own power instead of waiting here until somebody back home gets around to wondering what has happened to us and, later still, decides to mount an expedition to find out.

"But this has been a long day, and a wearing one. We should all of us get what sleep we can so as to be ready to start work at dawn."

She got to her feet, made her way to the hatch, crawled through it. Prenta followed her, and the two engineers.

"Where are you sleeping, Falsen?" asked Carlin. "You are welcome to share my cabin; fortunately it's on the *down* side of the ship and I've a mattress on the hull lining."

"I'll find a place," said Falsen shortly.

"As you please. Don't forget, you had the offer. A good night to you."

When she was gone Falsen arranged the cushions to form a bed. This compartment would be as good a place as any to sleep. He was in the process of settling down when, as he had known that she would, Linda joined him.

She looked disdainfully at the model.

"Are you taking your toys to bed with you?" she asked. "Personally, I'd prefer something more cuddly."

"It's not a toy."

"Whatever it is, it's in the way." She pushed it away with her foot, settled down beside him. She whispered intently, "Now, what are we doing? This could be our opportunity. Everybody disorganized . . ."

"No," he said. "*No*. We want the ship—but until she's been raised, made spaceworthy again, she's no use to anybody."

"But we could start reducing their numbers."

"The ship is sealed. Nothing, *nothing* could possibly get inside until the cargo port's opened again in the morning."

He curled up on the deck and she, behind him, fitted her body to his.

He was almost asleep and thought that she was already sleeping when she whispered, "Nicholas, I'm *hungry*. . . ."

"So am I," he grunted, "but there's nothing we can do about it."

CHAPTER 27

Falsen stood with the Lady Mother on the rim of the impact crater, looking down at the dozen crewwomen who, with shovels fabricated from sheet metal and tubing by Carlin's artificers, were trying to expose the broken stern vane.

It was a hopeless task. A persistent, drizzling rain was falling, drifting down from the ruddy sky. The exposed soil, no longer bound by the root-tendrils of the mosslike ground cover, was more liquid than solid. The workers, thought Carlin, looked like little girls playing in mud—but children so engaged would look happy, despite the filthiness of their bodies and clothing; these adults looked thoroughly miserable.

The Doralan captain said despondently, "Mr. Falsen, this is a hopeless task. If only this cursed rain would let up . . . ."

"It won't," Falsen told her.

He did not know how he knew, but he did. He was no meteorologist, but since his marooning on this dismal world, long-dormant ancestral senses had revived. He felt, somehow, that this precipitation would persist for days.

"There must be a way," she whispered.

"Lasers," he muttered doubtfully. "At low intensity, just to dry the pit out. . . . It could work. And there's all the fabric from the envelope of the dirigible, and the frames and struts . . . a sort of tent."

"Yes . . ." murmured the Lady Mother. Then, "Yes!"

She shouted an order into the trench. The workers stopped

plying their shovels. She shouted another order and, gratefully, they clambered out of the hole, their chubby feet and bare legs liberally coated with black slime, their once scarlet tunics filthy. The muck was even on their faces and in their hair. They put their shovels down near where Falsen and the Lady Mother were standing, trudged along the ridge to the ladder leading up to the open cargo hatch. They ascended this smartly enough. Even though the interior of the ship was comfortless, even though the air was tainted with the acridity of burning metal, it would be warm and dry. And there would be a respite from the back-breaking labor of ditch-digging.

Shortly after the last of them was aboard, Prenta emerged from the hull, made her way along the ridge to where Falsen and the Lady Mother were standing. She looked at the Earth-man with dislike, then addressed herself to her captain. She spoke in English for Falsen's benefit.

"You sent for me, Gracious Lady?"

"I did, Lady Prenta."

"But I am busy, Gracious Lady. You have no idea what it is like. Carlin's people are running around with their torches like madwomen, cutting and burning. I have to watch them lest they destroy the ship's internal strength entirely. . . ."

"The Lady Carlin is an engineer, Prenta. She knows what she is doing."

"Does she? *Does she?*"

"She does. And that metal we must have to patch the vane."

"If we are ever able to get to work on it, Gracious Lady." The chief officer stared down into the muddy pond. "Look at it. All morning, and twelve of my women who could have been better employed just wasting their time!"

"Mr. Falsen has thought of a scheme that should work."

"Mr. Falsen. Mr. Falsen. Oh, I do not doubt that the high and mighty Terrans are more used to coping with disasters than we are. Such representatives of the breed as we have here are very disaster-prone. But Jonahs must be used to catastrophes—and standing around to watch their betters cope with them!"

"I'll have no more talk of Jonahs, Lady Prenta. And, for your information, during this operation Mr. Falsen is to be regarded as one of my officers, as my aide. . . ."

"With all the authority that that implies?"

"Of course."

"Then, Lady Mother, I must register my protest. It is not fitting that personnel of the Pan-Doralan Interstellar Expeditionary Service should take orders from an alien being."

"They *will* take such orders, Lady Prenta. As *you* will, should the occasion arise."

There was what seemed to be a long silence during which the two women glared at each other. The Lady Mother's face was like steel—and Prenta's like cast iron, a hard metal but brittle. Suddenly it cracked.

"Very well, Gracious Lady," whispered the Doralan officer. "I will accept Mr. Falsen's . . . advice. And I give notice that a full report of this affair will be made by me to the Commissariat when we return to Dorala."

If you return to Dorala, thought Falsen.

"And now, Mr. Falsen," said the captain, "will you *advise* the Lady Prenta?"

Falsen explained what would have to be done, what would be needed.

"But the fabric," objected Prenta, "is buried under the stores. So are the stowbots. It will be impossible to get it out with the ship as she is."

"You have manpower—sorry, womanpower—don't you?" said Falsen. "And the mini-innies."

"They're Carlin's toys. She'll never let me use them. I wanted to borrow one to shift some crates that were blocking access to the helicopter hangar. She told me that control-room ornaments are incapable of handling any sort of machinery."

"She did, did she?" snapped the Lady Mother. "I could say that there are some people in this ship who are incapable of keeping machinery in running order. But this is an old vessel; she was old when we bought her. If we start blaming each other for our present predicament, we shall never extricate ourselves from it. Go back with Lady Prenta into the hull, Mr. Falsen. Find the Lady Carlin and tell her what you want. Tell her that I have delegated authority to you."

"That will please her," Prenta said.

And were the words ironic or not? Falsen wondered. How much did Prenta know?

•   •   •

He followed Prenta along the ridge of upflung earth, the rim of the impact crater. The soil was soft, wet, and his feet sank into it to above his ankles. They came to the foot of the ladder. Prenta went up it nimbly enough, Falsen followed more slowly.

They went down into the hold, to the chaotic jumble of stores and equipment, made their way over and through the over-turned crates and bales and drums, to an access door into the axial shaft. As they walked through the tunnel the acrid smell of burning metal became stronger and they could hear voices. Falsen recognized Carlin's distinctive tones; she was giving orders, he thought.

They emerged from the shaft into a compartment, brightly lit but obscured by eddies of blue smoke. Laser torches were wielded by white-overalled figures, the beams almost invisible but metal flaring into incandescence where they impinged. A mini-innie, buzzing like an enraged wasp, held an oval piece of plating in its claws, was lifting it and carrying it toward a hole that had been cut overhead. Watching carefully was a junior engineer with a control box in her hands.

Carlin was directing operations.

She was converting a bulkhead into a sort of web frame, her people cutting out marked ovals of plating. To judge by the expression on her face, she was enjoying herself. Man, thought Falsen, has always derived pleasure from knocking down the things that he himself has built. Presumably, the Doralan psychology was similar. But this was a careful, controlled destruction. There would be little loss of strength in the bulkhead, although it would never be an airtight one again.

He waited until Carlin had stopped yapping orders, then attracted her attention.

"What do you want?" she demanded. "Can't you see that I'm busy?"

"I'd like the loan of a couple of your mini-innies."

"You can't have them. I've already told Prenta. The helicopters can stay where they are until we've raised the ship."

"It's not to get the helicopters out, Lady Carlin."

"Then *what*, Falsen?"

Falsen told her.

"All right. I'll send Barli and Sula with you. I'll want them and their mini-innies back as soon as you've got your tent rigged." She turned to Prenta and said, "I can spare people and machines when it's for a worthwhile purpose."

Prenta snarled wordlessly.

Fortunately, the envelope fabric was in the storeroom that already had been opened. Unfortunately, it was now bottom stowage. But Falsen had already considered lightening the ship before attempting to raise her; now he was having to do just that to get to the material he wanted. Like a master stevedore, he stood on the axial shaft, directing the work of hoisting stores out through the open hatch. Some of the crates were so heavy that both mini-innies working in tandem were required for one lift.

Prenta stood with him, translating his orders when necessary. She was resenting him, resenting his authority, but did not let this get in the way of the work. He found that he was respecting her for this—how would he have liked being bossed around by an alien aboard *his* ship?—but he still did not have to like her.

It was late in the afternoon when the hold was at last cleared, all its contents piled more or less neatly outside the ship, except for the fabric and the metal struts.

Falsen ordered some of the fabric be used to cover the small mountain of stores against the rain. He suggested to the Lady Mother that work continue in shifts throughout the night, with searchlights mounted and guards posted in case of attack by the indigenous predators.

"No," she said. "We are all tired. Now we will get cleaned up as best as we may, and we will eat, then sleep. As you say on Earth, tomorrow is another day."

He found Linda in the little empty storeroom that they had used as a sleeping place the previous night.

"Where were you," he asked, "while everybody else was working?"

"I am neither an engineer nor a stevedore," she replied sulkily. "I would only have been in the way. Like Pondor, I had sense enough to keep from underfoot."

"I suppose that you kept each other company," he sneered.

"Not likely."

"I haven't seen him around," he said thoughtfully. "Have you . . . ?"

"No," she stated, "not yet."

She grinned wolfishly.

CHAPTER 28

Work was resumed at dawn after all hands had made a sketchy toilet and gulped a hot but unsatisfactory meal from cans of emergency rations. Falsen had not been happy about leaving the stores and the envelope fabric unguarded outside the ship but was relieved to find that nothing had been disturbed.

It was raining still, as he had known that it would be, heavier than on the previous day, but still little more than a drizzle. The air was warmer and he gratefully discarded his borrowed cloak, and then his shirt. He retained his shorts, although he would have been happier working naked. He did not think that the Doralans would have approved.

The work that had been done on the trench under the stern would have to be done again; slimy mud had trickled from the impact-crater rim back into the excavation. He stood there with the twelve unhappy laborers, with their shovels and baskets, looking down into it. One of them, who had a little English, asked in a despondent voice, "Start again? Now?"

"Wait," he told her.

The Lady Mother, Prenta following, came along the ridge. Both of them were carrying laser pistols, the captain holding one in each hand. She handed her spare weapon to Falsen. He looked at it, at the setting. It was already on wide beam.

"Shall we begin?" she asked.

"Yes," Falsen said.

The three of them lifted their pistols, aimed down into the trench. Water exploded into evil-smelling steam. There were

143

pops as unfortunate mud-dwellers, caught in the fire, burst. There were sparkles of ruddy incandescence glimpsed dimly through the billowing vapor. The sparkling became a continuous glow.

"Enough," said Falsen.

A slight, a very slight breeze slowly dissipated the steam and the smoke. The shallow crater was dry now, a depression lined with gray ash and crusty slag. Prenta yelped an order and one of the women, carrying a shovel, started down. She screamed, withdrew hastily. She sat down on the wet ground beyond the rim, rubbing her feet with both hands.

"They had better go back to get boots," Falsen said.

"You should have thought of that before," muttered Prenta.

"*You* should have thought of that, Lady Prenta," the captain told her. "Send them back into the ship to get dressed properly. And tell Klar to see the doctor. Meanwhile . . ."

"And pass word to Carlin that we shall be requiring the mini-innies again," said Falsen. "I told her last night, but she may have forgotten."

Meanwhile, the Lady Mother was playing the beam of her laser along the crater rim. It made sense, Falsen thought. He added his fire to hers, baking the walls of the pit into brick. He walked aft with her, then around to the other side. The two undamaged vanes, like great thick wide wings, towered over them, the pinions of some huge flying creature sprawled wounded on the ground, an enormous bird that could never fly again without the assistance of the tiny parasites that had infested its body.

They were almost finished when they heard the tinny clatter of the mini-innies emerging from the hatch in the ship's side. The little inertial-drive units hovered over the hull until their operators came out, clambered down the ladder to the ground. A third woman came after them. It was Pansir, the airship pilot. The engineers and the pilot walked slowly aft, Carlin's people with their control boxes in their hands. The mini-innies preceded them, flying about three meters above the ground, seeming to lead the way.

Falsen told Prenta, "I want them to spread out the largest sections of fabric. To lift them over the stern, over the vanes. . . . It may be necessary to join some sections. . . ."

"The Lady Pansir," said Prenta, "is quite capable of

dealing with anything involving envelope fabric. That is her job.''

One of the mini-innies was carrying, in its dangling claws, a large basket. It descended slowly, deposited its burden on the muddy ground, lifted again and hovered, muttering irritably, a stubby, meter-length spindle sprouting articulated appendages. Falsen tried to ignore it, looked into the open container. There were four fat squeeze-tubes, the labels of which he could not, of course, read. There were two pairs of shears, four pairs of gloves fashioned from a slippery-looking plastic.

The two engineers and Pansir talked briefly with Prenta, who seemed to be handing authority over to the pilot. Then the mini-innies flew noisily to the nearest roll of envelope fabric, while the hands of their operators played busily over the control boxes. Working in concert, they spread a square of the tough, silvery cloth over the wet ground. It was obviously too small. Another square was spread, and another, and another.

The crewwomen were back, booted now, all twelve of them; Falsen wondered if the one who had burned her feet was in the party. With a few exceptions—the Lady Mother, Prenta, Carlin (of course), Pansir and one or two others—all the Doralans looked the same to him. Prenta yelped orders, amplified in a calmer voice by Pansir. Four of the crewwomen took gloves from the basket, put them on. The pilot pulled her own pair from her belt, drew them over her hands. Two of the women picked up the fat tubes, the other two the shears. Led by Pansir, they walked to the outspread squares of envelope fabric.

''Pansir knows what she is doing, Mr. Falsen,'' said the Lady Mother. ''She knows how to use that . . . glue. It will bond almost anything to anything—cloth to cloth, cloth to metal, both to skin. But it will not stick to the gloves.''

Falsen, who had already guessed as much, asked, ''And will it work in these conditions? The wet ground, the rain getting heavier . . .''

''Of course. It is in bad weather that a dirigible's fabric gets torn.''

Pansir's party was working fast and efficiently, squeezing adhesive from the tubes, spreading a thin layer along the edge of the material with gloved fingers, pressing edge to edge with only a narrow overlap. The pilot fluttered about them

like an anxious mother hen. Now and again she would use a
pair of shears, trimming and fairing. Once she had to snip
away the hem of a tunic that had come into contact, perma-
nent contact, with a gummy surface. Falsen wondered what
she would have done had it been the pale skin of the wearer's
thigh rather than the fabric that was covering it.

The mini-innies spread two more squares of fabric, one of
which had to be cut to the proper shape. After they had been
secured to the others, Pansir walked around the rectangle of
silvery cloth, looking at it. She walked over it, examining the
seams. Satisfied, she went to talk with the engineers, then
came to report to the Lady Mother.

"All is ready, Gracious Lady."

"Very well, Lady Pansir. You may spread the . . . 'tent'?"

"As good a word as any," said Falsen.

There should have been four mini-innies, he thought, but
two would have to do. The pair of them positioned themselves over one end of the rectangle, at opposite corners.
They took a firm hold with their claws, then lifted high
enough but not too high, so that the free end of the fabric
remained on the ground. They just cleared the first of the
vanes, dragging their billowing train behind them. The cloth
fouled briefly but did not rip, pulled clear. They cleared the
second vane and then made their descent. All that remained
for the crewwomen was to spread the ends as far as possible,
to secure the edges to the ground with stakes fashioned from
the metal spars of the wrecked dirigible. It was not a tidy job
and looked, Falsen thought, like a towel flung carelessly over
the end of a long rock on some beach. But it would do, as
long as no wind blew up. It would keep the rain off.

The digging was going faster now, although water still oozed
up from the soggy soil, and every now and again the laser
pistols had to be used to dry things out. More and more of the
crumpled vane was being exposed. Looking at it, Falsen
doubted that it would be possible to repair the great shock
absorbers with materials available. In that case, those in the
other two vanes would have to be frozen, and any future
landing would have to be made with extreme care. He thought
that he would be able to cope when the time came.

He said to the Lady Mother, "Would you mind, Gracious

Lady, if I went back inside the ship to see how things are going?''

"Of course not, Mr. Falsen. The Lady Prenta has things well in hand. I will accompany you.''

They left the shelter of the tent, walked forward through the rain.

She said, "You have been a tower of strength, Mr. Falsen.''

If she knew, he thought, *if she* knew *she wouldn't be ladling out the praises. . . .*

She went on, "I don't know how we should have managed without your advice.''

He said, "You would have managed, Gracious Lady.''

"Would we, Mr. Falsen? After all, we are newcomers to space. You are the heir to many years of experience. . . .''

The heir to more than that, he thought, not without bitterness. If he had just been doing a job of spacemanship, helping this kindly, friendly woman to the best of his ability, he would have been happy. But, in the final analysis, it was not she whom he was helping. All that he was doing was for himself. And Linda. But Linda, especially since the wreck of the dirigible, had come to mean less to him than certain of the Doralans—the Lady Mother, Pansir, Carlin . . .

Carlin.

No. He did not like her, could never like her. She was as selfish as Linda. But he was stuck with Linda, whether he liked her or not. Fate had thrown them together and there was no choice but to stay together. They could never return to Earth or any Terran colony.

"You are very thoughtful, Mr. Falsen.'' She laughed softly. "I can almost hear your brain ticking over while you consider ways and means . . .''

He said, "Yes, there are problems.''

"There are indeed.''

They came to the ladder. She went up it. He followed her. They made their way over the slippery curve of hull plating to the open hatch. They paused when they heard the mechanical snarling of mini-innies, more than one of them, sounding louder and louder from the cargo port. The first of the machines emerged, two metal plates slung below it. There was a second one, a third and a fourth, all similarly loaded. The things hovered there until their operators, Carlin and three of her juniors, clambered up to the exterior of the hull.

The engineer said to the captain, "This is the first load, Gracious Lady. Then there will be more metal, then the welder and the power cells. How is the digging going?"

"Well enough now, Lady Carlin. You should be able to commence work shortly."

"That is good. Perhaps you would care to inspect what has been done so far to and about the main inertial-drive unit?" ·

"You have not severed the axial shaft, Lady Carlin?"

"I have cut no more than is necessary, Gracious Lady. I had considered bringing the parts of the drive through the shaft to this hold, but the main rotor is too large to be safely handled. It would have to be dragged—and could be damaged. We shall have to cut through fore and aft bulkheads and the hull itself." She grinned, a sudden lightening of her grease-smudged face. "Do not worry. I shall be able to make the damage good. I am as interested in getting the ship spaceworthy as anybody."

"I should hope so, Lady Carlin," said the Lady Mother stiffly.

She and Falsen waited until the engineers, with their airborne loads of material, were gone, and then descended into the ship, clambered down the ladder to the axial shaft. They had not far to go along this tunnel before they found themselves above the inertial-drive room. They looked down through the hole that had been cut through what was normally the side but which was now the floor of the shaft, to the cylindrical casing housed in its cylindrical compartment. Some of the thrust knees had already been disconnected, and a few of the casing plates had been removed, exposing camshafts and heavy rotors with off-center spindles.

"It looks like a lot of work still," said the Lady Mother. "Perhaps it would have been better to sever the shaft entirely and cut *big* holes in the bulkheads and the shell plating, to bring the unit out in one piece, under its own power."

"That would weaken the hull dangerously," said Falsen. "We might raise the ship only to have her break in two under her own weight."

"You are right," she said at last. Then, "I shall be very happy when this is all over!"

CHAPTER 29

By nightfall much had been accomplished.

The vane had been repaired, straightened and patched. It was not a sightly job but it looked strong enough, would do its share in supporting the great weight of the ship. The next day would be occupied by the taking apart of the main inertial-drive unit, transferring the components to outside the vessel and reassembling them. The day after that would see the ship raised and, if all went well, made spaceworthy again.

After an unsatisfactory meal, straight from a self-heating container, Falsen went to Linda, finding her in the cubbyhole that they had made their own until such time as the ship would be raised. He was feeling the need to unwind to discharge accumulated tensions in the time-honored manner. He was not prepared for the way in which she received him.

"So, here you are," she snapped. "The salvage expert. The way you've been carrying on, anybody would think that you're one of *them*."

"I've been doing what has to be done."

"Leaving me here, in this . . . kennel."

"You could have lent a hand."

"Doing what? The Doralans don't want me around. There's muttering going on about Jonahs. And what could I *do*, anyhow?"

"You could have lent a hand getting meals to us. That's in your department."

"The ship has a large enough catering staff."

"Most of them were out working. With shovels. Fetching and carrying for the engineers. Shifting stores."

"So what?"

"It has to be done, Linda. We want the ship. *We* want the ship. She'll be of no use to us the way she is."

"You'll never get her up. Forget about it. Why can't we carry on the way that we were doing at first? Before too long we'd have this planet to ourselves. There are worse worlds. . . ."

"Name one."

"There are worse worlds. *We* can survive here. Breed, even."

"Talking of breeding . . ."

He tried to pull her to him.

"No. I don't feel like it. I've got a headache, cooped up all day in this vile atmosphere."

"You could have been outside."

"In the *rain*? Are you mad?"

"Linda . . ."

"Leave me alone, damn you!"

So he left her alone.

He clambered through the hatch in the bulkhead, climbed one of the temporary ladders that had been set up throughout the ship to the axial shaft. Once inside this tunnel he made his way forward. He would talk with the Lady Mother, he thought. He would discuss with her what was yet to be done. He was rather surprised to realize that his conscience was bothering him. He was working for her, with her, and he was enjoying it—but when the job was done, there would have to be the betrayal. But need there be? Perhaps if he told her the truth—not all the truth, but some of it—she would be willing to take Linda and himself to some world upon which they could live out their lives with new identities. After all, if he succeeded in raising her ship for her, she would owe him something.

So thinking, he walked slowly through the shaft.

He was aware that somebody had come up into it through one of the side doors.

It was Carlin.

"I knew that you were coming this way," she said. "I want to talk to you. And you look as though you need a drink."

She had already been drinking; he could smell the alcoholic sweetness on her breath.

"Yes, I could use one," he said.

"Good. Come with me."

He followed her back through the door, dropped into a ring alleyway. They did not have far to go—Carlin walking, himself on his hands and knees, slithering down the slope—to the entrance to her cabin. She had rigged a rope, with knots at intervals, from just inside this doorway to what was now the deck of her quarters. She went down it with an agility that he could not match. He descended clumsily and cautiously.

Catlike, she made herself comfortable. A mattress and cushions covered most of the concave curvature of what would would be, until the ship was raised, the deck. The liquor cabinet was to one side of this area and easily accessible. Bottles and glasses were out, ready for use.

He sat down on the soft mattress, looking up at her. She had changed out of her overalls, was wearing her short scarlet gold-trimmed tunic. As on that other occasion when she had entertained him, she had nothing on under it. Alien or not, she was a woman, and available. Linda had made it plain that she was not available.

She stooped over, her back to him, to pour drinks. He admired the scenery while she was doing so. She straightened, turned, handed him his glass. She sat down beside him, leaned against him. In these circumstances it would have been almost impossible to avoid close physical contact; nonetheless, she seemed to be exaggerating the propinquity induced by the concave curvature of the surface upon which they were sitting. He enjoyed the warmth of her body against his—but . . .

But why the uneasiness that he was feeling?

She raised her glass, said, "Here's to us, Falsen."

"Here's to us," he repeated.

He sipped, cautiously at first. It was not gin this time. It was some golden spirit with which he was unfamiliar, spicy, mellow, yet fiery.

"We've earned this," she said. "We're the ones who're doing all the work. Up here." She tapped her forehead with the fingers of her free hand. "We're a good pair. I didn't think that I could ever like a control-room ornament, but I like you. Between the pair of us we'll get this big fat cow back on to her flat feet. We're the ones who count. The others? Pah! The Lady Mother is about as much use as that pampered cat of hers—or that bitch of yours. And where is dear Linda, by the way? Still playing the first-class passenger, not deigning to get her dainty paws dirty while the rest of us are sweating our guts out?"

"There's not much that she can do," said Falsen defensively. "After all, she's only a purser. . . ."

"And as I was saying, Falsen, we're the ones who count. Me, the engineer. You, the spaceman-navigator. Between us we could take this ship anywhere in the galaxy." She reached out for the bottle, refilled both glasses. "Mind you, I *could* manage without you . . ."

"And I without you," he said stiffly.

"As long as things didn't start breaking down," she said.

He laughed. "This is a rather pointless sort of conversation, Carlin. After all, we're all in the same boat."

"Some of us are," she said. "Some of us aren't. *You* could be."

"What are you driving at?" he demanded.

"Some of us," she told him, "are not at all happy about the Lady Mother's management of this expedition."

"I think that she is a very good captain," said Falsen stiffly.

"Loyal, aren't you?" she sneered. "In your book the spaceman branch of the service can do no wrong. Or the spacewoman branch, or the spaceperson branch. The Lord's Anointed, as I've heard engineers refer to you while I was doing my course at your Antarctic Academy. But there are other loyalties."

"Such as?" he asked curiously. "Such as?"

"Does the fact that you have made love to me mean nothing?" she asked.

Why should it mean more? he wondered. He suppressed a chuckle. If chance copulations engendered loyalty, then this quality would, as far as he was concerned, be spread extremely thinly over many worlds and ships.

It was her turn to laugh.

"Just a wolf," she said. (A wolf? How much did she know?) "A typical Terran wolf. On our world, where the male sex is kept under proper control, we don't have such animals. But I met plenty of them on Earth. Even so, we have—to use your peculiar euphemism—slept together. As

your first Doralan, I must occupy a special niche in your
murky memory.''

"That's it. We aren't even members of the same species.''

"More importantly, we aren't members of the same sex.
That's one of the reasons why I want you. One of the
reasons.''

"There are others?''

"Yes. You are a qualified, and presumably skilled,
navigator.''

"There are qualified and skilled navigators of your own
race aboard this ship. The Lady Mother. Prenta . . .''

"But what if their authority is stripped from them?''

He stared at her. She was more than half drunk, he thought,
and talking wildly. What was the old saying? "When the
wine is in, the wit is out. . . .'' Yet her words were not
slurred, and furthermore, she was talking with fluent ease in a
language not her own.

"What if their authority is stripped from them?'' she repeated.

Shocked (but why should he, of all people, feel shock?) he
asked, "Mutiny? Are you contemplating mutiny?''

"Mutiny? Whatever gave you that idea, Falsen? I'm no
expert on the regulations governing your space service, but I
know something of our own laws. Should a captain display
extreme incompetence, she may be superceded by a committee of her senior officers.''

"Oh? To begin with, I don't think that she has been
incompetent.''

"What about the mess that we are in now?''

"You asked the question, I shall answer it. This mess is
directly due to a breakdown of the machinery for which *you
are directly responsible*.''

"This is an old ship, Falsen, as you well know. Things are
liable to break down at any moment, as the Lady Mother well
knows. By making the landing approach that she did, she left
herself no options and did not have time to use emergency
reaction drive.''

"All right. You may, you just may, be right. But you will
still have your navigator, who's also next in line for captain.
Prenta.''

"Prenta!'' she spat.

"What about Pansir?''

"Her in charge of a *space*ship? Don't make me laugh, Falsen."

"All right, all right. Just suppose that your officers' revolt, since you don't like the word mutiny, comes off—whom do you see as captain?"

"Me, of course."

"You?"

He thought that she was going to strike him, her fingers clawed, but she held herself back with a visible effort.

"Why not?" she demanded. "I can command. I could even navigate after a fashion, although I'd like to have somebody more skilled than I to do it for me."

He said, "Yes, it would be rather embarrassing if you missed your home planet on the return journey."

"Who said anything about returning to Dorala?" she asked.

He stared at her.

"Who said anything about returning to Dorala?" she repeated. "Some of us aboard this ship are tired of the policy of our rulers, tagging along behind your mighty Federation like . . . like little dogs, grateful for the Federation's leftovers, such as this almost uninhabitable planet. We should strike out on our own, find our own worlds for colonization. Even found a colony . . ."

"And you have founding fathers, as well as founding mothers, aboard this ship," murmured Falsen, as much to himself as to her.

"Yes. We have. I know that you know. Garbill told me that you found him. Some of us wanted to . . . dispose of you and Linda before you could tell the Lady Mother, but I thought that the time would come when we should need you."

"Oh. And what if I tell her now? About the plot, about everything?"

"You will not, Falsen. I am sure that your story about how you and Linda came to be marooned on this world is not a true one, that you wish to return to Earth even less than we wish to return to Dorala. I offer you a chance to come with us, as navigator, to become a founding father of a new, biracial colony yourself."

"You must be drunk," he said harshly.

She smiled at him blearily—but there was a dangerous hardness under her soft expression.

"My tongue has been loosened," she said. "That I admit. But I am still in control, full control."

Suddenly she was perspiring profusely, sweat running in rivers down her face, soaking her hair. The efflux of fluid from the pores of her skin darkened her scarlet tunic almost to black. An acrid sweetness tainted the air.

"I *was* drunk," she said. "Now I am not. I know what I have been saying. My offer to you—and to Linda, if you must have her—still stands. And I warn you, Falsen, do not tell anybody, *anybody,* not even that bitch of yours. Of course, if you should blab to the Lady Mother, I doubt very much that she would believe you. After all, you are the outsider, the alien. Would she take *your* word against that of one of her most trusted senior officers?"

He said, "I must tell her."

"Then you'll not live long."

He laughed inwardly. It would take more than the combined efforts of Carlin and all her supporters to kill him. Unless they *knew*—but how could they?

"In any case," she went on, "you cannot tell her until the ship has been raised. Until that time we must all work together."

He said, "I make no promises."

She said, "But I am making threats." She stood up, steadily, and stripped off her sodden tunic. Under it she was naked. She went on, "I had intended that we would . . . make love? Yes, those words will have to do. But now I am sober and the very idea disgusts me. Get out, Falsen, back to your Linda. Have a good night's sleep so that you're ready for a hard day's work tomorrow."

He looked up at her. Now that she had spurned him, he was wanting her very badly. Suddenly he reached out, caught her ankle, tugged sharply. She fell and, with a speed that surprised even himself, he rolled over on top of her. Her claws ripped his shirt, scored his back. She tried to bring her knees, her feet up under his belly but he somehow forced her legs apart. Her sweat-slippery body writhed beneath him. In spite of her hostility, he knew that she was ready, as ready as he was, readier. She was unclothed; his shorts were still on, his erect penis straining at the material. But he needed his hands to hold her, to restrain her, to prevent her from doing more damage to him than she had done already.

One of her hands drove down to his groin and he flinched, expecting that she would savagely maul his genitals. But it was the sealseam that was the target for her fingers, that fell open, releasing his thrusting organ. He was into her, held closely to her by her arms and legs, imprisoned inside her by those tightly gripping, kneading protrusions.

Then, explosively, implosively, it was over.

He rolled off her, out of her.

They sprawled side by side on the damp mattress.

She asked lazily, "Has that helped you to make up your mind, Falsen?"

"I . . . I don't know." He was trying hard to be honest. "Perhaps . . . if you can take the ship without bloodshed, killing . . ."

She smiled smugly.

"I would never shed the blood of my own kind, Falsen."

And where does that leave me? he wondered. But should Carlin attempt to shed *his* blood she would have a surprise coming.

She said, "You had better leave now. I would like you to sleep here with me, but there are those who would not approve."

You can say that again, he thought.

"Where have you been?" demanded Linda. "What's happened to you? Your shirt, torn to shreds . . . And those scratches on your back . . ."

"That bloody Pondor," he lied. "He jumped me."

"And did he piss all over you? You *stink*." She wrinkled her nostrils. "No. It's not him, *not* tomcat. But . . ."

"I must have rubbed against something," he said.

CHAPTER 30

The next morning it was still raining.

Nonetheless the work went ahead, the reassembling of the inertial-drive unit. Like huge worker bees going about their business, the mini-innies flew into and out of the hole that had been cut in the shell plating, on each outward journey carrying in their clawed appendages components of the machine.

Prenta had succeeded in getting two of the little helicopters, the ones that had escaped damage in the crash, out of their stowage. Pansir was busy. There was the second airship carried by the space vessel to be gotten ready for flight, this one only a small nonrigid, little more than an assemblage of gasbags with a skeletal car. Grumbling to herself, annoyed at being taken away from what she considered more important work, Carlin had made the necessary modifications to the hydrogen-fusion power generator so that it now delivered a flow of helium as well as electricity for lights, machines and essential services.

Everybody, thought Falsen, was busy except himself. And, of course, Linda. He walked around outside the fallen ship, enjoying the feel of the warm rain on his naked torso, the moistness that squelched up between the toes of his bare feet. He accompanied the Lady Mother as, cloaked and hooded, she made her rounds of the various activities.

She expressed concern for his well-being.

"Are you not cold, Mr. Falsen, wearing only those shorts? I realize that your uniform is no longer wearable, but the ship's seamstress would be able to run up something suitable."

"She's probably doing something much more important, Gracious Lady. Isn't she working for Pansir?"

The captain laughed. "Oh, I suppose that the airship has rather higher priority than a new shirt for you, but there is no need for you to get wet. Should you not be keeping the Lady Linda company?"

Linda, thought Falsen, had made it quite plain that his company was not high on her list of priorities. She did not *know* what he had been doing with Carlin but she suspected. She had told him, "If I didn't know what you really are, I'd say that you were a two-legged tomcat. Get out of here and don't come back until the rain has washed the stink off you!"

Yet he was loyal to her, as he had to be. In the final analysis he had no option.

He said, "It is very stuffy inside the ship."

"Once she has been raised, the life-support systems will work properly." They paused by the tent under which Carlin and her engineers were working; the Lady Mother raised her voice to make herself heard above the racket of the mini-innies. "I really don't know how we should have managed without you, Mr. Falsen."

"You'd have managed," he said. "After all, spacemanship is no more than just doing the obvious thing."

"Space*woman*ship," she corrected with a smile. "But *this,* since it was your idea, *is* spacemanship."

From many people, thought Falsen, this would have been insincere flattery. Somehow, from the Lady Mother, it was not. All right, all right, he had slept with Carlin, now inside the tent bossing her juniors as they fitted part to part, as they maneuvered the mini-innies in the confined space to lift the heavier components into position. He may have slept with Carlin, yet he felt no affection for her, never could do so. But the Lady Mother . . . For one of his kind conscience was an expensive luxury; nonetheless, he possessed one. It was troubling him now, nagging him about the immorality of giving with one hand and taking away with both.

They watched the busy engineers and were ignored by them. Carlin made a major production of this.

They walked on toward the bows, out of earshot.

"What do you think of the Lady Carlin?" asked the Lady Mother abruptly.

"She is . . . very capable," said Falsen.

"Yes, she is. Otherwise she would not be a member of this expedition. Yet . . ."

"Yet?" echoed Falsen.

"Of late I have not quite trusted her. There are . . . undercurrents. Ponder has been talking to me—but can I believe what *he* says? After all, he is only a cat, and despite his command of language and his high opinion of himself has only a cat's brain. And a cat's jealousy and spitefulness. There are some of my officers whom he detests—and the Lady Carlin is one of them."

"I have gained the impression," said Falsen, "that he also hates Linda and myself."

"That is understandable, Mr. Falsen. After all, to him you are aliens. His ancestry may be Terran, but he is Doralan by birth."

Falsen inspected the huge towing lug. It was, in effect, an extension of the ship's longitudinal-strength members. He was reasonably sure that it would hold; his only worry was whether or not he would be able to apply sufficient torque when the time came. Without earthmoving equipment it would not be possible to fill the trench under the repaired vane in a hurry; to swing the ship around on the tip of one of the other vanes was the only solution.

And after that, when the vessel was again spaceworthy?

It almost seemed that the Lady Mother had been reading his thoughts.

"I rather fear," she said, "that after the ship has been raised there will be a demand by my officers that I return forthwith to Dorala. I shall not accede to it, of course. The survey of this planet must be completed and the nature of the dangerous carnivores determined. Also, I am required to avenge my people who have been killed by those animals."

My own hands, thought Falsen, *are clean. So far. But are Linda's? Even so, there are other dangerous forces loose on this world.*

He said, "But will not the slaughter of what must be a major life form have all sorts of unforeseen effects?"

"If we are to colonize this planet, Mr. Falsen, it must be done. After all, on *your* world the only lions and tigers and wolves left are in zoological parks. Pests such as the anopheles mosquito have been exterminated. Yet the complicated life-support machinery of the planetary spaceship still functions."

"It's just that the idea of *revenge* taken on unthinking beasts seems somehow wrong to me."

"Why should it, Mr. Falsen? While I was on Earth I saw films shot by anthropologists not very long ago, historically speaking. I saw the brutalities perpetrated by primitive fishermen upon captured sharks. We, at least, just kill. We do not torture first."

They made their way down from the ridge of the impact crater to level ground, walked aft to where Pansir and her gang were working. Most of the skilled airshipwomen had been killed in the crash of the big dirigible, so the pilot was having to do almost everything herself, running around the long gray sausage shape, tugging, adjusting, while the cells, fed by a long pipe running from the ship, slowly inflated. After making sure that the restraining lines were in place, Pansir greeted them cheerfully enough.

She said, using English for Falsen's benefit, "I shall soon be able to fly again, Gracious Lady."

"You are doing well, Lady Pansir."

They walked on.

"I wish that they were all like her, Mr. Falsen," said the captain. "She is the only one of my officers who does not delude herself that she could run a spaceship better than any captain ever appointed to that rank. Of course, she knows that she is the only one among us who can handle an airship properly. . . ."

They came to Prenta who, with a couple of crewwomen, was fussing around the two little helicopters. She raised her hand in salute to the Lady Mother, looked sourly at Falsen.

She said, "I shall be happy, Gracious Lady, if the Jonah will keep away from equipment for which I am personally responsible."

"Lady Prenta, must I order you again to stop making references to an absurd mythology, and one that is not even our own?"

"It is Terran mythology, Gracious Lady, and Mr. Falsen and Miss Veerhausen are Terrans."

There are worse beings in our mythology than Jonahs, thought Falsen.

"I am warning you, Lady Prenta. I shall be obliged to put you down in my confidential report as subject to xenophobia. Come, Mr. Falsen. The Lady Prenta will be happier when she is no longer obliged to look at you."

They strolled on towards the stern.

"You know, Mr. Falsen," she said, "your languages are much richer in picturesque sayings than any of ours. While I was at your Antarctic Academy, one of the courses I took was on the history of transport. I found especially fascinating the long story of wind-driven ships; on Dorala there are no great seas, so we ourselves have never known the need for such vessels. There was the period of the clippers, which reached their peak just as steam was coming in. There were all the sayings that were used aboard them. One, for some reason, has stuck in my memory. 'Growl you may, but go you must.' So it is with my people; Alida knows that they have cause enough to growl! But once the ship has been raised, the atmosphere will be back to normal. . . ."

You hope, thought Falsen. *Shall I warn her? Dare I warn her? If I put her on her guard against Carlin it will jeopardize my chances. Mine and Linda's. Carlin's vicious—and how much does she suspect?*

Then—*To hell with it,* he thought. *I'll get the ship up for them, and then I'll play it by ear.*

CHAPTER 31

The dismal day wore on.

During the afternoon Falsen spent much of his time with Carlin and her people although they, she especially, made it clear that his presence was not welcome. But he would be the pilot of the makeshift tug, and he was determined that everything would be constructed, as far as possible, to his requirements.

The drive unit was reassembled on a triangular platform standing two and a half meters clear of the ground. Secured to the three legs was another triangular platform, this one made from the glasslike material used for viewports. It was tough and would easily bear his weight and would afford him a clear downward field of view. There was a circular hole in the exact center of this deck, through which would run both the umbilical from the ship, carrying power from the hydrogen fusion plant, and the much lighter cable attached to the control panel that Falsen would be using. Aerodynamic qualities could not be hoped for in such an improvised craft, would not, in fact, be necessary. Nonetheless it was highly desirable to avoid any imbalance.

"I'm an engineer!" Carlin snarled at him. "Not a watchmaker."

"I'm riding this thing."

"Just don't get in my hair, Falsen."

The inertial-drive unit stood, a cylindrical tower of interlocking wheels and spindles, its core an enormous solenoid. It was the first time that Falsen had seen such a machine in its gleaming nakedness, with its featureless casing not in place. It reminded him of something that he had seen not all that long ago, during his last leave on Earth. Where had it been? Yes, in the city of Old Los Angeles, those fantastic constructions called the Watts Towers, steeples built from all sorts of metallic, glass and ceramic odds and ends. They were not the original towers, of course. They had been rebuilt more than once and improved upon every time.

"When you've finished gawking, Falsen," asked Carlin, "will it be all right with you if we get this baby dressed? I assure you that she's in working order; there aren't any parts left over."

"You're the engineer," he said.

"And you're the intrepid pilot," she sneered.

The mini-innies buzzed around, carrying their sections of curved plating. The artificers guided them into place, bolted the plates securely to the heavy framework. Finally, three enormously strong lugs were fitted to equidistantly spaced bearers.

"Is your lordship satisfied?" Carlin asked.

"There are still the power and the control cables to connect and my chair to fit."

"Rome wasn't built in a day, as you people say."

Falsen went out of the tent and looked up at the dismal, weeping sky. Its ruddiness was fading to gray, darkening. There wasn't much of this day left. But there was no hurry. He might need all the hours of daylight for the raising operation, starting at dawn. All manner of snags could—almost certainly would—develop.

He walked around the fallen hull. The two helicopters, now ready for flight, were covered with a light plastic sheet. Fully inflated, the blimp rode at the stubby mooring mast that had been erected, the skids on the underside of its car just clear of the ground. At the foot of the metallic skeleton pyramid the Lady Mother was talking with Pansir.

The airship pilot saw Falsen approaching, turned to him to enlist his support.

"Mr. Falsen," she said, "what do you think? I am not happy that my ship should be left out here during the hours of darkness, unattended." She managed a tremulous smile. "After all, I have already lost one airship."

Falsen sniffed the air judiciously.

He said, "There will be no wind tonight."

The two women took his word for it, but Pansir was still not satisfied.

"Even so, I think that there should be a guard mounted. We know that there are large, vicious beasts on this planet, and to leave so much valuable equipment outside the spaceship is just asking to have it damaged. Or destroyed."

"Even the hungriest carnivore," said the Lady Mother, "would not eat metal or plastic."

"One of them," insisted Pansir, "was responsible for the wreck of my big ship, as Mr. Falsen well knows."

"It was after the people inside the ship," Falsen told her.

"That is so," said the Lady Mother. "It is my feeling that the posting of sentries outside the hull would attract the things from the lake, from the caves, wherever it is that they came from. In any sort of a fight, with people firing wildly, things could be damaged. Not only your airship, Lady Pansir, but the helicopters and, even more important, the inertial-drive unit. What is your opinion, Mr. Falsen?"

"I think that you are right, Gracious Lady. But if a bio-sensitive radar scanner could be rigged, hooked up to an alarm system, we might all sleep easier."

"It is a long time," said the Lady Mother, "since I slept easily."

She was not complaining, was merely stating a fact. Looking at her tired, worn face Falsen felt a flood of sympathy.

"There is a curse on this world," she went on. "The only good thing about it has been finding you here. But come, both of you. We will see how the Lady Carlin is getting on."

Carlin had done as much as she could do before the day was over. Under its canopy stood the gleaming cylinder that housed the drive, squatting smugly on its stilted platform. A stout chair had been secured to the lower deck, just to one side of the hole through which the cables would pass. These, together with the control panel, would not be installed until the morning. The chief engineer and her people were now working on top of the spaceship's hull, spot-welding a cover over the hole that had been cut to remove the drive components. The ship was being sealed for the night.

"Aren't you going tomcatting this evening?" asked Linda.

"No. I want a good night's sleep."

"That will be a change. Aren't you going to let the Lady Mother cry on your shoulder before she goes beddy-byes? Or what about Carlin? Won't she be lonely?" She was watching his expression intently. "So it *is* Carlin, isn't it?"

He said, "Can't you see that I have to play along with these people? Once the ship has been raised and made spaceworthy, we shall be able to carry out our own plans."

Her mood changed abruptly.

"Yes. You're right. We must have a ship before we can get off this mudball to a decent world, one where we can live as we should. . . ."

"As we should?"

"Yes. We didn't ask to be made the way that we are. We didn't put in a written request to the Odd Gods of the Galaxy that some odd gene from way, way back be included in our makeup. Oh, we're luckier than our ancestors. We aren't slaves to the phases of the moon, as they were. We aren't even dependent now on the temporal precession field of the Mannschenn Drive. When we want to, we do. But I've been wanting to for a long time now, Nicholas. All this meat, this live raw meat rubbing shoulders with us—we can look, but we mustn't bite."

"There will be no more killing," he said. "We will seize the ship, but there will be no more killing."

"Who do you think you're kidding?" she asked scornfully.

"Let me get some sleep," he said tiredly.

CHAPTER 32

Daylight grew slowly and a steady warm drizzle drifted down from the heavy overcast. But there was no wind. Falsen was almost sure that it would stay that way, was hoping that his instincts were not misleading him. He stood by the inertial-drive unit, watching as the power supply and control cables were connected. He heard the clatter as, on the other side of the spaceship, the helicopters lifted, flying to a safe distance from the scene of operations. Pansir, too, was up, putting her fat, clumsy blimp through its paces, turning in lazy circles, dipping and soaring. She was to act as an observer, watching from the air, giving prompt warning should anything unnoticed by Falsen, invisible to those stationed on the ground, go wrong.

Three mini-innies brought carefully measured and cut lengths of the enormously strong towing wire from the ship, each with a ferruled eye at both ends. Six pieces had been prepared. Two lengths were shackled to each of the lugs on the drive casing. The free ends dangled to the damp ground all around the lower platform onto which the pilot's chair had been secured.

The Lady Mother said doubtfully, "I still think that the towing wires should be longer, Mr. Falsen. . . ."

"If they were, I should find it very hard to apply sufficient torque. And that I must do in the final stages."

The mini-innies flew out from under the canopy and stationed themselves around the edge. Their metal claws took hold of the fabric. The noisy machines lifted, and the huge

166

sheltering sheet came clear of its metal supports, was carried away and then dropped to the ground.

Falsen pulled his laser pistol from its holster, looked—not for the first time—at the gauge on its butt. According to this, the weapon was fully charged. Just to be certain, he pointed the weapon at the ground, pressed the firing stud briefly. There was an explosion of steam and the rim of the hole that had been bored glowed briefly. He reholstered the pistol and then stepped onto the triangular platform between the three supporting legs. He sat down in the chair—it had been re-made to accommodate his Terran bulk—and made the seatbelt fast about his body. He reached down for the combination control box and radio-telephone transceiver, set it on his lap. He switched on. Green *ready* lights glowed all over the panel.

He turned to Carlin and said, "Make sure that the power cable is clear at all times, hanging straight down."

"Just do your job, Falsen," she said, "and I'll do mine."

"Good luck, Mr. Falsen," said the Lady Mother. "And good luck to all of us."

Falsen had a last look around. Everybody, except for the two engineers who would be tending the hydrogen-fusion power generator, was out of the ship. He did not envy them. He, at least, would know what was happening. All that they could do was to keep things working and hope. He saw Linda, standing well back, keeping herself apart from the Doralans. He waved to her. She half-heartedly lifted her hand in reply.

He spoke toward the microphone of the transceiver.

"Falsen to Lady Pansir. I am about to lift off."

"I hear you, Mr. Falsen," came the reply. "I am watching."

His fingers went to the control panel. Over his head the inertial-drive unit grumbled, and he could feel the vibration of the framework supporting it. Something started to rattle. He hoped that it was nothing important. Around him, on the mossy ground, the film of moisture that had formed after the removal of the tent quivered, took on the appearance of widening concentric circles like the ripples on the surface of a pond marking the impact of a flung stone. He moved the control knob clockwise and the clangor of the drive became deafening. He was well clear of the ground now, looking down at the team of scarlet-cloaked crewwomen who, under Carlin's energetic direction, were tending the umbilical cable that ran from the cargo hatch in the ship's side to the make-shift tug. They were making sure that there was plenty of slack.

Carefully he put his clumsy craft through its paces—vertical thrust, lateral thrust and torque. When he was satisfied he flew slowly towards the stem of the spaceship, reducing altitude as he did so. Beneath him trudged Carlin and her crew, tugging the power cable, aided by the mini-innies.

Then he was over the control room and the ground party was scrambling down into the impact crater, accompanied by the mini-innies. One of these was carrying a huge shackle and bars and hammers. Falsen applied lateral thrust cautiously, edged forward until the eyed ends of the six towing wires were dangling around the lug at the very end of the stem. Securing them, he soon realized, was not going to be so easy as either he or Carlin had hoped. That part of the ship, a sharply tapered cone of metal and transparent plastic, rain-slippery, afforded very insecure footing. Three of the crew women slipped, fell heavily into the mud. There was an interlude of floundering confusion until Carlin got things under control. She had a mini-innie pick her up by the belt while another carried the heavy shackle. The operators of the machines seemed to know what they were doing.

One by one the towing-wire eyes were passed up and around the arms of the shackle. Falsen applied lift gently so that the metal U was dangling, its open jaw downward. Then, millimeter by millimeter, he reduced altitude until Carlin could maneuver the shackle into position over and around the towing lug. She was joined by one of her crew, carried by another of the mini-innies, herself carrying the shackle pin. She inserted this. It was a snug fit and there was more delay until the heavy hammer could be passed to her. She dealt the end of the pin a blow—and became living proof of Newton's Third Law of Motion, swinging out and away from the point of impact. After this there was a transferring of positions, with the junior engineer holding the shackle steady while Carlin drove in the pin with a series of decisive taps. When the job was finished she inserted the forelock into its slot at the protruding end and used a light hammer to knock it into its securing position.

She looked up to the hovering Falsen and shouted, her

voice barely audible above the clatter of the drive, "Take her away, Falsen, as soon as we're clear!"

In less than five minutes the Doralans and their machines were away from the spaceship's bows and standing by the heavy power cable.

The Lady Mother's voice came from the transceiver, "Are you ready, Mr. Falsen?"

"All ready," he replied.

The cacophony of the drive increased in intensity. The tow wires tautened. The measurements had been accurate, Falsen noted with satisfaction. All six parts were bearing an equal strain, and there was clearance, very little but enough, between them and the edges of his platform. They should hold if the Safe Working Load Certificate were to be believed. After all, they would never have to support the full weight of the ship; at all times her tonnage would be supported by the surface of the planet. Once he had her up to an angle greater than forty-five degrees it would be a piece of cake.

Slowly, slowly, he built up the lift. The wires were thrumming, a disquietening sound that was audible even above the increasingly noisy hammering of the inertial drive. He looked down. The ship had not budged. It was not only her weight that was holding her down; it was the suction of the mud in which she was resting. He thought briefly of reducing thrust, allowing the wires to slacken, then piling on maximum vertical thrust. He decided against it. That would be too much even for these cables.

But lateral thrust might be the answer. He applied it, first one way and then the other. He repeated the maneuver, and again.

"She is moving!" came Pansir's high voice from the transceiver.

"So . . . Vertical thrust again . . . A slow buildup of thrust . . . The wires resumed their ominous singing.

And would the wires, the eyes, hold? Would the cut ends pull clear of the ferrules? He looked down. There were no indications that this was about to happen. He looked up but, from his almost central position on the platform, could not see how the eyes shackled to the towing lugs on the drive casing were holding.

"She is lifting!"

He could not tell if the voice from the transceiver was Pansir's or the Lady Mother's, but the information was all that mattered.

She was coming up, slowly at first and then faster and faster as the angle made by her long axis with the ground increased, as her weight was being borne more by the surface than by the tow wires.

"About forty-five degrees . . ." the Lady Mother was saying. "Fifty . . ."

"Lady Pansir, how do things look to you?" Falsen asked.

"Very good, Mr. Falsen. The weight is coming onto the repaired vane. From up here I can see no signs of buckling."

"The vane is taking the weight," came Carlin's voice. She added smugly, "It is stronger than it was before."

He maintained vertical thrust while increasing the lateral component. He was pulling the stem of the ship horizontally now as much as he was lifting it. And the wires were holding.

Looking down through the transparent deck, he could see for himself. He was hovering noisily above a great leaning tower of metal—a leaning tower that still would topple if his support were to be removed. It would not be long now before the great feet of the other two vanes made contact with the ground. But then the third one would have been lifted clear, would be hanging, unsupported, above the trench.

"Contact!" cried the Lady Mother jubilantly.

The tower was no longer leaning, was upright—but it would have to be tilted again before full stability could be achieved.

Falsen used lateral thrust again, pulling the ship away from the vertical until her weight was borne only by one of the undamaged vanes. Now was the time to use the torque control, turning the drive unit about its vertical axis, hoping that the ship would follow. But she resisted, the foot of the vane gripped firmly in the mud. The towlines began to twist.

There was no longer clearance between them and the edge of the platform. The transparent deck began to buckle, to crack. "You're breaking up!" came Pansir's voice. "You're breaking up!"

Pieces were coming away from the edge of the platform, falling like glittering dead leaves, those of them hitting the spaceship shattering into smaller fragments. Falsen cursed—and turned the torque control to its maximum setting.

Suddenly the ship began to swing, to turn, teetering on the single vane. As the tow wires straightened, untwisting, they pulled away more of the platform into which they had embedded themselves. The cracks extended to the very center of it and Falsen's chair was left dangling over nothingness, held by only two of its legs. But the ship was still turning, had turned. Falsen was hanging on to the power cable with one hand, had both legs around it. With his right hand he pressed the control box to his chest and, straining, could just reach the torque-setting knob with his fingers. He turned it back, then looked down. The ship was resting on all three vanes, the repaired one now just clear of the impact crater.

"Can I help?" somebody was asking. "Can I help?"

It was Pansir. The blimp was hanging only ten meters from him, and the airship pilot was leaning out of an open window in her cab, megaphone raised to her mouth.

There was nothing that she could do, Falsen thought, although he appreciated the offer.

"Just keep handy!" he shouted.

He managed to get his fingers onto the vertical-thrust control, reduced lift until the two wires were barely taut. Then he lowered the box until it was dangling by its cable, let go of it. He hoped that the wires would be strong enough to support its weight; he would be needing it again. He managed, with one hand, to unbuckle the belt with the pistol-holster attached, brought it up to his mouth, got a strong grip on it with his teeth. Unsnapping the seat belt was next. He suddenly realized that he had been supporting the chair, not it him. It dropped away, narrowly missing the control box in its descent, bounced, fragmented and twisted, off the bows of the spaceship.

But he would need two hands to get the belt around him and the umbilical cable. He dare not let go of this, fearing that should he do so he would fall over backward, losing the grip that his legs had upon the thick insulated wire. Something hit him sharply on the shoulder. He looked around. The blimp was very close now and Pansir, still leaning out of her window, was pulling up, hand over hand, a light heaving line with a weight on the end of it. She threw again, skillfully. The weight missed him—then whipped around the umbilical, continuing to take a turn around his body. It would hold him—perhaps only briefly, but for long enough. With both hands free, he was able to secure himself with his belt and then pull the control box up to where he could handle it.

All the indicator lights on the panel were glowing; it was still in working order.

Falsen pulled the laser pistol from its holster. He took careful aim at one of the tow wires. There was a coruscation of blue incandescent sparks, but the wire was tough. It parted at last. Then the second wire was dealt with, and the third, and the fourth. . . . But by this time the charge in the pistol was almost depleted, could produce no more than a dull red glow from the surface upon which its beam impinged.

But Pansir had been watching.

Handling her clumsy aircraft with consummate skill, she brought it around to a position from which she would have a clear field of fire, could bring her own hand laser to bear upon the remaining towlines without hitting Falsen or cutting the vitally important power cable. Her aim was good—but the range was comparatively long. It seemed an eternity before the last of the wires, dripping gobbets of molten metal, parted.

"Thank you, Lady Pansir," said Falsen inadequately.

She circled above him as he dropped slowly to the ground, to the waiting Doralans and to the solitary figure, in a sodden white uniform, that was Linda. With sudden bitterness he asked himself what she had done to help in raising the ship. The alien women—the Lady Mother, Carlin and Pansir especially—had proven their worth, while she had just been standing around, doing nothing.

But there was the ship, a great gleaming tower almost ready for her natural element again. One side of her was still covered with black, dripping mud but it didn't matter. The rain would soon wash it off, and if it didn't it still wouldn't matter.

Below him, with her ground crew and the busy mini-innies, Carlin pulled the dangling umbilical clear of his line of descent.

CHAPTER 33

Falsen sat with the Lady Mother in her day cabin.

There was little evidence of the crash in this room; either no furniture had been broken or it had already been skillfully repaired. But the cups from which they were drinking the hot aniseed-flavored tea were of thick plastic, not thin porcelain, as were the plates on which were displayed the little, too-sweet cakes. There had been breakages.

They sat there, nibbling, while Pondor, at his mistress's feet, glared balefully at the Earthman.

"You did very well, Mr. Falsen," said the Doralan captain.

"So did your people, Gracious Lady," he said. "Lady Carlin, Lady Pansir . . . If it hadn't been for Pansir I'd have suffered a nasty fall. . . ."

She smiled and remarked, "That is an understatement."

Falsen suppressed a smile of his own. Understatement it had not been. Losing his grip on the power cable would have meant a nasty fall, no more. But it was not necessary to tell the Lady Mother that.

She asked abruptly, "Have you considered how you and Miss Veerhausen are going to make your way back to Earth?"

The question took him aback, and he thought hard and fast before replying.

He said at last, "Well, Gracious Lady, I assumed that you would be giving us passage to Dorala in this ship. Then, of course, we should have to see the Terran ambassador to arrange a DTS passage home."

"DTS?"

"Distressed Terran Spacepersons."

"Of course." She sipped from her cup. "But, Mr. Falsen, do you really wish to return to Earth?"

Again he was taken aback. How much did she suspect, or know?

He said, rather lamely, "I was born there."

"But what will be waiting for you there, Mr. Falsen? You're a spaceman, and a good one—as I have learned—but your career is finished." (*How much* do *you know?* he demanded silently.) "You must know of Lloyd's Black Book. In the event of any major disaster in space—and the loss of your ship, *Epsilon Crucis*, must be classed as such—the names of survivors, if any, are recorded. As yours will be. Even though you, as a control-room officer, cannot be held responsible for the breakdown of the ship's Mannschenn Drive, you were there when it happened. Perhaps you are accident-prone. No . . . that's not quite right. Perhaps, they reason, you are one of those beings around whom things 'just happen.' "

"What your Lady Prenta would call a Jonah," said Falsen.

She smiled at this, then went on, "I have no doubt that you would be cleared by a court of enquiry. Your certificate of competency would not be canceled, or suspended. But who would employ you? What shipping company would be prepared to pay higher insurance premiums on one of its vessels to which you have been appointed?"

"I've heard of Lloyd's Black Book," said Falsen.

"And you must be in it," mewed Pondor suddenly.

"Quiet, cat!" snapped the Lady Mother. Then, to the man, "Do you *want* to return to Earth, Mr. Falsen?"

Earth wouldn't have me, he thought.

He said, "The way you put it, Gracious Lady, my prospects don't seem at all rosy."

"They are not, Mr. Falsen. And it is a great pity that your talents should be allowed to go to waste. Some more tea?" She poured from the metal pot. "I'll be frank with you. To begin with, I am very grateful to you. And I am a woman not without influence on my own world. My elder sister is High Mother of the Department of Interstellar Shipping—what in your parliamentary system would be called a minister. Among her many responsibilities is the establishment of our own Astronautical Academy. You are, of course, aware that ours is a matriarchal society. Even so, we look upon Earthmen, Earth *men,* as our mentors in astronautical matters. You must have noticed how, despite your sex, you have been accepted aboard this vessel. That is because you are a spaceman, a *space* man. If you'd been just a man, perhaps a passenger cast away as you were, you would have been regarded as . . . as . . .'' She struggled to find a telling simile, came out at last with, "Something that the cat brought in.''

"*I* wouldn't touch him,'' mewed Pondor.

"*Quiet!* I say.''

"Not everybody has accepted me,'' said Falsen.

"The Lady Carlin respects your competence, as does the Lady Pansir.''

"Prenta still hates me.''

"That has nothing to do with your sex, Mr. Falsen. Officially, she is my second-in-command. Even before we found you she resented my putting the Lady Carlin in charge of extravehicular activities. And lately she has resented, even more strongly, your being in virtual full control of the raising operation. She is very jealous.''

"I guessed that, Gracious Lady.''

"At our Academy you would have to cope with similar jealousies as well as sexual antagonism—but I am sure that, once the story of what you did for this ship has been widely publicized, you would be accepted by the majority.''

Falsen sipped his tea thoughtfully. The idea was not unattractive. Dorala was not Earth—but to Earth he could never return. Could he adapt to an utterly alien culture? Why not? Others before him had done so. He recalled how, during one of his leaves on Earth, he had visited Japan and had been taken to the tomb of the Anjin Sama, still after many centuries venerated almost as a shrine. This Anjin Sama had been Will Adams, the first Englishman in Japan, by the standards of his time an extremely competent navigator, by the standards of any time an outstanding seaman. He had never returned to England. He had become a *daimyo,* a Japanese nobleman and an admiral. In those long-ago days the Japanese culture had been as strange to a European as the Doralan culture would be now to a Terran. Stranger, perhaps . . .

A shore job, and a job that he would enjoy . . . that could be the answer to his problems, to Linda's problems. Once they were away for a long period from the temporal-precession field of the Mannschenn Drive, surely they would no longer be subject to their own peculiar regression, even though at times they might will themselves (as they could now) to regress.

But why should they wish to do so?

"You look interested, Mr. Falsen," said the Lady Mother. "Or should I call you Captain-Professor Falsen?"

"I haven't got the job yet, Gracious Lady," he said. "I haven't said, even, that I want it."

"I became quite expert in reading Terran expressions while I was on Earth, Mr. Falsen. You have your doubts—as who would not?—but you are tempted."

"I am," he said.

"Then, think about it. There is no hurry. There will be the remainder of our stay here and then the duration of the voyage back to Dorala. Talk it over with the Lady Linda." She smiled knowingly. "You will need her with you. I know, from my own experience, that sexual release of tensions is not possible between members of our two species. And sex—as even we in our matriarchal society acknowledge—is essential for physical and mental health."

I wonder who you tried it with on Earth, thought Falsen. Possibly it had been with some crudely masculine type who had been determined to demonstrate to this woman, from a world where women ruled, the God-given superiority of the male. And what would she think if she found out about him and Carlin?

"And now, Mr. Falsen, please excuse me. I must prepare a rough draft of my report on the raising of the ship and on the events prior to it."

This, obviously, was dismissal.

Falsen finished his tea, got to his feet, thanked the Doralan captain and left.

He hoped that Linda would be as sympathetic to the Lady Mother's proposal as he was.

CHAPTER 34

"*You,* a schoolmaster!" she sneered.

"Why not, Linda?" He tried to make a joke. "The Odd Gods of the Galaxy know that there are enough wolves on the tutorial staffs of colleges and universities."

"There are wolves, and wolves. Listen to me, Nick. We're almost there. Soon we will be able to get what *we* want. We. Us. And to hell with these bloody Doralan pussycats. A world of our own is what we must have, some planet out towards the Rim that the Federation hasn't stumbled on yet, won't stumble on until it has been populated by our descendants."

"A dream. A good one, perhaps, but only a dream. Whatever else we might be, we're a civilized man and woman. We could exist without the comforts to which we are used, the comforts deriving from modern technology, but it would be no more than an existence. . . ."

"It would be life!" she almost shouted. "Life as it should be lived!"

"Quiet, Linda! Somebody might hear."

"There's nobody out in the alleyway, not even that bloody Pondor. Nick, drop this crazy idea."

"It's not crazy. We would have a good life on Dorala. You'd have even less to worry about than I would—after all, you're of the right sex to get along in a matriarchal society. Oh, we'd find it hard, at first, to restrain ourselves—but we're used to doing that. And I'm sure that once we're away from the Mannschenn Drive, from the temporal-precession field, we shall revert to . . . to normality.''

"Normality? What is normal? I prefer to think that the way we are now is normal. For us.''

He said, ''The Lady Mother is offering us an ideal solution to our problem. We should accept the offer.''

"The Lady Mother. Carlin. Pansir. All the pussycats, and at least one of them a pussycat in heat. I'm disgusted with you, Nick. You aren't fussy, are you? Well, *I* am. These Doralans are good for only one thing—and that's not screwing. Don't tell me that you didn't enjoy your share of . . . of . . . Dimilin, wasn't it? She was quite good eating.''

He got up from her bunk, where he had been sitting beside her.

He said, ''Think about it. I've already decided—and you have to go along with me. I'm the spaceman, the navigator. Without me you can do nothing. You'll come to realize that we shall be doing the right thing.''

"Where are you going, Nick? To Carlin, I suppose.''

"No.''

"Or is it her high and mightiness now? Is she trading in her pet cat for a pet . . . poodle?''

"*No*. Unlike some people I've had a heavy day. I want to get some sleep. By myself.''

He let himself out into the deserted alleyway, walked the short distance to the open door of his own cabin. As soon as he entered the room he was aware of a familiar scent. *Carlin!* he thought at first—then realized that it was not. The aroma was essentially male. It was coming from his bed. Sitting on the couch, his green eyes luminous in the semidarkness, was Pondor.

"Do you mind if I come in?'' asked the man sardonically.

"You may enter,'' replied the animal.

"And you may get the hell out of here.''

"With pleasure, but not yet. Shut the door. There are keen ears aboard this ship.''

Falsen shut the door.

"I do not like you, Mr. Falsen,'' said the cat, ''but there are those aboard this ship I like still less. And we do have something in common.''

"Something in common?'' echoed Falsen.

"We are males, both of us, in female territory. More, we are Terran males. . . ."

"I thought that you regarded yourself as Doralan."

"By birth, but not by ancestry. I am loyal both to my sex and to my planet of origin. I am loyal, too, to the Lady Mother, as I think that you now are. There are loyalties—and loyalties. . . ."

Falsen stared at the animal, wondering just how much intelligence was housed inside that tiny skull. Many a human of his acquaintance could not have expressed himself so well.

He said, "Yes. I am loyal to your mistress."

"I believe you. I am sure that you will help her to get the ship back home. You are loyal, and I am loyal—but there are things I know that I have not told her. I am loyal to my sex. I know that should she discover that there are males aboard this vessel, in addition to yourself and myself, she would take severe disciplinary action—and not only against the officers responsible for their presence. That I do not wish to see." He continued with quite surprising but quite natural coarseness, "As long as Carlin and certain others are getting well-fucked when they want it, it will keep them quiet." Cats, even mutated, highly intelligent and multilingual cats, could not laugh, but Pondor managed a derisive mewing sound. "I have reason to believe that you have been a pacifying influence."

"That's none of your business!"

"But it is, Mr. Falsen. I want a quiet life. I don't want to stir up more trouble than there has been already. You do not want any more trouble either. You just want to do your work. But be careful, at all times. Do not trust the Lady Carlin. Do not, especially, trust the Lady Prenta. She is jealous of you."

"And Pansir?"

"She likes you. And many people who, at first, were suspicious and contemptuous of you—an alien male!—now respect you. As do even I."

"Thank you," said Falsen without sarcasm.

"So, do your best, and guard your back at all times. Now I will go."

Falsen opened the cabin door. The animal jumped down from the bunk and, tail held high, stalked out into the alleyway.

CHAPTER 35

The next day was, by the standards of this world, fine.

It had stopped raining and there was no wind. The ruddy sun, glaring through the high overcast, was a clearly defined disk rather than a fuzzily amorphous ball of dull incandescence. Outside the ship the air was unpleasantly hot and steamy, heavy with the cloying reek of rotting vegetation. Moist vapor eddied up from the stagnant pools, from the wet ground itself.

It was not a day for hard physical work, but the work had to go on. There was the inertial-drive unit to be dismantled and its components to be carried back inside the vessel for reassembly. There was that minor mountain of assorted stores to be shifted back into the holds from which they had been off-loaded. There was the integrity of the ship's structure to restore.

Falsen was one of the lucky ones. He, together with the Lady Mother, Pansir and two airshipwomen, was up in the blimp, away from the worst of the heat, well clear of the organized confusion, the shrill orders, the continual clattering buzz of the mini-innies as they fetched and carried, obedient to the control boxes of Carlin and her engineers.

Linda was not with him. She was sulking somewhere inside the spaceship. He had seen her at breakfast and, after the unsatisfying meal, had asked her if she had given further thought to the Doralan captain's proposal. She had told him that she still had to make up her mind. And then a junior officer had come knocking at her cabin door, telling Falsen that the Lady Mother wished to see him.

So, now here he was, seated in relative comfort in the rather cramped control cabin of the blimp, enjoying the motion-engendered breeze that blew in through the open windows. He looked down at the ship, at the tiny scarlet-uniformed figures scurrying around her like a swarm of ants. No doubt Carlin and Prenta would be fighting like cat and dog—or like two cats each obsessively jealous of the other. When he boarded the blimp a quarrel had been developing over the use of the mini-innies.

"We have been taking risks," said the Lady Mother. "All the stores and equipment left outside overnight. We are fortunate that the . . . beasts left us alone. Is your bio-sensitive radar functioning, Lady Pansir?"

"Yes, Gracious Lady. It was not too badly damaged when the big airship crashed, and was easily repaired."

"Good. Then, we shall fly over the lake and see what we can see."

Pansir took the controls from the crewwoman she was training as coxswain, brought the airship around until it was heading for the distant hills. After the alteration of course she called the novice back to the wheel, issued brief orders in her own language.

She smiled at Falsen and said, "I was telling her to keep her steady as she goes."

Falsen looked into the screen of the bio-sensitive radar. It was alive with little flecks of light, especially as the blimp passed over the pools. He remembered the arthropod that Linda had caught on his first morning on this planet. So much had happened since that day. And how much more would happen before the Doralan spaceship, her survey mission completed, lifted off on her homeward voyage? Very little, he hoped. In spite of Linda's objectives, he had made up his mind to revert to true humanity, even though it would mean living out his life in an alien culture. The alternative no longer appealed to him.

The blimp flew steadily on.

They were fast approaching the hills that rimmed the lake. There was turbulence over the ridge, and Pansir was obliged to take the controls again. But it was nothing serious, little more than a strong updraft. Maintaining course and altitude was child's play for Pansir, who had demonstrated her ability in the big airship to cope with far more severe conditions. If it had not been for the great leech's revival the dirigible might never have been lost.

They were over the lake now, engines stopped, drifting. The mirrorlike surface of the water was unruffled, perfectly smooth. Yet the body of water was swarming with life. Shoals of gleaming specks swam in the screen of the bio-sensitive radar with, now and again, luminous blobs that indicated the presence of something much larger. Falsen left the screen, joined the Lady Mother at one of the side windows, looked directly down. With this line of sight he could see a few meters below the surface, although not with any great clarity; the water was too muddy.

Something big swam into his field of view. It was one of the giant leeches, moving slowly and sinuously. It vanished in the murky depths. Then there was a shoal of tiny beings that might have been either fishes or arthropods. Pursuing them came another of the leeches.

"But where are the things that come out onto dry land?" asked the Lady Mother.

"They must be nocturnal animals," said Falsen.

"When I put in my report," she said. "I shall say that this world is not suitable for our use and urge that we endeavor to discover planets approximating more closely to our own—or more exploitable. After all, Mr. Falsen, your Survey Service made the first landing here, took one look and said, 'Not for us!' And then somebody high in your government said, 'Let the Doralans have it.' "

"But you've paid for it now," said Falsen.

"We have, and that is the tragedy of it. Lives, valuable lives, have been lost. But did not one of your poets write, 'If blood be the price of admiralty, Lord God, we have paid in full . . .'?"

"Something like that, Gracious Lady," said Falsen.

"But somebody—or something—must pay their share," she went on.

He said, "I still find it hard to understand your desire to take revenge on mindless predators."

"Mindless, Mr. Falsen? Individually mindless, perhaps—but there is the planetary mind. Perhaps the concept is unfamiliar to you, perhaps not. A dim yet powerful intelligence resenting outsiders—resenting, even, such beings who have evolved in its own territory and who have attained real intelli-

gence of their own and are using this tool to engineer changes
in the environment. Your own history has examples enough
of such resentment—earthquakes and freak storms, plagues
. . . attacks both biological and physical upon those whom the
world mind considers undesirable.

"The pattern, here, can be discerned. There have been the
raids made by the beasts upon my people. There was the
freak storm that destroyed the airship."

"I could have brought the ship through the storm, Gracious
Lady," said Pansir stiffly from behind them. "If it had not
been for that leech running loose. . . ."

"Still inside the pattern, Lady Pansir," said the captain.

Falsen turned his head to look at her. He had realized
suddenly that she was a religious fanatic and therefore
dangerous. If she knew of his and Linda's true nature, she
would have them destroyed without compunction—*if* she
knew how to do it. Almost certainly she did not; that was
some consolation. But it was a great pity that she was this way.
He had not only respected her but felt a growing affection for
her. He would have to comport himself very carefully if he
were ever to take up that promised appointment at the Doralan
Space Academy.

"Yes," the Lady Mother went on, "before we leave, the
act of revenge—retribution—must be taken. This world mind
must be taught that we Doralans are not to be trifled with."

"We have a saying on Earth," said Falsen, "that seems
opposite. It points out the futility of farting against thunder."

The Lady Mother was not shocked. She smiled at him
tolerantly, condescendingly.

"Futile or not, there are some gestures that must be made.
Even if my ecologist were still living, the gesture would be
made." She turned away from the window. "Very well,
Lady Pansir. You may take us back to the spaceship."

CHAPTER 36

When they flew over the spaceship they could see that much had been accomplished during their absence. The mountain of off-loaded stores had been diminished and the inertial-drive unit reduced to a scatter of component parts, already being carried, piece by piece, through the reopened hole in the shell plating, back to their proper place inside the hull. The buzzing clatter of the mini-innies, handling both the pieces of the drive and packages of stores, was clearly audible in the blimp's cabin, as were the orders being shouted in high, clear voices by Carlin, Prenta and other officers.

At the controls again, Pansir drove the little dirigible down, slowly circled the spaceship at control-room level. Most of the big viewports were clear; only one was obscured by mud, the black ooze that had now dried to a crinkled crust. The Lady Mother stared, almost wistfully, into what was the throne room of her little realm. Falsen could almost read her thoughts. Soon now, she had to be thinking, she would be sitting there in state, fusion power at her fingertips, directing the ascent from this dismal world, the escape to the clean emptiness of interstellar space.

For her, thought Falsen, the voyage back to Dorala would not be her last one. Her powerful friends and relatives would see to it that she was not grounded. But for him it would be his last trip.

He could see quite well into the control room.

Already, much of the instrumentation had been restored to working order; telltale lights glowed—red, green, white and amber—on panels. A scarlet-uniformed junior officer was working on something, making adjustments.

The captain said, "Soon I shall have my ship back. There is the inertial drive to be reassembled but that should not take long. The integrity of the hull must be restored. And, of course, the Mannschenn Drive controls must be recalibrated. Do you know anything of the correct procedures, Mr. Falsen?"

"Only what I have read in textbooks, Gracious Lady."

"A pity. I was hoping to be able to avail myself of your expertise again."

Not in anything involving the Mannschenn Drive you won't! thought Falsen. He knew what recalibration entailed, working at the control panel in the Mannschenn Drive room in close proximity to the uncannily precessing rotors, exposed to the full intensity of the temporal-precession field, an intensity far greater than that experienced while the Drive was working normally in deep space. Should he be involved too closely in the operation, there would be the very real danger that he would not be able to control himself. And that would mean good-bye to his dream of starting a fresh life on Dorala.

"If all goes well," went on the Lady Mother, "we should be ready for the recalibration late tomorrow afternoon."

Meanwhile, Pansir had taken the blimp still lower, holding it so that they could peer into the hole cut in the shell plating, the aperture through which the mini-innies were carrying the components of the inertial drive. Buzzing angrily, one of the little machines, a gleaming spindle grasped in its claws, flew past the control cab with only millimetres of clearance.

An angry voice, Carlin's, burst from the speaker of the transceiver. The only word that Falsen could distinguish was a name, Pansir's. The pilot looked enquiringly at the captain, who issued a brief order in her own language. The airship rose steeply.

The Lady Mother smiled and said to Falsen, "We were getting in the way, it seems. The Lady Carlin said, 'Get that bloody gasbag out of here!' "

"Shall we land now, Gracious Lady?" asked Pansir.

"Yes." She smiled tiredly. "If the Lady Prenta can let us have a ground crew, that is."

There were further exchanges on the radio telephone, after which six crewwomen detached themselves from the gang working around the stores, walked to the stubby mooring mast.

Not long thereafter Falsen was assisting the Lady Mother down the short ladder that had been set up from the ground to the door of the blimp's control cab.

Together they walked back to the ship.

CHAPTER 37

"They are recalibrating the Mannschenn Drive tomorrow afternoon," said Falsen.

"So what?" said Linda.

"So, we'd better keep out of sight. Either shut ourselves up in our cabins or get well clear of the ship."

"Why?"

"During recalibration, the field builds up, for short periods, to abnormally great intensity. During such . . . flashes, we may not be able to control ourselves."

"I'm tired of controlling myself," she muttered sullenly. "If you hadn't let yourself be conned into taking this schoolmastering job, there'd be no need for us to control ourselves."

"In any case," he told her, "we should have to control ourselves until the ship is spaceworthy."

"I'm sick of this charade!" she flared. "And I warn you now, I'll be sicker still when I try to settle down with you as an instructor's wife in that bloody Academy!"

"You'd be sicker still if we had to live like wild animals on some savage world. Oh, you might like to revert every now and again, just as any human enjoys a holiday away from the big cities, in the woods or on the seashore. But all your life? You wouldn't like it. Even people like us need the attention of a dentist now and again, are subject to failing eyesight and deteriorating digestive functions, and all the rest of it. There's one killer who's bound to get us in the end: old age."

"Old age will get us no matter where we are—either on Dorala or on a planet of our own choice."

"On a planet of our own choice—and we might be years finding it!—it'd be much faster than on a world with a well-developed medical science."

"Would you live forever?" she sneered.

"Given the chance, I'd like to try," he said.

CHAPTER 38

They had gotten away from the ship, were standing, watching by a wide, stagnant pool three kilometers from the vessel. The sun was sliding slowly down the western sky.

The Lady Mother was disappointed when Falsen did not volunteer to help with the recalibration.

"But I am not an engineer, Gracious Lady," he had said.

"And certain of my engineers," she had told him, "have given, as *their* excuse, that they are not navigators. I had hoped that you, who have already displayed your versatility, would assist . . ."

"I should only be in the way. With your permission, Gracious Lady, I should like to take a stroll outside the ship. After all, we shall not be staying on this world much longer. And by day it should be safe enough."

"All right, Mr. Falsen. But take a side arm with you."

So, he was standing here with Linda, looking at the ship. He could visualize what was happening inside her, in the Mannschenn Drive room. There would be the complexity of gleaming gyroscopes, planes of rotation set at eye-baffling angles each to each. There would be the monitor screens exhibiting not the normal wave forms but luminous straight traces. There would be the Lady Mother with the Mannschenn Drive Manual opened to the right page. Somebody would be at the main switchboard, other officers would be watching the monitors.

Better them than me, thought Falsen.

Beside him, Linda cried out sharply.

The ship was wavering, dimming. It was as though some internal illumination had been switched off. The air seemed to crackle with strain as the very fabric of the continuum was warped; beneath their feet the ground undulated and the surface of the pool was whipped into a brief frenzy, although there was no wind.

And then the ship was as she had been, standing proudly luminous.

"Is that all?" asked the girl.

"No," said Falsen. "That was only the first step, just finding out if the Drive works. The next steps will be to find out if it can be controlled."

"And what if it can't be?"

"From our point of view, there'll be an implosion—the air rushing in to occupy the space where the ship was."

"And from the viewpoint of those aboard her?"

"I don't know. There have been accidents during calibration—but nobody has ever come back from wherever and whenever it was they were flung. One theory is that the ship digs her own black hole and then falls into it."

"But a black hole? Surely that would destroy the planet. . . ."

"By the time temporal precession has built up to such a level, the planet will have left the ship far, very far, behind. In any case, there are safety devices, cutouts . . ."

"Which might not work."

Again there was the feeling of unbearable tension, but this time the ship did not fade but shone brighter and brighter, a dazzling column of incandescence, orange, white, dazzlingly blue. And there came the compelling sensation of *déjà vu*. It was experienced by all spacemen at the beginning of every voyage, when the Mannschenn Drive was started, when the temporal-precession field built up, when the tumbling gyroscopes began their long fall down the dark dimensions through the warped continuum, dragging the ship and all aboard her with them. Sometimes there was prevision of an actual future (at the start of the journey in *Epsilon Crucis* Falsen had *seen* the dismal landscape of this planet but, after trajectory had been set and things in the control room were back to normal, had shrugged it off as some odd vision with no foundation in reality); sometimes a probable or only a remotely possible future was glimpsed; sometimes, and frequently, whatever was seen was an hallucinatory experience.

And now . . .

It was bitterly cold and, high in the sky, a huge full moon was pouring silvery radiance down onto the wide, almost featureless white plain. Ahead of Falsen as he ran, with Linda beside him, was a sort of open carriage on runners, drawn by three horses. The hooves of the galloping animals broke the surface of the snow, making the going difficult for the pursuers. Falsen stumbled, uttered a wordless curse. Recovering, he pulled out to the left, clear of the runner tracks, the hoof marks. Linda pulled out to the right.

He ran, his feet silent on frozen surface.

From ahead he could hear the cracking of a whip, the pounding of hooves, a terrified whinny. The horses had to be at the very limit of their endurance; surely they could not maintain this speed for much longer. Falsen was gaining on the sleigh, as was Linda. He could smell fear, equine and human. . . .

Human?

But it was an oddly familiar smell nonetheless.

Closer was the sleigh, and closer, and the cracking of the driver's whip was a continuous fusillade. Inside the vehicle, at the back of it, somebody was standing up. Falsen expected to see the gleam of a leveled weapon, to hear the sharp report of its being fired, but was surprised when something—someone? —fell or was pushed from the rear of the sleigh. It—he? she?—sprawled blackly on the white snow, arms extended. The scent was warm, sweet.

Linda got to it first, was tearing at it hungrily. Falsen roughly pushed her to one side. He was the male; she would have to be content with his leavings. He shook it angrily, lifting it up from the ground with ease. It was a long coat tailored from some dark fur. It was empty save for the odor of whoever it was that had worn it.

Falsen dropped the garment, resumed the chase. Linda had already done so. Slowly he overhauled her, drew level with her. Louder and louder he could hear the cracking of the whip, the thudding of the hooves. He laughed as more garments were jettisoned; their emptiness was so obvious as they fluttered down to the snow. He was gaining on the sleigh— slowly, slowly, but still decreasing the distance between pursuers and pursued.

Suddenly the vehicle lurched, swinging broadside onto Linda and Falsen. A horse was down, neighing shrilly, its flailing legs sending up a flurry of snow crystals that glittered in the blazing moonlight like tiny diamonds. Another horse was down, felled by a wild kick. The remaining beast plunged frantically and ineffectually in its restraining harness. It was screaming.

Somebody jumped down from the sleigh to the ground, was walking, slowly yet unafraid, towards Falsen. It was a woman. She was quite naked, small-breasted and heavy-haunched. A smile curved her wide, sensual mouth.

Falsen snarled.

She he must have.

He advanced to meet her. His nose told him that she was in heat.

He . . .

Abruptly the scene faded as though it had been switched off.

Falsen realized that he was on his hands and knees on the muddy bank of the pond, looking across the smooth dark surface of the water at something big and pale, some animal, on the further side. He got hastily to his feet, knew that they were bare when he felt the slime oozing up between his toes. A very slight stirring of the air was suddenly cool on his skin. Not only his feet were naked.

He stared across the pool at . . . Carlin.

She, too, was unclothed, was just coming slowly erect from a crouching posture. Her scent, carried to him by the merest ghost of a breeze, was that of the woman in his precession-induced dream.

"Carlin!" Linda called sharply.

Falsen turned to look at her. She was as naked as he was.

"Carlin!" Linda cried again. "What are you doing here? Spying on us?"

"Spying, Miss Veerhausen? I thought that you were about to take a swim and would not mind if I joined you. . . ."

"Come on in," shouted Falsen. "The water's fine!"

It was not.

It was dirty, and it stank, but he struck out for mid-pool, making a great show of enjoyment. Carlin met him there while Linda splashed unenthusiastically in the shallows.

Treading water, he asked, "I thought that you'd have been helping to recalibrate the Drive controls."

She said, "The Lady Mother thinks that she knows everything. I left her to it. But I suppose that I'd better get back on board now."

She swam sinuously to her side of the pool, clambered out and walked away. She must, thought Falsen, have shed her clothing some distance from the water.

CHAPTER 39

Falsen stared at the ship. She looked normal enough now. All the tension had gone from the air; there was no longer the sensation of being poised, tottering on the brink of some abyss, some rift in the very fabric of space-time.

Linda asked, "Have they finished the recalibration?"

"I think so," he said.

She began to pick up her discarded clothing. "We . . . we must have changed," she muttered. "It is a good thing that Carlin didn't come upon us when we were . . ."

"If she had," said Falsen, "it would have been too bad for her."

"Did you . . . dream? I did. But it wasn't a prevision. It was more like a reenactment of something in the past. The distant past. There was moonlight, a full moon. But the moon was wrong. No. Not wrong—but the way that it must have been. A long time ago. . . ."

"Without the scars of the open cast-mine workings around Tycho," he said. "Without the reflection of the sunlight from the colony domes."

"How did you know?"

"You were in my dream. We must have shared it."

"Do you have any Russian ancestors?" she demanded.

"Yes. Do you?"

"Yes." She smiled suddenly. "It's a small universe, isn't it?" Then, "But Carlin can't possibly have any Russian ancestors. And she was in *my* dream? Was she in yours?"

"Yes," he admitted.

"And what was she doing running around naked, both in the dream and in real life?"

"I don't know."

"You don't know. You wouldn't. Oh, no. Not you. Could it just possibly be that she was living through some occasion in the past when you screwed her—or some occasion in the future when you'll be screwing her again? Why else should *she* strip off?"

"It's the usual thing to do before you have a swim," he said.

"It's the usual thing to undress on the bank, not at least half a kilometer from the water."

"She must have found a dry place to leave her clothes."

"Just for a change, it's not raining—or hadn't you noticed?"

"Carlin is an alien," he told her patiently. "You just don't know how her mind works."

"But you know how her body works."

He said sullenly, "Isn't this rather a pointless discussion?"

"You might think so."

She turned away from him, began to dress. She must have disrobed hastily; her uniform shirt, already several times repaired, was again no more than tatters topped by a pair of gold-braided shoulderboards. His own shirt, as he discovered when he put it on, was no better.

They began to walk slowly back to the ship, keeping behind those of the Doralan crew who had not stayed on board during the recalibration. Some of them, he noted incuriously at first, looked almost as ragged as himself and Linda. His imagination was stirred by the sight of naked shoulders and rumps gleaming through the rents in the scarlet fabric. He wondered what their own precession-induced visions had been, visualized some sort of Lesbian orgy. Or not, perhaps, Lesbian . . . The presence of those male stowaways was proof enough of the heterosexuality of some, if not of all the Doralans. A matriarchal society must breed female chauvinist pigs.

But what of the Doralan males? he wondered. They had been obliged to remain on board, in hiding, during the recalibration of the interstellar-drive controls. Would there not have been a danger of their reverting to a period in history when their sex had been dominant and running amok? But there must have been that danger every time that the

Mannschenn Drive had been started up—and it was a danger that could be coped with, quite easily, by a heavy dose of some sedative.

They came at last to the foot of the ramp, mounted it to the after air lock. Prenta was standing there, a clipboard in her hand, obviously keeping a tally of the returning personnel. She was as sour-faced as ever, made the final ticks as Linda and Falsen boarded.

She snarled, "With the Jonahs off the ship, the recalibration went smoothly."

"We are not Jonahs," said Falsen.

"Then, if you aren't, what are you?" she retorted.

"A good question," said Linda sweetly before Falsen's elbow in her ribs could stop her.

But Prenta merely sneered at the riposte.

CHAPTER 40

Falsen found it hard to sleep that night. Although his belly was full, the food that had been served at the evening meal, nutritious enough, failed to satisfy. There could be no meat until the tissue culture vats, themselves damaged and their contents ruined at the time of the disastrous landing, were restocked. And restocked they could not be unless some suitable indigenous meat animal were found. There was a perfectly good way of growing a fresh supply of edible flesh, of course, one that would entail only a minor sacrifice by one or two of the Doralans, or from Falsen or Linda, but it was not likely that the Lady Mother would tolerate cannibalism, even though there would be no real victims, no taking of life.

He could not sleep and at last gently disentangled himself from Linda, who was twitching and whimpering as she dreamed. He pulled on his shorts, let himself out into the alleyway. He hesitated at the door of his own cabin, then went on to the nearest entry into the axial shaft. He pushed the button for the elevator. He waited only seconds before it came. Once inside the cage, he hesitated again. Should he call on Carlin? Would she welcome him? More importantly, did he feel like another torrid session with her? He did not, he decided. It would be far too soon after his brief but savage coupling with Linda. But he might, he just might, be able to scrounge a drink from her, although Carlin almost certainly would be reluctant to give away anything unless she received something in return. He remembered, then, that Pansir had the control-room watch—and the airshipwoman would almost certainly have cigarettes with her. Perhaps a smoke would have a soporific effect upon him.

He took the elevator up to the captain's deck, then climbed the short ladder up to the hatch that gave access to the control room. As on a past occasion, it was quite light inside this compartment, reflected illumination pouring in through the big ports as the blazing searchlights probed the terrain around the ship. The air smelled of burning tobacco, the sweetly acrid fumes drifting from the scarlet-uniformed figure seated by the display of the bio-sensitive radar.

Falsen walked slowly towards the Doralan, making a slight scuffling noise as he did so. The glowing tip of the cigarette suddenly vanished as it was snuffed out before Pansir swiveled in her seat to see who it was approaching her.

She said sharply, "Oh, it's you, Mr. Falsen. I thought that it was the Lady Mother. She does not approve of smoking. . . ."

"And this is her control room that you're stinking up, Lady Pansir, not the gondola of your airship."

"Is there a . . . stink? I shall have to increase the revolutions of the extractor fans."

"And for a consideration I'll promise not to tell the Lady Mother that you have been smoking in here."

"A consideration? Oh, of course." She laughed, extended the packet to him. "Now I have bought your silence."

She took a fresh cigarette for herself. They both lit up, smoking in companionable silence, he standing just behind her, looking with her into the screen, almost hypnotized by the steady rotation of the sweep, the tiny bursts of scintillation that indicated the presence of life forms on the ground surface, all of them small.

She said, "A quiet watch. The way that all watches should be." She laughed again. "A year ago I never dreamed that I should be standing a watch in the control room of a spaceship—even one not in space but sitting quietly on a planetary surface. I was happy then, flying my mail and passenger route from Dwill to Kandoor and back, threading my way through the passes in the Tevenal Range. Oh, we had some storms among the high mountains and some anxious moments, I admit. It's because I was an experienced captain on that run that I was selected to be this expedition's airship pilot. But I'm an airwoman, Mr. Falsen, not a spacewoman. It's the

only life for me. I suppose you find my attitude strange.
You're a spaceperson and that's your way of life."

"It won't be for much longer, Lady Pansir."

"I am sorry, truly sorry. The Lady Mother has told me of
her proposal to you. I think that you will be wise to accept."

"Perhaps I shall see something of you on Dorala after I
take up my appointment."

"Of course you will. And you will always be an honored
passenger aboard any airship that I command."

"As long as you don't have any giant leeches running
loose through the aircraft," he laughed.

She said nothing, in a way that was more meaningful than
words could have been.

"I'm sorry," he told her at last. "That wasn't very funny."

"It was not," she said. "Was that an example of what you
Terrans call black humor?"

"I suppose so."

He stubbed out his cigarette in the empty container that she
had been using as an ashtray. She followed suit, then offered
him the pack. He was about to accept when his hand froze in
mid-motion. In the screen there had suddenly appeared six
large blobs of luminescence, moving fast, obviously not tiny
ground-crawlers.

"Look!" he almost shouted.

Whatever they were, they were heading toward the ship.
But there was nothing to worry about. She was tightly sealed
and, pursuant to the Lady Mother's orders, the air-lock doors
were not only shut but spot-welded on the inside. There was
to be no repetition of that massacre when the predators had
got inside the hull.

"Wait here, Mr. Falsen," said Pansir, "while I call the
captain. I do not think that there is any need to sound the
general alarm."

She got up from her chair, went to a telephone. Falsen
continued his watch on the screen. The things had slowed
down, had stopped. They seemed to be milling around. Perhaps they had caught something, were tearing it to pieces,
devouring it. But any large animal would have shown up in
the display.

Pansir, who had been talking rapidly and urgently, came
back, joined Falsen at the radar.

"No!" she cried. *"No!"*

"What's wrong? They can't do any harm out there."

"But they can! They can! Cannot you see where they are?"

She dragged the man to one of the viewports, pointed.

"Look!" she screamed.

There was the blimp, riding at its stubby mooring mast. There were the pale figures, kangaroolike, leaping up and trying to reach the fat, silvery sausage with their foreclaws. It made no sense at all. Why should flesh-eating beasts be so intent upon destroying a lifeless construction of metal and plastic? But whether it made sense or not, they seemed determined to vent their animal fury upon the airship.

The Lady Mother joined them at the window. She was carrying a pair of binoculars, raised the glasses to her eyes.

"This must be stopped!" she said. "Lady Pansir, sound the general alarm, then tell the Lady Carlin to unseal the after air-lock door at once! Tell the Lady Prenta to go out with an armed party to kill the things!"

"With your permission, Gracious Lady, I would go out. It is *my* ship that they are attacking."

"As you will. But sound the alarm. *Now*!"

Bells sounded throughout the ship, shrilling and clanging. There was a high clamor of frightened voices. Officers tumbled up into the control room like disturbed, angry ants pouring out of their nest. The Lady Mother was issuing short, sharp orders.

Somehow, almost without volition, Falsen was caught up in the flurry of events. He was riding down to the stern in the elevator, crammed into the cage with Pansir and five crewwomen whom he did not know. With them he piled out into the air-lock vestibule, where the acridity of burned metal mingled with other, organic scents—of fear, of anger, of excitement. Carlin was there, the welding torch with which she had unsealed the door still in hand. Prenta was there, handing out belts, each with a holstered hand laser attached. Surprisingly, Linda was there, an expression of wolfish anticipation on her face.

Prenta operated the manual controls of the outer door. It opened, and damp air gusted in, its swampy reek mingling with all the other scents. Pansir ran out first, her hand laser already out of its holster. Falsen and Linda followed close behind. He was conscious of others crowding after him. They clattered down the ramp into the artificially bright night. The searchlights were no longer sweeping, and such of them as could be brought to bear were concentrated upon the blimp, their harsh glare reflected from the silvery lattice of the mooring mast, from the condensation-slick envelope. It was reflected too, although less dazzlingly, from those pale, leaping bodies, the savage animals that were either unaware or contemptuous of the commotion they had initiated.

Pansir ran, easily outdistancing all the others save for the two Terrans. She still had breath to scream. Falsen wondered what she was yelling but was sure that it was bloodthirsty imprecations. She was firing already, wasting the charge of her weapon at this extreme range. A low shrub, caught by the slashing beam, burst into smoky incandescence.

They were ugly beasts, these things that were attacking the airship, tailless but with heavy, oddly jointed hindlegs almost like those of a Terran kangaroo. Their forelegs were short, but only relatively so, terminating in handlike claws, their heads round, vaguely feline but with long, protruding fangs.

"*Them* . . ." panted Linda. "It's them . . ."

Surely they must be within range now. Falsen pulled his pistol and fired. He must have missed, although he did not think that his aim was all that bad. Others were firing. He winced as a poorly directed beam scorched his back. People were screaming, *things* were screaming. Here and there the vegetation underfoot was smoldering, the thick, evil-smelling smoke adding to the confusion.

Pansir flung herself at one of the animals just as it launched itself in a fresh leap aimed at the vulnerable underbelly of the blimp. Freakishly, she caught not a leg but the brute's sex organ, her hand gripping its penis and testicles. It squawled like an enraged tomcat, fell heavily and clumsily to the ground with the airship pilot sprawled under it, still hanging on desperately. It brought its viciously clawed hind feet up to slash and to disembowel, but Falsen flung himself on it, got his own hands about the thick neck. He almost . . . reverted; that way he would have been better able to fight, to use his teeth as well as his other merely human equipment. But even in the confusion somebody would be sure to see.

He wrestled with the animal, trying to choke it. Pansir at last had relaxed her grip, and together, man and beast, they rolled off her, away from her. Falsen was conscious of the outcry all about him, the screams and the bestial snarls. He caught confused glimpses of laser beams blaring as they explosively ignited smoke particles, of leaping and pouncing carnivores, of female bodies half-naked and completely so. The scent of newly shed blood was thick in the air. It was like some medieval painter's vision of hell.

Suddenly there was darkness.

Something must have happened aboard the spaceship, perhaps nothing worse than a temporary power failure. Falsen hoped that this was all that it was. When the lights went out he was taken unawares, relaxed his grip. His enemy broke away from him, threw him off. He staggered to his feet, looked wildly about. He could see little; nobody yet had thought of switching a laser pistol to wide beam.

From the ship came a vastly amplified voice, the Lady Mother's.

"Divenoo . . . Divenoo . . ." Then, concerned even now for the welfare of those whom she regarded as her guests, "Return . . . Return . . ."

Falsen could see the space vessel now, but dimly. A circle of faint illumination must be the open air-lock door; another glow, high up, must be the control room. There was power of some kind for emergency lighting and for the loud hailer.

"Divenoo . . . Divenoo . . ."

Which was all very well, as long as the predators allowed them to break off the engagement.

But they, too, had stopped fighting, must have run back to wherever it was that they had come from. Laser pistols were now being used as torches, and the beams showed nothing but Doralans—the living, and two or three dead. Falsen feared that Pansir was among these latter but, when the light fell upon her, she put up a hand to shield her eyes. She tried to get to her feet. Falsen helped her.

But she refused to leave the scene of the fight until she was sure that her precious little dirigible was undamaged.

CHAPTER 41

Power had been restored and all services were now operating normally. A heavily armed party had gone out from the ship to the scene of the fight, had brought the bodies of those killed back to the vessel. The air-lock door had been shut, but the welding had not been renewed; soon it would be necessary to open it again.

All officers, with the exception of the few with important duties, had been summoned to one of the general rooms. On a low platform to one side of it stood the Lady Mother. Behind her was a screen, a square of black emptiness, and to one side of this an almost featureless control box. A junior officer, holding a bundle of slides, was standing by.

The Doralan captain could have been a university professor about to give a lecture, the long pointer that she was holding adding to the illusion. But, thought Falsen, no academic about to address her students would have looked so weighted down by tragedy, would have been so burdened by the responsibilities of command. She gravely surveyed her audience, then rapped sharply on the platform with the butt of her pointer. The twittering whispers of the officers suddenly ceased.

"Ladies," she began. "Ladies, and Mr. Falsen. I shall address you in English, which language most of you know. I shall pause frequently so that translations may be made for the benefit of those few of you who have no English. . . ."

"Why talk to us in a foreign tongue, Gracious Lady?" demanded Prenta.

"Lady Prenta, I hardly need to tell you that the Lady Linda

and Mr. Falsen are, to all practical intents and purposes, members of our crew. They have shared our perils.''

She paused to allow the voluntary translators to do their work.

''I am not going to ask you to decide what must now be done,'' she went on. ''I have made my decision. But I want you all to know what is to be done, and why. I have heard the reports of most of you; the written reports I have yet to receive.'' She looked sternly at Carlin. ''I especially require yours, Lady Carlin. The failure of the ship's power supply might well have have resulted in an even greater disaster than it did.''

Carlin stared back at the Lady Mother. Defiantly? Insolently? Looking at her, Falsen could not be sure.

The captain looked at a list that she was holding in her left hand.

''The dead,'' she announced gravely. ''Junior Powermistress Delai. Senior Spacewoman Adar. Tank Attendant Goren. And one unidentified person. No doubt the Lady Prenta, after making a more careful check of the crew list, will be able to tell me who she is.''

''Everybody has been accounted for, Gracious Lady,'' said Prenta sourly.

''Nonetheless, Lady Prenta, a mistake or an omission must have been made. But its rectification can wait until matters have been brought to a satisfactory conclusion.

''And now I shall show to you the photographs taken from the control room, using a telephoto lens, during the action. You will all agree, I think, that they are evidence of a most remarkable case of parallel evolution. The similarities, of course, may be no more than superficial. Mr. Falsen will tell you that in the seas of his planet there are creatures that even from a short distance look remarkably alike, the sharks and the dolphins. The shark is a very primitive, almost brainless fish, the dolphin a highly evolved mammal, now recognized by Man as a fellow intelligent being. . . .''

She should have been a schoolmistress, thought Falsen admiringly.

The junior officer inserted a slide into a slot at the side of the control box. The screen was no longer black, had the appearance of a brightly lit tank in which was standing a ferocious beast in an attitude suggesting that it was about to leap. Its mother, thought Falsen, must have been a kangaroo that couldn't run as fast as a saber-toothed tiger—or, perhaps, it had been the other way around. It was a short-haired animal with a dappled hide.

He had seen the things, of course, had grappled with them, but all the time they had been in violent motion. Now, looking at this frozen presentation, he could appreciate what he had been up against.

A second slide was inserted, this one showing an animal in mid-jump. It was indubitably male.

"These," said the Lady Mother, "could almost be pictures of the *simbor*." She looked at Falsen and Linda. "The *simbor* is one of our greater carnivores. It is almost extinct, save for a few specimens in zoos and reserves. But these . . . things, of course, cannot possibly be *simbors*, tens of light-years from their native habitat. There can be no *simbors* here. . . ."

Or if there are, thought Falsen, reviving in his mind a tired old joke, *you brought 'em here yourself.*

A note of fanaticism was becoming evident in her voice.

"Some of you," she said, "believe as I do, that every world is a living being with its own soul, a spirit that is a dimly intelligent yet enormously powerful deity. The god of this planet, the god that *is* this planet, hates us. It has thrown against us the storm that wrecked the big airship and has attacked us with its armies of vicious beasts. Perhaps their resemblance to the *simbor* is not coincidental. Perhaps it had foreknowledge of our coming, and bred especially, over many years, simulacra of the animals most feared and detested in our history and mythology. . . ."

She paused for breath and to allow the translators to do their work.

"Ladies, and Mr. Falsen, this is my intention. I shall hit back, and hard, before I shake the dust of this world forever off my feet." She was not entirely humorless, even now. "Perhaps I should have said 'wipe the mud of this world forever off my feet.' As some of you know, we carry aboard this ship two—if I may employ the Terran euphemism—nuclear devices. Bombs." She looked at Falsen. "They were manufactured on Earth, as a matter of fact. I am going to use them. If I had more than two I would use them all. No more than a gesture, perhaps, but one that must be made if we are to lift off from this planet with our honor intact.

"We know little about these *simbor*like beasts—but this we do know. They are nocturnal in their habits. They seem, unlike our own *simbors*, to be of an aquatic nature. They have been traced to the cave and to the lake connected with it by tunnels.

"Shortly after dawn, when the predators will be sleeping, we shall attack. Two helicopters, sharing the load, will carry one of the bombs. This they will drop in the lake. The airship will carry the other one, together with a party who will take it down through the tunnels into the big cavern. Each bomb will be fitted with a time fuse and these fumes will be synchronized, set so that the explosion will take place when the aircraft are well clear."

She spoke briefly to the young officer in charge of the projection apparatus. Another slide was inserted into the box.

"Some of you," said the Lady Mother, "may think that I am being vicious. But I ask you to look at these pictures."

In the tanklike screen a body appeared, that of a woman with her throat torn out, her belly ripped open.

"Your shipmate," said the Lady Mother softly. "Junior Powermistress Delai." The presentation faded, was replaced by one almost identical. "Senior Spacewoman Adar." Then there was the third one. "And Tank Attendant Goren." Goren, in addition to her other injuries, was lacking her right hand. It seemed to have been bitten off. "And now," went on the captain, "we have the unfortunate whom the Lady Prenta has not yet been able to identify. . . ."

Apart from the torn-out throat, the unidentified Doralan's wounds were different from those of her fellow victims. Where the face should have been was just raw flesh, and the skin, together with the nipples, had been ripped off the chest. Between the legs was a gaping, bloody cavity. It looked more like the work of a homicidal sex maniac than that of a wild animal, however vicious. A gasp of horror went up from most of the assembled officers.

"Look!" declaimed the Lady Mother. "Look! And if you have held doubts until now, you must surely lose them. These people, my women, *our* women, must be avenged!"

Somebody had come into the big room, a long white

laboratory coat over her uniform, a garment with stains and spatterings upon it, some of them blood.

She spoke urgently to the captain, who said, "Please speak in English, Doctor, out of courtesy to Mr. Falsen and the Lady Linda."

"Very well, Gracious Lady." The medical officer cast a baleful glare in the direction of the two Terrans. "I have made the . . . autopsy . . ."

"Surely," said the Lady Mother, "the causes of death were obvious in all four cases."

"They are. But . . ." The doctor pointed dramatically at the three-dimensional picture in the screen. "But that is not the body of a woman. That is the body of a man!"

The captain broke the shocked silence.

She said at last, "Once we have lifted off from the surface of this accursed planet a full enquiry will be made. Somebody— officer, petty officer or enlisted woman—must have been harboring a stowaway, her"—the voice oozed contempt— "*playmate.* But we must not be uncharitable. He was loyal. Clad in a borrowed uniform, he rushed out at the side of his mistress to fight alongside her. He died. He has paid the penalty for his presence. And I promise you that whoever brought him on board will also pay.

"My apologies, Mr. Falsen, for having spoken unkindly of your sex. But Terran men are different from ours. You are more than mere strutting phalluses. And now, ladies, you have heard what I have had to say. I will leave the details of organization to department heads. I wish the punitive expedition to be ready as soon after dawn as possible.

"That is all."

CHAPTER 42

"It must have been one of the stowaways," she said. "One of those tomcats the tabbies brought along to satisfy them. But what was it—he—doing outside the ship?"

"Getting killed," said Falsen.

"Answer my question properly, please."

"All right. I go along with the Lady Mother's theory. But why the mutilations?" He looked at Linda suspiciously. "It wasn't . . . you?"

"It was not. I had my hands full fighting the local beasts. Oh, I admit that after the lights went out I slipped out of my uniform so I could change. I fight better that way. I did rip the throat out of one of the *simbors,* if that's what they are. And then when Her High and Mightiness started screaming for us to return, I wiped my mouth on the rags of somebody's tunic, found my own shirt and shorts and made myself respectable."

"What happened to the *simbor*'s body?" asked Falsen.

"How should I know? One moment the things were there, the next moment they weren't. They must have taken the dead one with them. After all, it's meat. . . . I should have taken more of it while I had the chance."

"A pity," agreed Falsen. "The last chance you'll be getting, probably. When we're on Dorala we shall have to watch our step. If there's anything suspicious about us, somebody is bound to run screaming to the Terran Embassy—and once *they* get into the act there'll be urgent correspondence with Earth, and records will be checked, and everybody will know who and what we are."

"Oh, all right, all right. I'll be a good girl all the voyage to Dorala and all the time that we're there." She stared at the deck of her cabin sulkily, then raised her head to look at Falsen. "Being a good girl has its drawbacks, though. When you're a good girl people expect you to do things for them. Why did *she* insist that we accompany the punitive expedition, as she calls it, to help to plant the bomb in the cave?"

"We've been there before, you know."

"Why not Carlin?"

"The Lady Mother thinks that she'll be better employed making sure that all the machinery works properly on lift-off."

"She has something there. But why are *we* supposed to lug that bomb into the bowels of the earth?"

"Because we're bigger than the Doralans," he explained. "Stronger. The two of us can carry it—one at the front, one at the back. It would take four Doralans—and that tunnel's narrow in places."

"I still don't like it."

"Neither do I," he said. "But as long as we stay on this world, we shall never run short of things not to like."

CHAPTER 43

Falsen and Linda walked out of the ship into the warm drizzle, the gray, dismal morning. They had scorned the offer of waterproof Doralan cloaks; such garments would have been too small for them, would have hampered their movements. When they reached the foot of the ramp they paused, hearing the clatter of mini-innies overhead, looked up and back. Two of the noisy little machines flew out of a cargo port high on the towering hull; between them they carried a dull-gleaming cylinder. Peering out of the aperture was the operator, her hands on the control box as she steered the lifting devices towards the blimp at its mooring mast.

"The bomb," said Linda glumly.

"One of them," said Falsen.

"And we're supposed to carry it through the tunnels into the cave. It takes *two* mini-innies to lift it—or hadn't you noticed?"

"One could handle it easily," said Falsen. "The Lady Mother is just being careful, that's all."

"I wish that your precious Lady Mother would be as careful with us!"

"As far as we are concerned there's no danger."

"How do you know, Nicholas? How do you know? Has it ever been put to the test? There weren't any nuclear weapons when the legends were born."

He would have replied but he heard somebody coming down the gangway. He turned, saw it was Prenta, her scowling face framed by the hood of her cloak. Behind her came three crewwomen.

She said to Falsen, "All right. Let us get the show on the road."

With her followers she began to walk briskly toward the blimp. Falsen and Linda set off after her, pausing briefly when a second pair of mini-innies, burdened as the first had been, came out from the cargo port. These delivered their load to the waiting helicopters.

"Come *on!*" Prenta called back irritably from ahead.

After a trudge through the saturated, ankle-deep moss they came to the mooring mast. Pansir, who had come out to the blimp earlier than the others, was supervising the stowage of the bomb in the small cargo compartment abaft the control cab, snarling at Prenta when she attempted to take charge of this operation. She saw Falsen, flashed him a brief smile, said, "You and the Lady Linda may board, to get out of the rain."

"Thank you," said Falsen.

Linda clambered up the short ladder into the cab. He followed her. Before long Prenta joined them, found a place as far from them as possible. A crewwoman came up and in. Her face was vaguely familiar. One of those who had been in the cave system before, Falsen thought. A member of the stretcher party that Carlin had organized to bring out the bodies.

Pansir was the last to board, pulling up the ladder and closing the door after her. She opened a window so that she could shout down to the ground crew, ordering them to release the blimp from the mast. Before she could speak, an increasingly loud clangor assailed the ears of all those in the cab. It came from the spaceship. It was the big vessel's inertial drive being started up.

The pilot's face showed alarm.

Prenta's voice, as she spoke in English for the benefit of the Terrans, was heavily condescending. "Do not worry, Lady Pansir. The Lady Mother is not about to maroon us on this world, even though that should be the fate of some of us here. We are, as you have been informed, going to explode two nuclear devices, one of them underwater, one underground. There could be severe tremors, possibly even an earthquake, with the risk of the spaceship's being overturned. So, until

things have . . . settled down, the drive will be in operation
and the ship, to all intents and purposes, almost as weightless
as your gasbag.''

"This, Lady Prenta, is more than an assemblage of gasbags."

"As you will," sneered Prenta.

Pansir shouted shrilly through the forward window. Audible above the metallic clangor from the ship was the sharp
clink as a hammer struck the quick-release gear at the head of
the mooring mast. The blimp drifted slowly sternward. Pansir
shut the window, put one hand on the wheel, the other on the
engine-control lever. The motor started, humming loudly.
Wheel and rudder hard over, the airship turned. To port, the
mooring mast slid by. On it, halfway down, a scarlet-
uniformed figure waved.

Ahead the hills were dimly visible, a blackness almost
obscured by drifting veils of faintly ruddy gray. Pansir held a
steady course but used the heaters to increase the lift to
maintain clearance from the gently rising ground. There was
no further conversation in the cab. Falsen sat on the deck very
close to Linda, gratefully conscious of the warmth of her
body. He was feeling an increasing uneasiness. His instincts
were telling him that there was something wrong, very wrong.
It was not the nature of the blimp's cargo that was worrying
him, although many men would have been terrified at being
obliged to ride in close proximity to such awesome destructive
power.

He looked through a side window. To starboard he could
see two of the little helicopters, on a divergent course. Between them they carried in a sling the twin to what was in the
blimp's cargo compartment. No, he thought, not a twin. That
one was the slave, the one in the airship was the master. That
way the explosions would be simultaneous, triggered by a
single timing device. That way the party in the airship, who
would have much more to do, could be sure of being well
clear when the big bangs happened.

Pansir spoke over her shoulder.

She said, "When I come in for a landing, I shall valve gas.
I can afford it, as a considerable weight will be discharged. I
shall want two of you to jump out to handle the mooring lines
and the quick-release grapnels. You must make sure that . . ."

"Lady Pansir," said Prenta, "as part of my training for
this exploratory and survey expedition, I underwent a course

in airship handling. Although I do not pretend to be a flying mail-van driver, I do know something about the techniques.''

''Just jump when I tell you to, Lady Prenta!'' snapped Pansir.

The hills were very close now, and the airship was nosing downward at a shallow angle.

''Come and stand with me, Mr. Falsen,'' ordered the airshipwoman. ''You have been here before, as I have. Together we shall be able to recognize the place where I brought the big ship. . . .''

The blimp circled slowly over the slopes, boulder-strewn and with clumps of low, struggling bushes.

''Can we have the window open again?'' asked Falsen.

''Of course,'' said Pansir.

But there was no scent, as there had been the first time that he had been out here. There were no easily identifiable marks. But . . . his memories were growing stronger and stronger. This, surely, was the place. He pointed.

''Perhaps . . .'' said Pansir doubtfully. ''Perhaps . . . yes, you could be right. . . .'' She turned. ''Lady Prenta, Spacewoman Durl, are you ready?''

''Of course,'' snapped Prenta.

The ground was close now, the wide clearing among the outcroppings of rock almost level. Engines stopped, the blimp settled slowly. There was a very slight jar as the skids kissed the ground. She began to lift as Prenta and Durl jumped out, then steadied as they caught the dangling mooring lines, one on either side of the cab. The quick-release grapnels were driven into the ground.

''All fast!'' called Prenta.

There was a door into the cargo compartment at the after end of the cab. Falsen went through it, stood looking at the almost featureless metal cylinder, checked the carrying slings at either end of it. He took hold of one, lifted. The thing was not overly heavy. He lowered it carefully and then opened a side door. Outside it and a little below him the two Doralans were waiting.

''Let us have it,'' called Prenta.

Slowly, carefully, Falsen got an end of the one-and-a-half-meter-long cylinder out over the door sill. The Doralans took hold of the dangling sling, walked away with it, taking small, gingerly steps. Falsen, at his end, lifted again, eased the bomb out through the opening. His hands on both parts of the sling, yet to be adjusted for carrying in a confined space, he lowered away, millimeter by cautious millimeter. Prenta and the other woman were trying to be as careful, but the weight was too much for them. There was frantic fumbling and their end dropped to the wet ground with an audible thud. Durl let go of her part of the sling and actually started to run. Prenta cursed her shrilly and she stopped in mid-stride, crept timorously back.

Falsen returned to the control cab, where Pansir was speaking into the transceiver, reporting to the spaceship. When she was finished he asked, "Is it all right for the Lady Linda and I to disembark?"

"The Lady Prenta is in charge of operations now," she told him. She looked at him worriedly. "Be careful, please. I do not like this business."

"Expect us when you see us," he told her. "And thanks for the ride."

Scorning the ladder, he jumped down to the ground. Linda followed him. With a shock he realized that both Prenta and Durl had drawn pistols from the holsters at their belts. Then he saw that they were not holding weapons but large electric torches—although the butts of hand guns were visible as their cloaks opened at their waists as they moved. He should have brought a laser himself, he thought. Anything, *anything* might be waiting for them in the cave.

"Durl will lead the way," said Prenta. "She has been here before. You and the Lady Linda will follow, with the bomb. I shall bring up the rear. The bomb will not be armed and its fuse will not be set until it has been placed in position."

"And you will be doing the arming and the fuse-setting?" he asked.

"Of course. Now let us get going."

Durl led the way.

Falsen was next, his hands behind him, firmly holding the now shortened sling. Linda was at the other end of the cylinder. Prenta brought up the rear.

They passed through the cave entrance, into the narrow, descending tunnel. The Doralans' torches gave adequate illumination; even so, it was heavy going for the two Terrans, burdened as they were. Before they had gone many steps,

Falsen's arms were aching. He could hear Linda panting behind him, could smell her acrid sweat.

Down they went, and down, negotiating with difficulty the bends, the narrower passages, wincing as, now and again, the bomb casing clanged against rocky projections. Even though the thing was not armed, all four of them knew its terrible potentialities.

Still they descended. Falsen considered calling a halt before his arms fell off but doubted that he would be able to pick up the cylinder again should he do so. The sooner this job was over the better, he told himself. *Something* was going to happen, and he wanted to get out of the caves and well away before it did.

They emerged from the tunnel into the great cavern with its black mirrorlike subterranean lake. With a gusty sigh of relief Falsen set his end of the burden down on the fine, gray sand. Linda dropped hers as though regardless of the consequences, then emitted a little scream as she realized how careless she had been.

The man turned to face the Doralan officer, blinked irritably until she moved the beam of her torch away from his face.

He said, "This will have to do."

"It will do," said Prenta.

Falsen flexed his cramped fingers, rubbed his aching arms. He walked away from the bomb, sat down heavily. Linda joined him. He watched as Prenta gave her torch to Durl, who turned both lights full onto the sinister, gleaming cylinder. There was enough reflected illumination for Falsen to see Prenta throw open her cloak, put one of her hands to her belt. She was, he thought, carrying around quite an arsenal, tools as well as weapons. It was a powered screwdriver that she selected. She walked slowly to the bomb, squatted close by it. The screwdriver hummed as she removed the securing studs of the panel, dropped them onto the sand. Why, he wondered, did she not put them down on something to avoid the clogging of the threads by grit?

He asked as much.

"What does it matter?" said Prenta. "There will be no need to put the cover back. Once the bomb is armed and the fuse is set, that's it. And I, for one, don't want to waste any time putting the lid back on once the ticking has started!"

She returned the screwdriver to her belt, selected another screwdriver, a much smaller one. She pushed it into the opening, turned carefully. There was a series of clicks that she seemed to be counting. She looked at her wrist chronometer, the face of which was a blackness in which oddly shaped squiggles danced. Again she used the special tool, in a different place. There were more clicks.

She got slowly to her feet.

"There," she said in a smugly satisfied voice. "There."

She made as though to return the small screwdriver to her belt, and as she did so the spacewoman, Durl, swung the beams of both torches full on Falsen and Linda, shocking and dazzling them. Yet Falsen was not entirely blinded; he saw Prenta drop the tool and snatch from its holster a pistol with a bell-shaped muzzle. She fired without bothering to aim properly. There had been no need to take careful aim; the missile exploded before it hit them, bursting into a net of fine, springy wire that wrapped itself about them like an enormously strong cocoon.

Prenta laughed shrilly.

"I could have used my laser," she said, "but I want you to know what's happening until the very end. . . ." She returned the net-throwing pistol to its holster. "Talking of lasers," she went on, "I'd better make sure that you can't use yours. You just might be contortionists enough to reach them. . . ."

She approached them cautiously. She had in her hand the large screwdriver. She switched it on, set it to full power. The whirling blade, rotating at full speed, would function as a drill of sorts.

She inserted the shaft through an opening in the mesh. Falsen could feel the vibration at his hip as it made contact with his holstered pistol. He heard the sharp crack of shattering plastic, a sputtering of sparks. He smelled the acridity of ozone. He saw Prenta move away from him slightly as she dealt with Linda's weapon.

"There," she said again, still with insufferable smugness. "Two birds with one stone, as you Terrans say. You, the Jonahs, who have brought us nothing but misfortune since we found you and brought you aboard our ship. You, *and* whatever the beasts are that infest these caverns!"

Falsen found that he could speak in spite of the difficulty of moving his jaw.

"The Lady Mother . . ." he began.

"The Lady Mother will believe what I and Durl tell her. We were attacked down here by *simbors*. The two of you, hampered by the bomb that you were carrying, were killed. I and Durl drove them off and escaped injury."

"And . . . Pansir . . ."

"The same story will do for her. Come, Durl. And happy waiting, Mr. Falsen and Lady Linda."

Then she was gone, and Durl with her.

CHAPTER 44

The bomb was humming softly to itself.

During his last Survey Service training cruise Falsen had watched, from a safe distance, the test-firing of such a device. He had seen, through almost opaque glasses, the burgeoning fireball, bright as a thousand suns, heard the supernal thunder, felt the shock wave. He remembered the words of the instructor who had lectured the young officers on the capabilities of such weapons.

"If you're ever involved in a shooting war," the elderly commander had said, "you'll find that there are quite a few situations in which presence of mind will save your skins. But when those things are being slung around, absence of body is the real lifesaver."

And his body, thought Falsen, his strange body could save him yet, could get him out of here.

He hoped.

He willed the change.

Bound as he was, enmeshed by the binding net, he could not remove his hampering clothing. But this did not matter. He could move his head. His muzzle pushed at the strands of wire. He got his mouth open, felt a metallic filament between his sharp, strong teeth. His enormously powerful jaws closed and he worried the strand, snarling wordlessly as he did so. His lips were cut and he could taste his own blood. Such minor wounds were nothing to worry about, would heal almost at once. Fortunately the alloy, whatever it was, from which the wire had been drawn contained no silver.

The strand parted.

With the first one gone the rest were relatively easy. He tore away at the mesh furiously, ignoring the pain from his bleeding mouth. Suddenly the net slackened about his body, their bodies. He changed again, although reversion to human form seemed to require a far greater effort of will than it had ever done before. He used his hands to pull the still clinging wire strands away from himself and from Linda.

The cavern was in pitch-darkness and he had no means of making light with him. He could not see, but he could smell. There was the mingled scent of Linda and himself, of Prenta and the spacewoman Durl. He followed it, running rather than walking, Linda close on his heels. He grazed his shoulder on one side of the tunnel entrance but kept on going, not daring to slacken speed. It was essential that he and Linda get outside the caves before the lift-off of the blimp. Perhaps Pansir would refuse to believe Prenta's story about their having been killed by the indigenous predators, would be insisting on waiting for them. But this was unlikely. Nobody likes to hang around when a nuclear bomb is liable to go off at any tick of the clock.

They ran on, frequently scraping skin on the rough rock walls of the tunnel. He briefly considered abandoning his tattered clothing and continuing the journey on all fours. He decided against it. If—*if!*—the blimp was still there when they got outside, it would not do for the Doralan women to be made aware of his true nature. If there were only Prenta and her henchwoman to worry about, it would not matter so much; they would have to die anyhow. But Pansir was different. He hoped that she would be among the survivors of this ill-starred expedition.

He came to a fork in the tunnel, hesitated.

The scent in the right-hand branch was the fresher—but it was of Prenta and Durl only. To the left it was a compound of Terran and Doralan odors, male and female. Perhaps the Doralans, having taken a wrong turning, were now hopelessly lost. It would serve them right.

"Come on!" he shouted to Linda as he followed the old scent.

The air was fresher now, moisture-laden. There was light, dim but bright enough to make the going easier. Falsen ran faster. He could hear Linda panting behind him.

And there was the Doralans' scent again, strong, overlaying the older traces. They must have rejoined the main tunnel. They could be in the cab of the blimp before Falsen and Linda were clear of the caves, might even now be casting off. Falsen ran as he had never run before, his pumping legs driving him up the last uphill stretch. Suddenly the light coming from ahead was dazzlingly bright. The other bomb, that dropped in the lake? Had it been detonated already? There was darkness, then another flash. Lighting, it must be. There were reverberations of thunder, accompanied by a steady drumming noise.

He burst out into the open, was almost flattened by the torrential downpour that flailed his skin. The visibility was minimal, but he could see the blimp. Two moorings were still out, one on either side of it. On the side of the cab that Falsen could see, a hand was out the open window, gripping the tripping line to that grapnel. It must belong to either Prenta or Durl—and on the other side either Durl or Prenta would have a hand out, waiting for Pansir's order. And the pilot herself would be at her controls. If she knew that Falsen and Linda were safe, she would delay the lift-off.

Falsen shouted, shouted again. He knew that it was hopeless; inside the cab the noise of the rain drumming on the airship's envelope had to be deafening. The hand that he could see jerked upwards and the grapnel came free, its claws folding downward like the frame of a blown-inside-out umbrella. Almost simultaneously, the other anchor pulled clear of the sodden ground. The blimp began to lift sluggishly, struggling upward against the weight of the water pouring down on it from the dark sky. The skids were not yet impossibly high above the rain-filled depressions in which they had rested.

Falsen jumped. His outstretched hands caught one of the vertical struts of the undercarriage. He hung on grimly. From the corner of his eye he saw Linda leap, her arms upraised. Her clawed fingers missed the skid by millimeters and she fell, sprawling facedown in the mud.

But the blimp was dropping again; the man's weight was too much for it. A vent opened in the underside of its envelope and a stream of water gushed out; Pansir was jettisoning ballast. Linda was on her feet. She caught Falsen's dangling legs, clambered up his body. The airship was still falling despite the outflow of water ballast, a torrent that diminished to a trickle. It increased again; Pansir must be emptying another tank. But before this could take effect, Falsen's feet had touched the ground and he was able to pull himself into a more secure position, sitting on one skid, hanging onto a strut, facing Linda who was sitting on the other.

The blimp rose tiredly—then, as the downpour became even heavier, sagged to earth again.

Something was going on overhead, in the control cab. There were scufflings, thuddings. An object fell heavily to the ground, barely missing Falsen in its descent. It was Pansir. She sprawled there on her back, unmoving. The front of her scarlet tunic was charred, as was the body beneath it.

Prenta, who knew too well how little time was left, had done her own dumping of ballast.

CHAPTER 45

Again the blimp lifted sluggishly. The ground, and the sprawled figure of the murdered Pansir, fell slowly away and astern. The rain seemed to be easing, but there was wind—gusty, backing and veering. Presumably, Prenta was at the controls; she might, as she had claimed, have taken a crash course in the handling of lighter-than-air craft, but she was no airshipwoman. She was progressing in a series of swoops, yawing to port and to starboard. All too frequently the framework on which the Terrans were insecurely seated shuddered violently, almost shaking them off.

Dipping and rolling, maintaining an uneasy course, the blimp blundered on. The driving rain soaked and chilled Linda and Falsen, the wind's insistent fingers tried to rip the rags of their uniforms from their bodies. They clung to their struts with numbed hands, looking down at the dreary, waterlogged landscape, staring ahead every now and again into the wind wondering if they would ever see the tower that was the ship breaking the monotony of the distant gray horizon.

Falsen thought longingly of the warmth and dryness of the cabin over his head. He might be able to climb up to it, might be able to force open the door from the outside. Prenta and Durl were armed, but that would not worry him unless that net-throwing pistol was used again. He would kill the pair of them—Prenta especially—with pleasure. Her murder of Pansir had been inexcusable. But suppose he did dispose of the two Doralans—what then? Prenta might be a barely competent airship pilot; he would be completely incompetent.

"There she is!" called Linda, her voice barely audible above the creakings of the undercarriage structure, the whining of the wind.

Falsen turned his head, screwing his eyes up against the lashing rain. Yes, there she was, a tiny uplifted finger seeming, as streaming moisture blurred his vision, to beckon—and then to burst into incandescence. Intense light blazed down from the overcast sky, was reflected from the pools of water on the ground as well as from the metal hull of the distant spaceship. The very raindrops were arrows of flame.

The glare faded from blue-white to yellow, to a sullen crimson, and as it did so the mind-numbing thunder of the atomic blasts hit the airship, buffeting it, slamming it up and forward. Falsen looked astern. The hill was still there and, in the relative safety of the blast shadow, the airship had survived almost unscathed. Beyond the hill the fireball was rising from the lake, from what had once been a lake but was now a burning crater. But the silhouetted outline of the rocky eminence was changing, slowly at first and then with frightening speed. It was like watching the birth of a mountain. Then all collapsed suddenly, as the towering walls of new rock fell in upon themselves.

It had not been a birth after all, but an abortion.

There was warm rain, hot rain, falling in sheets. There was increasing turbulence. The blimp was lifted as though by a giant hand, then dashed downward. A low shrub snatched at Falsen's dangling ankles, almost dragged him from his perch. The airship struggled to regain altitude, was caught by a sudden updraft and snatched to safety. She was off course, spinning about her vertical axis. It seemed that Prenta would never be able to get her under control again, but at last she did so.

The spaceship was closer now, still standing, apparently unaffected by the cataclysm ordered by her captain. And the mooring mast was still there, some distance from her, a skeleton-pyramid of gleaming metal. Falsen wondered what the ground crew would think when they saw Linda and himself sitting on the skids. Prenta must already have made her report by radio-telephone to the Lady Mother, must have told her that Linda and Falsen—and Pansir—had been killed.

And now, thought Falsen grimly, she would have some explaining to do.

But there was no ground crew. Even in these vile weather conditions the scarlet uniforms should have been cleary visible. Perhaps they were waiting inside the spaceship until the rain stopped and the wind died down. From their viewpoint this was all very well, but from that of those aboard the blimp the situation was far from satisfactory.

A port was opening high on the side of the spaceship, a circle of darkness in the sheer cliff of metal that was reflecting the dreadful, lurid light from the sky. Something came out of it—a helicopter. It was followed by a second machine. There were only two of the little aircraft—which meant that, between them, they would be carrying only four women. Such a small number of people might be able to moor the airship at her mast, but it would be a struggle.

The helicopters flew swiftly toward the blimp, rising to meet her, making no attempt to come in for a landing by the mooring mast. Their intention, it became obvious, was to pass on either side of her at control-car level. They drove in steadily. Falsen could see the pilots hunched intently over their controls and, behind them, the passengers. And what were *they* doing? They were leaning out from their seats, and weapons glittered in their hands. As they roared past the airship, they caught her in a crossfire of laser beams, slashing through the thin walls of the cab. There was a sudden acridity of hot metal and burned meat.

They came back, the gunners still firing. Falsen's shirt burst into flames. He tore the blazing rags from his body with his free hand, dropped them. With this second assault the wordless screaming that had been coming from the beam-riddled cab suddenly ceased.

Astern of the blimp the helicopters turned again, made a final pass. This time they concentrated on the envelope. There was a soft thud of exploding gas cells. There was not enough whole fabric left to function even as a crude parachute. The airship fell heavily, faster and faster, struck and threw up a brief fountain of water and mud.

It was no more than a tangle of twisted metal and smoldering rags.

Within seconds the rain put out the last embers.

CHAPTER 46

Falsen crawled out of the wreckage.

He stood up slowly, stretched his limbs cautiously, took a deep breath. There was nothing broken. (There should not have been, if the old legends were true. He already knew that there was some truth in them.) He fell to his hands and knees, began to burrow into the debris. One hand made contact with warm, living flesh. It was Linda. He got his shoulder under one of the skids that was pinning her to the ground, strained upward to release her. She scrambled free, wriggled past him out into the warm—the radioactive?—rain.

He let the skid drop, backed out to join her.

They stood there, letting the downpour wash the mud from their bodies. They looked at each other, each seeking reassurance from the other's breathing presence.

She said at last, shakily, "Just what the hell was all that about? She must *know*, that precious Lady Mother of yours. She tried to have us killed. She probably ordered Prenta to do away with us in the cave, and then when she saw that we were still alive, sent out the helicopters to finish us off."

"No," said Falsen. "No. Those flygirls were out to get everybody and everything—the blimp, Prenta, Durl, Pansir even. I doubt if they knew that she'd already been murdered."

"It must have been *her* that sent the helicopters out."

But it couldn't have been her, Falsen thought. What was happening? Who was giving the orders?

He could guess.

"Give me a hand," he ordered.

225

He began to clear the tatters of balloon and envelope fabric from the crumpled car. It had fallen onto its side. All the windows had shattered, and it was easy enough for him to get in.

Prenta was dead, of course, as was Durl. Each had been hit several times by the flashing laser fire, mainly about their heads and chests, although Durl's right foot had been burned off at the ankle. The middles of their bodies were untouched.

He took Prenta's hand laser from the assortment of tools and weaponry at her belt, passed it out to Linda. Durl's pistol was already drawn; she must have been making a futile attempt at defense. He pried it out of her dead hand. He saw that, according to the meter set into its butt, it was almost fully charged. Nonetheless, he loosed a brief pulse at the instrument panel, adding to the considerable damage that it had already suffered.

He clambered out through the broken window, rejoined Linda.

He said, "We have to be ready for anything. To fight. This will be our last chance to take the ship. . . ."

She looked at him, grinning wolfishly.

She said, "So you've come to your senses. You've dropped that mad idea of becoming an academic on Dorala."

"It would never have worked," he said, but not without regret.

He fingered the sealseam of his shorts, stepped out of the garment as it fell about his ankles. Should it become necessary for him to . . . change, he wanted to be completely unhampered. Apart from his near-invulnerability, it would not be a fight against hopeless odds. If his suspicions were correct, the number of the spaceship's crew must have been considerably reduced.

But how close was she to lift-off?

The inertial drive, which had been running when they left the ship for the caves, was silent now. The ramp, he could just see in spite of the distance and the rain, was still out, the after air-lock door still open. The glow from the fireball, the mushroom cloud, had died and, although it was not yet sunset, a murky darkness had fallen. Lights were on within the spaceship, bright in the gloom. A single searchlight was commencing its sweep. It would be easy enough for him and Linda to avoid its probing beam.

And the bio-sensitive radar?

But he and Linda were not the only relatively large living things abroad in this unnatural night. Not far from them something big broke from one of the pools, writhed over the wet ground to another stagnant mire. The pond from which it had emerged was steaming, its surface bubbling. The subterranean blast must have had all manner of disastrous effects.

They moved as fast as they could over the sodden ground, falling to their faces as the searchlight beam swept in their direction and then, before they got to their feet, rolling in the mire to coat their pale, naked bodies with the black muck. They were careful to keep their weapons clear of the mud.

As they got closer to the ship they moved more cautiously, frequently pausing to renew their coatings of camouflage. They could see, as they approached, that Carlin had no sentries out—but there was one member of the vessel's complement who sat miserable and terrified in the mud, staring towards the bright lights that marked what had been, what never again would be, his home. Linda pounced on him before he was aware of their coming, held him high, squeezing him with deliberate cruelty.

Pondor spat and tried to scratch, screamed something in Doralan. He glared wildly at Falsen, recognized him in spite of the mud covering his body. He mewed, "I warned you . . . *They* are killing, killing . . . The Lady Mother . . . dead . . . The others . . . ,"

Carlin . . . thought Falsen. The mutiny of which she had talked . . . The elimination of the captain and all loyal crew members . . . The shooting down of the returning blimp . . . *very well,* he told himself. He and Linda should be able to deal with the mutineers, and then the ship would be theirs.

But it was a pity about the Lady Mother.

"Be careful!" squealed the cat. "They are . . ."

He was not allowed to finish; his voice died in a choking gurgle as Linda's teeth found his throat. The girl swallowed noisily, then threw the little lifeless body to one side.

She muttered, "I needed that. An apéritif, shall we say?"

"You fool!" snarled Falsen. "He was trying to warn us of something."

She shrugged and said, "I hated the beast, anyhow. As well kill him now as later."

He looked at her, standing defiantly in the glare of the

lights from the ship. The rain had washed her pale naked body clean again. She was far too conspicuous—as he must be.

He said, "We must change again."

"For dinner?" she asked sardonically.

"That's not funny."

"What about our pistols?" she said.

"Carry them in our mouths. And be careful not to break anything."

He watched her, saw her white flesh creep and shift, darken and change, her graceful limbs shorten and warp. And as his own metamorphosis was initiated, he felt the pain that was somehow not a pain, the sense of freedom from the laws governing the conduct of civilized man. He dropped his hand laser when his forepaw could no longer grip it, fell to all fours and picked the weapon up from the mud with his teeth. *So I'm a retriever now!* he thought sardonically.

Crouching low, moving swiftly and silently, a gray shadow among the gray shadows, he streaked towards the circle of bright light that was the air-lock door. The smell of warm machinery and lubricants, of lifeless, inanimate metal, was stronger and stronger, repugnant in his nostrils. There was the smell, too, of alien flesh and blood.

And of violent death.

He made the last few meters of the journey on his belly. At the foot of the ramp he froze, listening and . . . feeling.

Carlin, he thought, must be lax. Not only were there no sentries outside the ship, but there was nobody in the air lock. And why had this means of ingress been left so invitingly open? Probably, he told himself, during and after the general confusion of the mutiny, nobody had gotten around to closing it.

He ran up the ramp into the brightly lit chamber, Linda after him. The inner door was open, too, giving access to the vestibule. Reluctantly, he decided to change again; human shape would be more efficient for the negotiation of the spiral staircase around the axial shaft. After picking up his pistol from the deck, he watched Linda as her body shuddered, warped and shifted, its mass redistributing itself until she became again, outwardly, a fully human woman.

She made for the elevator shaft, her finger already extended to the call button.

"Hold it!" he snapped. "We take the stairs."

"Why?"

"I don't want to run the risk of being trapped in a cage between decks."

"You're right," she admitted.

Still he hesitated before setting foot onto the first tread of the spiral staircase. There was something wrong, very wrong. There was the smell of violent death—itself not frightening to such as him—but the ship herself was far from dead. It pulsed with unseen life, whispered vaguely yet threateningly of the menace that was waiting on the next deck above, or on the deck or decks above that.

Linda looked at him, fear plain on her face.

"Come on!" he said. "They can't hurt *us*. Come on."

And so they climbed, deck after deck, resting now and again to recover breath. They came upon evidence of the fate that had befallen those loyal to the Lady Mother. There were splashes of almost dried blood, but there were no bodies. Here and there paintwork had been blistered and metal scarred by laser fire. There must have been a fight, but who had won? *Pondor's already told us,* he thought. Then, with a flash of sympathy, *Poor bastard!*

Lured by the scent of fresh meat, they left the axial shaft at one of the "farm" levels, ventured outboard. They expected to find corpses, but there were none. There were only the tissue-culture vats, the ranked, gleaming, upright cylinders, each with its gauge glasses, its systems to supply nutrients and to carry away waste products. Pumps were softly throbbing and sighing.

"The vats have been restocked," Linda said flatly. "There's protein enough here for the voyage—a voyage to anywhere. . . ."

I shouldn't feel shocked, thought Falsen. *I, of all people, shouldn't feel shocked.* Yet, illogically, he did.

They returned to the axial shaft, the spiral staircase. They continued their ascent, more cautiously now. They made brief explorations of storerooms and work shops. They were not surprised to find in one of the cold stores the hanging, naked, mutilated bodies. There were burn wounds, which was to be expected. There were ragged, eviscerating gashes.

They must have fought with knives and axes, Falsen thought. Vaguely he wondered why this had been so.

"Come *on*!" snarled Linda. "If you do find your precious Lady Mother or your darling Carlin among that lot, they'll be of no use to you! Or only for eating, after they've been thawed."

Creeping rather than running they completed their journey, came at last to the captain's quarters. The door of the day cabin was open. They could hear voices, low and indistinct, speaking Doralan. They approached the doorway, their bare feet silent on the soft plastic deck covering.

"Come in!" called a voice, Carlin's, speaking in English.

Hand laser ready for use, Falsen erupted through the doorway.

"I could kill you now!" he snarled, his weapon covering those behind and around the big desk. "I *shall* kill you soon, but first I want you to know who is killing you, and why. It should help to make your last moments uneasier."

He stared contemputously at them, and they stared back at him and Linda with matching contempt—Carlin lolling insolently at ease behind the desk; five other women, two junior officers and three enlisted women; and the five whose uniform tunics could not conceal the fact that they were males. None of them was armed. He hated them all, the fat, satisfied sleekness of them, the treachery which had brought them to where they now stood and sat, mistresses (and masters?) of a huge, sky-cleaving ship, a vessel in which, had it not been for his intervention, they would have escaped just penalties for the crimes of mutiny and murder.

Carlin sneered.

"You," she stated, "are as bad as we."

"No," said Falsen. "We would never have murdered the Lady Mother and her people. . . ."

"Speak for yourself, Falsen."

"I would never have shot down an unarmed blimp."

"Prenta had to go, and her little bedwarmer, Durl."

"Your fellow conspirators," he said disgustedly.

"Whatever makes you think that, Falsen?"

"Prenta and Dural tried to kill us. They murdered Pansir."

Carlin laughed. "Pansir got in the way, I suppose. And Prenta thought that she would be doing the Lady Mother a favor by getting rid of the two Jonahs responsible for all our misfortunes. Tell me, did she use that fancy pistol I made for her? She told me that it was for catching one of the beasts alive, but I suspected that she really wanted it for you. She left you trussed up in the cave, didn't she, just waiting for the Big Bang?

"But you got away, as I knew that you would. Your kind aren't easily killed. . . ."

Your kind.

The way that she had emphasized the words was significant.

"So you *know*?" demanded Falsen.

"Of course I know. We aren't all fools, Mr. Falsen. We aren't all like our late, unlamented Lady Mother. Some of us did more on Earth than study astronautics. Some of us read widely—your history, your myths and legends. And we know, as you know, that the interstellar drive does queer things to time as well as space, and that some people, when exposed to the temporal-precession field, revert. Revert with improvements, no nonsense about having to wait for the full moon and all the rest of it. While I was staying at your Academy I read the Dennison Report. It's supposed to be 'Top Secret, Destroy By Fire Before Reading'—but I was enjoying, or not enjoying, an affair with an admiral with exotic tastes. The fat old fool was quite besotted and let me paw through his papers. . . ."

Falsen's hand tightened on the butt of his hand laser, his thumb on the firing stud.

"You were marooned, of course," went on Carlin, "from your ship. Or ships. The normal humans in the crew should have killed you. But they didn't, which was our good fortune. Your activities, at least until you became the Lady Mother's pet puppy, put up a smoke screen behind which we would get to work. It is a pity, though, that one of you killed Garbillen when he, with the other males, was outside the ship. We had to make his body look like that of a woman—not too successfully, as it turned out. But it doesn't matter now. What does matter is that we have an imbalance of the sexes.

"So, Falsen, again I make you my offer. Come along with us, as navigator, to help us to find our own world out towards the Rim. As navigator, and . . ."

"What about Linda?" he demanded.

"Linda? I'm not spiteful, Falsen, though I have cause to be. She'll be quite happy left on this world, running wild and hunting food animals. . . ."

Behind Falsen, Linda screamed viciously and fired her

pistol, keeping the firing stud depressed so that it emitted a continuous, energy-wasting beam. The thin pencil of almost invisible light splashed across Carlin, igniting the material of her tunic, swept up to the grinning cat's face, down to the lower part of her body. The big desk burst into flames, flared briefly, smoldered ruddily and smokily. Falsen was firing too, directing his aim at the other Doralans—all of whom just stood there, staring at him unblinkingly.

The air stank of charred wood and fabric, hot metal, scorched paint.

And that was all.

Through the slowly clearing acrid fumes he glared at the hateful face before him—the supercilious cat's face, the big, unwinking eyes.

"Have you quite finished?" asked Carlin at last. "As you may have noticed, your weapons are useless. I will tell you why. Some of our myths and legends are almost echoes of yours. Or is it the other way around? Some of us, like some of you, are affected by the temporal-precession fields of the Drive. But there is a difference. Our authorities are not yet aware of the danger. They do not know, as you know and we know, how short a way we have come from the frontier of the dark. . . ."

"I don't know what you mean," said Falsen sullenly.

But he did. He did.

"If you don't know," said Carlin, "you soon will."

Two of her people, a man and a woman, were tearing away the scorched, still smoldering remnants of their clothing. Falsen stared at them while Linda repeatedly pressed the firing stud of her useless, charge-depleted pistol. He saw the firm, golden flesh creep and shift and change, watched the terrifying metamorphosis of almost-human humanoid into *simbor*. Standing erect, the tigerlike, kangaroolike animals snarled wordlessly, unsheathed the long, razor-sharp claws of all four paws. Growling, Falsen hurled his useless hand laser at the male. The beast evaded the missile easily, fell into a crouch preparatory to the killing spring.

Falsen bared his teeth, snarling back at the *simbor*. At his side, Linda screamed ferociously. He fell to all fours as the change came over him, as he sloughed off the remaining shreds of his humanity. But he was still thinking like a man.

There's still a chance, he told himself. *We already know that we can kill them. And, after all, they're only . . . cats. . . .*

Beside him, Linda was changed. The fur of her body was erect and bristling; her lips were drawn back from her sharp teeth as she growled deeply and ominously.

Yet Carlin laughed, then snapped a brief order. The *simbors,* which had been about to leap, settled reluctantly back to their haunches.

She said, almost regretfully, "It would have been a good fight and could have gone either way. But I have so few, Falsen, with whom to start my colony. . . ."

Her hand came up from beneath the smoking ruins of the desk, holding a pistol—not a hand laser but a big, clumsy-looking weapon that could well have been copied from something in a museum.

She went on, "I made this myself, in my workshop. And the ammunition. Luckily the cartridges didn't explode when you burned the desk." Then, as she began firing, the noise thunderous in the confined space, "Silver bullets, of course."

The larger of the two werewolves died before he could get to the door. The other, his mate, vainly attacking, was slammed down in mid-leap.